CHILDREN OF THE STARS

CHILDREN OF THE STARS

NEIL V. YOUNG

atmosphere press

ACKNOWLEDGMENTS

It is said that writing is a lonely profession. I have found that's not always the case. Since embarking on my writing career, I have met many wonderful people, my friends, who have helped me become the wordsmith I am today. To that end I have a list of the wonderful individuals without whose support I wouldn't have made it this far.

This list is, however, far from complete. And to anyone who I might have left off, I do apologize. Your help was no less valuable to me.

I would like to thank, in no particular order:

Elaine Ash, whose experience and talent was fundamental in making my manuscript everything it could be. Brennan and Dava White Harvey, for pointing out that I needed a plot. My writers critique group and writer's society friends who helped me hammer the copy into the work it became, including Patrice Hickey, Rose Molina, Leif Bailey, Susan Buckner, as well as a posthumous shout out to my friends George Snyder, Darlene Quinn, Tony N. Todero and Deryl Quick. To Larry Porricelli, Steve Hutson, Kathy Porter, Jeff Michaels, who kept me going with their positivity and enthusiasm, as well as the Westside Weird crew of Neil Citrin, Chrome Oxide, Marco Subias and John Gwinner. And William Kirkland who was there with financial aid and friendship when I needed both.

ONE

Some cycles, it didn't pay to get out of the sleep capsule.

Dayton Murdoch lumbered his way down the canyon floor, his space suit keeping him warm despite the minus-sixty-three degrees Celsius of a trace atmosphere. His crewmate and friend trudged along behind him, the reddish rocks and sandy soil crunching beneath her sealed boots in the low gravity.

Periodically, Dayton would stop to catch his breath, only to hear Zara stop several feet behind him. He looked up, past the rock spires and vaulting formations that low gravity seemed to encourage. The stars shone, dominated by a gaseous purple nebula. It filled the skyline.

"So anyway, Trenton in the service bay was talking my ear off all through the prep today." Zara's voice came in over Dayton's helmet mic. "He's a pretty prepped guy, right? He said you were really into that girl from the old mining outfit."

"Uh huh."

"What? Am I boring you?"

"Oh, no! This is incredibly fascinating."

"You're not serious."

"No, I'm not."

"Well, you should be," Zara continued. "Trenton said he spoke to some of that mine crew, and they said she was kind of …"

"Kind of what?"

"Well, you know."

"No, I don't." Dayton turned to face her, only to see her some three meters behind him. With suit comms, you never knew how far away the other person was.

Zara was petite, with pale white skin that contrasted with

her jet-black hair and almond eyes. A stripe down her bangs rotated colors, fading from ice blue to bright red, to neon green, then back again, thanks to bioluminescent programming. Her hands were large and calloused.

By comparison, Dayton stood nearly two meters in height, which was tall for his sixteen years. His hair was dark as well, which served in sharp distinction to his cobalt-blue eyes. He'd been careful, and few of the solar flares he'd encountered left blemishes.

Zara wasn't unattractive. He just didn't feel anything romantic.

"Take it easy," Zara said. She crossed her arms in front of her face, the traditional sign of friendship among belters. "I am just trying to be a good partner here. You know, trying to warn you about stuff. I doubt your new partner in Recon would be like this."

"Look," Dayton said after a long and very frustrated breath. "It seems like you're only looking out for me when I meet someone, and then you're always finding something wrong with them."

"Most guys would appreciate someone looking out for them. You think anyone's gonna look out for you when you make Recon next mission?"

The thought brought Dayton a rush of pleasure to his whole being. Zara was wrong about a lot of things. But she was right about him wanting Recon. He had only fourteen flight hours left to go, and then he would be qualified. Out of Survey. No more mapping. No more scanning. Recon was the exploratory wing. The exciting stuff.

Soon, very soon, Zara would be assigned another Survey pilot. This was both bad and good news. Good in the fact he wouldn't have to listen to her impetuous prying into his life. Bad because, when it was all told, she was a good scan op.

"Cut your thrusters," Dayton said. "We've got a downed survey probe around here, and the background radiation is making a lock too difficult."

Like himself, Zara had been born to her parents onboard *Venture* as it took a twenty-year-long trip to Earth. The ship represented the financial and labor efforts of a dozen countries, sent to explore the galaxy, as well as perform various assists to existing colonies. With its new light-drives, it really covered a wide swath of the stars.

Now, it sat in orbit around OPL549 while the surveyors, engineers, and techs scoured the far side of the planet. Since the *Venture* had left twenty years earlier, the Chinese had set up a large mining colony on OPL549, but the planet was far from completely surveyed. It was overflowing with all kinds of subsurface minerals.

"I think it's over there." Dayton pointed his scanner in the direction of a column of smoke that rose into the thin, purplish sky of OPL549. Direct vision was blocked by a slight hill, but Dayton was sure that was where the probe had ended up. The amount of radiation indicated that the probe was likely damaged. The casings holding the power supplies of those old type-R probes weren't very tough.

"That's where it crashed," Dayton said as he pointed west.

"Oh really?" Zara said sarcastically. "You think so, huh? Is that your training talking, or maybe it's that smoldering crater up ahead?"

"Yeah," Dayton tried to sound like he wasn't frustrated. He failed. "Cracks like that are why I don't make small talk."

"Oh, come on." Zara touched a thick, gloved hand on his shoulder. "I'm just having fun with it."

"You want excitement, play more grav ball."

That comment silenced Zara for the moment.

At the hilltop, a prime view of the impact site spread before them. Rocks of all sizes and shapes were scattered in every direction from a smoldering, black crater several meters across. The texture and color of the soil was darker red, meaning it had been tossed out as well.

"Just when I thought this place couldn't have any more rocks," Dayton said. He adjusted his scanner through the acrid smoke.

"I'm reading increased radioactivity." Zara stepped up to his side.

"Yeah, I got that too."

He began sidestepping his way down into the smoke. Soon, he found himself at the bottom of the crater, next to the shiny metallic silvery ball that was the probe. The rads were high here, but his suit would keep him safe.

"What do you see?" Zara's voice cackled to life in his headset. Dayton looked around. She was still up on the ridge.

"Why aren't you down here?"

"You don't need me."

"Uh, this is a probe recovery?"

"I can't see anything through the smoke."

"Oh, boohoo. I made it down here. Just follow your scanner."

"You know, you are not much of a gentleman."

"Excuse me. You volunteered for this assignment. Now you want special treatment?"

A wave of grumbling and huffing filled Dayton's ears. *Fourteen hours*, he told himself. Fourteen measly hours was all that kept him from a Recon patch. He'd be the youngest pilot to ever get that patch! There were pilots in their middle age that didn't have that.

And not for the first time, his mind wandered back to the Wall of Honor on the bridge. Every pilot that made Recon was there, with their image and record. It was something every crewman walked past at one time or another. And Dayton's name would be there, listing him as the youngest pilot to have made Recon—ever! He'd be immortalized and at only sixteen!

Focus, he reminded himself. *Eyes on the prize.*

"That casing is hot." Zara read from her scanner. "How are we going to open it?"

Dayton examined the probe. It was cracked and dented,

but he did see that the indicator lights were on. This meant the power was still flowing.

"By not touching it," he said, punching the security code into his handheld. He waited while it synched up with the probe.

"So far, the radiation isn't a problem," Zara said. "But we will probably have to go into decon anyway."

"Wouldn't be the first time."

"Do you ever talk about anything but business?"

"All the time."

"But not with me."

"Yeah, that's right."

A full schematic of the probe took shape on his hand mirror-sized screen. Sure enough, it was damaged.

Dayton tapped the touchscreen right over the equator of the silver sphere. Recognition codes flooded into the scanner from the probe. He was in.

"Now, if we can just download what we need."

"I'm getting a power surge," she said as her own scanner emitted a high-pitched electronic squeal. "That thing is not liking you accessing it. Let's get out of here."

"Almost there," Dayton said. The progress line showed ninety percent complete. The data was transferring.

"The casing is breaking apart." Zara's voice carried equal parts of worry and fear. "I'm reading minor pulses in the power core. We need to leave!"

Ninety-eight percent.

"Not just yet," Dayton answered. He'd known Zara had a flair for the dramatic. Given that, he probably had a few more minutes than she let on.

"Yes! Yet!"

Ninety-nine percent.

"Only telemetry is left," he said. "That always takes longer to load."

"It'll do." She grabbed his suit's shoulder handle. "We go now!"

Dayton glanced up, turning to face Zara, when his eyes locked onto the probe. The burnt metallic ball was red with heat, and a stream of black smoke with silver highlights shot out of the cracks in the thing's skin.

"Okay, now maybe we'll leave." He turned and ran up the trench. Zara beat him to the rim by a mere two seconds.

The thing exploded.

A huge shock wave hit Dayton from behind, forcing him to the rocky ground. His suit's computer blared a small klaxon that rang like a cacophony in his ears. His faceplate had a spiderweb crack in the lower right corner. It was spreading. Bits of radioactive metal, electronic circuit board fragments, and chunks of black rock rained down around them. Garbage, large and small, bounced off his suit, but its protective carapace held.

He turned to see a column of fire shoot into the thin air and die down. "Zara?" he called out over the comm.

"Yeah?"

"Sound off. You okay?"

"Scanner got shattered in that shockwave," she said. "Or the fall. I'm not sure which. You?"

"Faceplate crack. But I'm on it."

He pressed the right side of his helmet. The blast shield slammed down over the faceplate. This effectively sealed his helmet from caving in and decompressing him, but it was like wearing dark goggles.

"Can you see?" Zara said, waving her hand back and forth in front of his faceplate.

"Yeah, I'll be fine," he said, pushing her arm away. "Let's get back to Old 21."

"Fine. I'm flying."

"No."

"So, you're willing to risk our lives just to get another flight hour in?"

"Enough already."

"You'll never make Recon if you're dead."

As if on cue, Dayton stumbled over some rocks the size of twenty-five-liter fuel cans. He recovered before falling, but the point was made. He couldn't see well enough to fly.

Another hour. Another hour closer to the wall. Another hour closer to immortality. But it was denied. He finally had to admit that. At least for now.

"All right," he said in a defeated whisper. "You take the controls."

"Come on. I'll lead you back."

She placed his hand on her right shoulder-mounted hand-hold.

Even through the blast shield's darkness, Dayton could make out the form of Old 21. A Planetary Survey Vehicle, or PSV, it resembled those old Lamborghinis in movies they showed in the cinema wing. Except this Lamborghini had anti-gravity plates to allow it to fly through atmospheres and a boxy back where the main thrusters were located.

Old 21 had micro pits, burn marks, and dents from a thousand missions to every barren, volcanic, vacuum, and toxic planet it had visited. Before the PSV became his, it had been too close to a spewing volcano. This burned off most of the recognition numbers of the PSV, leaving only the last two numbers, 2 and 1, recognizable. It got the nickname "Old 21," and it stuck.

"Operator Two-Two-Seven-Alpha," a familiar voice crackled in Dayton's earpiece. It was Milly, a nickname given to Millard Harbison, the man who ran the small craft bay aboard *Venture*.

"Two-Two-Seven-Alpha, go." Dayton tried to sound professional.

"Murdock," Milly said. "I picked up a blast in your area."

"Umm, yeah," he answered, trying not to sound out of breath. "That probe went up."

"You owe me a report." Milly's voice came on, more irritated, if that was possible. "I want you in my office for debriefing."

Uh oh. Dayton knew the sound of trouble, and this was it.

TWO

Milly's office was at the end of the most well-lit and well-maintained corridor in the *Venture*. The ship was over seven kilometers long and full of corridors that were efficient but sterile and cold. A lot like the man in the office.

"I want to see my mom," grumbled Zara. "I wish my parents were back from their explorer duty already. "

"It'll happen," Dayton replied. "They'll get back. They want to see Earth more than anyone else."

They entered Milly's office.

Milly sat behind his desk, looking angry as usual. His hair, or what was left of it, was graying and making a full retreat from his temples and crown. The lines on his face were long and deep. He wore a uniform that may have fit him in his youth, but now it strained under the bulge of his pot belly. He had square, blunt facial features with dark, puffy bags under his beady eyes.

"You two." Milly looked up at the duo with a tired expression. "Sit." It was as if he wanted to be angrier but was too tired to muster the effort.

Dayton and Zara took the uncomfortable metal chairs.

"You two have been busy," Milly said. "I understand you caused that probe to explode."

"Sir," Zara said. "The probe was like that when we found it. We got the data and came right back."

"Yes," Milly tilted his head back. "And one of my probes is destroyed. Then, you return the surveyor to maintenance, and they report there is undue wear on the scanners, the shield emitters, and the bottom of the hull of Surveyor One-Zero-Three-Two-One."

"Old Twenty-One," Dayton said.

"You don't designate vehicles, Mister Murdock," Milly somehow summoned the energy to admonish him. "Or do you think nearly being a Recon pilot gives you that right?"

"I do not," Dayton said. "That damage must have been from the explosion."

"Or solar flares, or radiation," Zara was quick to throw in.

"Yes, yes." Milly waved the excuses away. "You know what I think? I think that you two were careless in your procedures. You openly admitted in this report that you rushed the data retrieval."

Dayton tried to keep himself steady. His eyes wandered to the metal sipper bottle on Milly's desk. It sat there, held in place by its gravity-secure lock. The top of the bottle resembled nothing so much as a disgusting volcano eruption of dried spittle.

"Sir—" Zara started to say.

"Don't even try it, missy," Milly glared at them both. "You thought that by destroying another probe, you could somehow flip me, and the whole ship, off. What is it? Some kind of rebellion?"

"How could I destroy the probe?" Dayton knew every word he said could be explosive, but with Milly, explosions were the norm.

"What the Hell are you talking about?" Milly's beady little eyes narrowed on Dayton. "You're a genuine troublemaker, as is Little Missy here. In fact, I don't think that probe was damaged at all."

"Damaged at all?" Dayton raised his voice, then calmed it. "The probe fell from orbit. Of course it was damaged."

"It was a thin-atmosphere reentry," Milly smiled, revealing a mismatched row of yellowed, browning teeth. "Not much could happen."

"Well, sir, I don't know what to tell you," Dayton fumbled for the right response. "It must've landed hard. I mean, the probe was leaking radiation like an unshielded jump conduit.

Its casing was cracked and getting worse by the second."

"So?" Milly's tiny, almost pupil-less eyes bulged as he spoke. A thick vein crossing his bald pate was pulsing like a hydraulic piston. "You were just looking for another hour to burn off till Recon, right? You just want what you want."

"I have the maintenance records right here." Milly held up his data tablet. "That probe was checked out fine during the first duty cycle. Those type-Ajax probes are made of an alloy they use on boring equipment. It is several times harder than even the densest rock."

"That may be!" Dayton threw up his hands. "The probe was in bad shape. I stayed till the last possible millisecond downloading the data. We barely escaped."

"Okay, gentlemen," Milly stood, revealing his rotund form as his bulk heaved him to his feet. "I think I see what's going on here."

Not by the length of a comet's tail do you know what's going on here.

"Sir," Dayton said the word with as much faux respect as he could muster. "What was I supposed to do? Sit there and soak up the radiation, maybe burn my suit open and die from exposure?"

The vein in Milly's head nearly popped as he shook with anger.

"I do have one punishment in mind for you two." Milly produced a pair of duty cards and handed one to each of them. "I've been saving these for a special occasion. You just gave me that occasion."

Okay, Dayton thought. This might not be all bad. A flight punishment still counted as logged flight hours.

Milly thrashed open the steel drawer in his desk, and it gave way with a scrape. He produced two cards from it. However, these plastic pass cards didn't have the black stripe of a Survey mission. They didn't have the purple stripe of a cargo run. No. These were red striped.

Maintenance.

"I'll inform your parents," Milly said with malicious pleasure.

Zara slumped in her seat.

Dayton felt his spirit crushed by the sight of those two card keys. There would be no extra mission time. No more flight hours for now. Dayton cursed himself silently.

Recon had to wait.

***

After a long pull through zero-G sections of the ship, Dayton and Zara made it to the deployment bay, the site of their punishment. Their job was to get at least six of the defunct mining "Crabs" working again as soon as possible. Crabs were named because of their resemblance to the Earth-ocean creature. They drifted about with their many arms full of drills and nets and blasted chunks off asteroids.

Luckily, Zara had swiped a couple of nutricubes from the galley. A simple orange square, a nutricube had a spongy texture, but just one could satisfy a human's nutritional needs. Older crewmembers longed for the days of "real food," but Dayton was happy with the nutricubes.

Dayton looked up from the workbench, peering over the disassembled Crab he was working on. Zara was a meter away, working on her own Crab, which was also in pieces. The humans weren't dejected, but they weren't thrilled either.

A deep rumbling, almost a grinding, beneath the deck plates shocked them both.

"I've never heard that before," Zara said with alarm.

Dayton looked at the deck, feeling the vibrations under his boots. Over the years, he had developed an almost engineer-like feel for the *Venture*. He knew when she was straining. He knew when she was in trouble. Now, the grinding intensified, and then hundreds of small dings began echoing off the bay doors.

"Meteor shower?" Zara asked.

"Maybe. Meteor showers don't make the bulkheads creak, though." Dayton noticed the bulkheads and deck were flexing. "We're out of here."

"No arguments."

Dayton and Zara made it as far as the access tubes when they saw the emergency crash doors slam shut and block their way. A warning klaxon boomed from the overhead speaker system.

"Warning, this is a stage-one emergency jump. Time to opening of quantum corridor is fifteen minutes. All crew shifts report to safe areas immediately."

"I thought we were cycles away from entering a tunnel," Zara said. "What's up with this?"

"I don't know." Dayton could feel the deck sliding around under his boots. The thought of activating his boot magnets shot through his mind, but he didn't do it since the gravity was still working. At least at present.

"We're a long way from the nearest safe zone," Zara replied.

Dayton punched up the comm line on the computer panel, hoping to get his father or at least comm central. Hell, even Milly would have been welcome. Instead, all that glared back at him was a ship's logo screen with the red words "ALL CHANNELS LOCKED" flashing across it.

"Great." Zara stared at the screen. "What are we supposed to do now?"

"Calm down," Dayton said. He switched from the comm channel to a schematic of their area of *Venture*, a long, rectangular room that was the Crab bay. A couple more keystrokes, and a single area highlighted in blinking green. "Okay, we have an emergency escape pod adjacent to this bay. Those things are shielded. See? We're good."

"That?" Zara said. "My old bunk has more room than that thing."

"If you have a better idea, I'd like to hear it." Dayton wasn't thrilled at the prospect of being locked in one of those cramped cylinders either, but their options were limited. "C'mon, it's right at the end of the Crab parade."

The area at the front of the Crab bay hadn't been organized in a long time. Over the years, crewmen had moved an old Crab engine, a pile of detached Crab arms, and several dented cargo containers in front of the entry hatch to the escape pod.

"No way we can move all this stuff in less than twelve minutes." Zara kicked one of the old cargo pods. It bonged in return.

Dayton pulled open a gravity control panel on the rust-stained bulkhead. "Turn on your boot magnets."

Three keystrokes and a handle pull on the control panel, and the whole bay was floating in zero-G. "Start pushing," Dayton exclaimed as he clanked-stepped over to one of the now floating cargo containers. A quick push and Dayton sent the old bin tumbling across the length of the bay. It clanged against several of the Crabs.

Zara rapidly tossed the arms, and in a matter of minutes, everything that had been blocking the escape pod was floating and banging around the opposite end of the bay. Dayton marched back over to the control panel and brought the gravity back online. The flotsam at the end of the bay came down with a series of resounding crashes that nearly ruptured their eardrums. But it worked.

"Warning, this is a stage-one emergency jump. Time to opening of quantum tunnel is five minutes. All crew shifts report to safe areas immediately."

"See?" Dayton shrugged. "Plenty of time."

"I'll feel better once we're inside that pod." Zara hit a sequence of keys on the emergency pod's access hatch. The hatch opened only a few centimeters.

"Why doesn't this surprise me?" Zara smashed her fist against the keypad. "Is there an emergency hydraulic handle?"

"I'm on it," Dayton said. An aged pump handle sat in a

grimy and unused alcove just to the right of the hatch. Dayton grabbed the metal handle and felt the oozing spread of grease on his palms. He steadied himself and pushed the handle up. It didn't seem to move. He re-gripped and pushed again, only this time, his greasy hands nearly slid off the handle.

"Ouch," Dayton looked around and saw an old, stained towel plopped on the deck plates by his feet. He snatched the rag and wrapped it around the handle. With a deep breath, he pushed upward until his muscles ached in protest.

The old handle eventually surrendered, and Dayton pumped it three times until he saw a grimy "all-clear" green light illuminated at its base. "Try it now."

Zara hit the keypad again, and this time, the hatch door opened. The two were through it in seconds. Dayton slammed the red button on the inside of the pod, and the hatch doors eased shut.

"All right, flight leader." Zara looked around at their surroundings. "At least we won't go hyper-happy."

Dayton glanced around the pod. It was designed for six people. There were six acceleration chairs mounted to the bulkheads, three to each side, and a small storage locker that held some emergency space suits. A few metal boxes were welded to the center of the pod. The air was stale but breathable.

Zara fiddled with the control panel, and air began to rush from the overhead ducts. "Maybe we can get the air a little fresher."

Zara opened the comm panel with her torque wrench and began working on the exposed circuit board.

"You're better at this than I am," Dayton said.

That was something he knew too well. Zara was brilliant with the systems. She had proven herself again and again by fixing everything she came across. No broken comm unit was too damaged. No junction box too neglected. The only drawback was that she thumbed her nose at authority. Dayton tried to help her stay on course, but she was a wild one.

Dayton unlocked the survival kit in the middle of the pod. He needed to keep himself occupied. He pressed the power button of an e-reader and watched as the text of the latest shipboard-approved survival manual scrolled on its screen.

***

Days passed with nothing to do but stare at the quantum tunnel. It was a wormhole created by the ship that allowed them to travel faster than light. Oscillating blue, gold, and red hues swirled past the small porthole, doing an intricate dance. It passed for entertainment. It was day three.

Zara bounced a grav ball against the bulkhead, quickly catching it every time. "Want another survival bar?"

"Thanks," Dayton waved the possibility away. "I've already had like twelve of them. Those things taste like carbon filters."

"Arrggh." The ball careened off and landed among the space suits on the far rack. Zara didn't make any attempt to retrieve it. "This place is driving me nuts. Can't they at least stop at a jump point already? What about your dad? What about my parents? They're still out there in the lab shuttle."

Dayton didn't answer. They had opened a locker, the contents of which were now scattered across the pod's interior. Manuals, distilled water tubes, those awful ration bars, oxygen tanks, a flare gun, thermal tarpaulin, a survival knife, a length of nylon rope, and a flashlight. There was also the chemical toilet, which made things awkward when one of them used it. Lucky for them, Dayton was able to activate the gravity in the pod.

"What if this is it?" Zara kicked at the toilet and plopped herself down in one of the seats. "I miss Res Hab quarters. I miss my parents. I miss Toki."

"I miss my dad, too. Toki, even. He can be a pain and a bug, but—"

"I worked so hard to grow a few flowers in our Res Hab quarters. I hope Mom gives them some water."

"I miss eating nutricubes. Watching old Earth movies with Dad and Brock."

"Brock is only thirteen; He's so immature."

"Toki's six. That's immature."

They lapsed into silence. Zara broke it, "What if we don't come out of the tunnel?"

Dayton thought before answering. *What would Dad say? Keep calm. Remember your training.* "I doubt that," he said, with more confidence than he felt. "After they find clear coordinates to exit the tunnel, they'll stop, and we can get out of here. Usually a week."

"How did we get here? What happened to the ship in the first place?" Zara asked.

"Someone really blew it. It felt like a storm to me. With all those micrometeorites hitting the ship, what else could it be?"

Zara tossed the last of her survival bar down the toilet in disgust. "They should have seen a storm on scanners. I mean, *Venture* isn't the most maneuverable thing in the universe, but she can avoid a storm with some warning."

"Then I guess that's why they entered the tunnel." Dayton sat down in one of the acceleration couches. How long had it been since his last sonic shower? Since before their mission to retrieve the probe. He supposed the pod was getting smelly, what with two occupants in such a small confinement. But he'd gone nose blind some time ago. Probably just as well.

Where would *Venture* end up? The captain didn't tell them their next stop. Hopefully, one of the lightly-settled systems. Maybe something with a lot of asteroid fields that needed surveying. That would be great. Just one of those assignments would log him sixteen hours. He'd come out of that with two to spare.

Dayton imagined what it must feel like to walk the corridors with a Recon patch. He thought he had earned respect before. No, this would be beyond that. Within a few years, he could be posted to another explorer ship. He'd heard tales of Recon pilots with planets named after them. Truly, that would be immortality.

"Hey," Zara said as she messed with the comm unit. "I got it working."

"I knew you would," Dayton said. "Let's access the main communications channels."

"They're locked out," Zara shifted her head to watch the comm unit screen. "It says it's on Command Override."

"Why?"

"I have no idea," Zara said. "There's only one record of a communication, but it's a Threat Level Omega."

"That means you can't access it?"

"Oh, please," Zara rolled her eyes. "Let me download it to my portable unit, and in time, I can descramble it."

"Will anyone know you're there?"

"No. I'll cover my digital tracks."

Zara downloaded the file, shoved the mess of wires and circuit boards back into the wall panel, and slammed the face shut.

"Screw it," Zara said. "Maybe we should just send one of the Crabs up with a note saying we're fine. At least then they'd know."

"That's a good idea," Dayton said. "But we'd have to open the hatch and reactivate one of those Crabs. I don't relish the idea of going space-happy."

"Do you think space-happy is even real? I mean, can people really go crazy from being in a quantum tunnel?"

"Right now, I think I'm about to go space-happy in this pod. Let's open the hatch; it's worth a try."

"Do you have the remote-operations control pad?" Dayton popped open the access panel. A coil of multicolored wires fell out.

"Right here somewhere." Zara dug in the mess she had

made around herself and produced the control pad, which resembled a portable tablet, only about half the size and with a joystick.

Dayton plugged the wires into the back of the ops controller and flipped it open. The screen read that all the systems were in working order. One after the other, it ticked down the list of available Crabs, finally settling on a total of thirty.

"Thirty?" Zara tapped the side of the unit with her forefinger. "Do we need that many?"

"No, but we have that many to work with." Dayton punched up command instructions for the Crabs. They sat there, unmoving and at attention in the bay. "Number Twelve looks good. Let's try him."

"Fine." Zara peered out the escape pod hatch window into the Crab bay. "Can you record a message?"

At the cue, Dayton spoke into the panel's intercom. "This is Survey Flight Pilot Dayton Murdoch, serial number Zero-Four-Five-Seven-Niner-Two-One. With me is Flight Technician Zara McCulloch, serial number Delta-Mike-Zero-Five-Two-Two-Four. We are currently trapped in Escape Pod One-One-Four in Crab Bay Fourteen-Alpha Forward. Please send us any information you can about this unscheduled quantum tunnel jump. We estimate we have enough supplies to last us another two weeks. Please respond by logging a voice message and sending this Crab back to its origin."

With a few more keystrokes, Number Twelve activated and rose less than a meter from its cradle, its thruster modules keeping it surprisingly stable despite the rocking of the ship.

Using the main entrance was out of the question, Dayton knew. The main clamshell was locked down during tunnel voyages. Crab Number Twelve obediently moved to the side access airlock. The airlock was designed for nothing larger than one or two humans. Dayton grunted in frustration as he tried to get the Crab into the narrow entrance. It bumped repeatedly against the opening without luck.

"That Crab ain't going nowhere," Zara motioned at the hapless Crab banging against the airlock entryway.

"Actually, I think I can make this happen." Dayton hit a few more keys. Upon hitting the *Enter* button, the Crab's drills and mining shield disconnected and floated away, leaving it a good deal thinner.

With its reduced size, Dayton guided the Crab into the airlock and closed the entry door. It was a close fit, but Dayton made it work. Dayton cut the thrusters, and the Crab crashed onto the deck with a resounding thud. The Crab just sat there as the pressure equalized.

"All right." Dayton hit the remote activator for the exit door on the airlock. "Let's send him on his way."

The door slid open, and in a millisecond, the Crab was sucked out of the airlock and into the oscillating colors of the quantum tunnel.

"What the—" Zara pounded her fist against the bulkhead. "I thought Crabs could do all the extravehicular stuff in quantum tunnels."

"I think we should have secured him," Dayton said. He tapped the keys on the panel, and the airlock slammed shut.

"Do we have anything to secure him with?" Zara looked around the bay, within the limitations the porthole on the pod's hatch afforded her.

Dayton said. "Every crab comes with a tether hook. Let's hook up a spool."

"Will that work?"

"I don't know."

"Only one way to find out."

"Actually, no," Dayton said. "It won't work."

"But we have spools."

"Not a kilometer's worth."

"So?"

"The nearest habitation ring is a klick away."

"Oh," Zara's voice sunk, along with her spirits.

"Nothing," Dayton said, turning to watch the oscillating colors of hyperspace shooting by. "Ride it out is about all we can do."

THREE

A deep, massive grinding sound echoed all around them. It was day five. "I think we're coming out of the quantum tunnel."

" 'Bout time." Zara got up and raced to the porthole.

The tunnel faded. Dayton saw the clear, unmistakable stars of normal space. Standing out from the blackness was a sight he had seen only in videos and still images. The Earth was huge, with blue oceans with white streaks and golden landmasses. It was bigger than he had imagined, and the sight made his heart race.

Zara looked down at the planet and shook her head. "That can't be Earth. We were only in the tunnel for a few days. No way we could have made it this far."

"Yeah, we have three, maybe four years yet." Dayton's eyes took in the sight. "We're not supposed to be here till I'm twenty. I'm only sixteen. It's not supposed to be like this."

Did they cross some time rift? Like everything else about quantum tunneling, Dayton had heard stories. And was he still considered sixteen? What now?

"Then we're out of here." Zara hit the hatch control, and the doors whooshed open. Fresh air rushed in. Even the metallic, over-cycled air of the Crab bay was a welcome change from the staleness of the pod.

The deck plates shook and rolled under them. Dayton could hear Zara fall down behind him. Her trademark cussing told him she was okay. He turned and helped her up anyway. The habit of having your partner's back died hard in the Reaches, and she was still his partner. Sparks ignited from overhead lighting panels; *Venture* shuddered to its spine. Almost in response, the klaxons began wailing, and the overhead digitized voice returned.

"Warning, Emergency decompression imminent, sections Yankee-Twelve through Zulu-Thirteen. All personnel evacuate immediately."

"Oh, what now?" Zara shouted, as if the computer voice could hear her. "What section is this?"

"Zulu-Eleven."

"So, are we pretty much flatlined?"

The two sprinted down the bay, only to find the crawl tubes were still blocked by emergency doors.

"Back in the escape pod," Dayton said.

"Uh, no." Zara shook her head. "We just left that thing."

Dayton leaned against the bulkhead as the deck swayed. "We don't really have a lot of choices right now. An explosive decompression pretty much makes up my mind. We'll need to jettison."

"You remember how to do that?"

More sparks cascaded down from overhead. Wall panels exploded.

"Back to the pod."

Deck plates shifted uncontrollably. They half ran, half jumped their way through the pitching deck plates, Crab rows, and loose cargo containers. It was more of an obstacle course, but Dayton had run his share of those in training. This wasn't too different.

Once inside, Dayton reclosed the hatch.

Several pieces of *Venture's* hull snapped off and fell prey to Earth's gravity, plunging down toward the planet. As they disappeared into the blue-white and gold color of the planet, they hit the atmosphere and lit brilliant, fiery trails.

Dayton jumped to the nearest couch and strapped himself in. He opened the armrest panel and punched in the prep codes. The computer began ticking down the pre-flight checks. Dayton felt as if things were moving in slow motion. The computer was just running its programs, unaware of the unfurling chaos around it.

"Well, look at the bright side," Zara cracked through gritted teeth. "You're gonna end up piloting something after all."

When the panel status read "READY," Dayton looked at Zara. She had already strapped herself in. Dayton took a deep breath, closed his eyes, and hit the launch button.

Dayton was pinned against his seat as the pod blasted from *Venture*. He gripped his handrests. The pod spun. Through the porthole, he thought he saw more pods leaving the ship. All hands were bugging out.

What of his father? What of Turco, his pilot mentor? Where were they?

Zara, for once, was quiet. Dayton had only seen that happen one other time, back when a burst propulsor had left them stranded in deep space. This was worse.

Moments later, the ride started to get bumpy, and it sent all the survival gear they'd scattered around the pod flying in different directions. Dayton had to duck a medical kit that came hurling his way. Zara wasn't so lucky with a bundle of nylon rope. They must have hit the outer atmosphere. Dayton could feel the pod slowing down.

The gear tumbled like garments in an ancient clothes-drying machine. Dayton himself was struck by a water purifier. A portable heater backflipped into Zara's lap. "Owwww." She threw it off. Dayton punched up the telemetry data on his chair's armrest. "We've fallen about twenty kilometers since hitting the atmosphere."

"Weren't the chutes supposed to deploy?"

"I don't know."

Dayton's armrest panel was blinking with a red wrench icon. He pressed it, and the bad news displayed—the parachute mortars were jammed.

"We need to get out of this thing," Dayton said.

Zara hit the quick release on her straps and made her way across the pod to the suits. The centrifugal force slammed her into the bulkhead. Her tough frame struggled as she crawled to the suit rack.

Zara tossed a suit, reentry pack, and helmet to Dayton in

rapid-fire succession. He managed to catch them in the chaos. He undid the straps but stayed on the couch. Dayton stepped one leg into the suit, then turned over on the couch, trying to get the other leg in. He lost his balance and fell out. This was an improvement, so Dayton twisted and tugged at the space suit until, at last, he had it on.

He looked to see if Zara was ready. Her suit hung a bit large on her, but it would do. She gave a thumbs up.

Hearing only his own labored breathing inside his helmet, he struggled to his feet and made it to the control panel on the bulkhead.

Dayton blew the hatch.

Before his next blink could complete, he was sucked out of the pod like a grav ball through an acceleration tube. He looked around, turning his helmet in every direction. He was falling, tumbling. He couldn't see Zara anywhere, though it was such a shaky blur she could have been two feet or two kilometers from him.

Was his own reentry kit going to work? The mortars in the pod had failed to fire, and they had been sitting unused probably for as many years as the thing on his back. Where was the pull chord?

He heard a whistle. No, a beep. It was his own helmet beeping, first in a slow, barely discernible tone, then in a rapid series of beeps. Another mechanical voice came from the helmet's internal speakers.

Automatic activation device deployed.

The chute unfurled above him like a stack of clothing tossed into the air, then ballooned into a spectacular elliptical ram air chute. "Zara!" he yelled, seeing contrails in every direction. He dreaded the thought that Zara might be plunging out of control only to crash into the Earth.

He was many kilometers up. Below him, there was an ocean. He'd seen videos and still images of the various water bodies, but from here, it looked so humongous and blue. The area of the ocean nearer to shore had a distinctive, yellowish tint to it. That wasn't in any of the database files about Earth's oceans.

From horizon to horizon, Dayton could make out thick contrails of other pods and debris cascading toward the surface. Some seemed to have parachutes deployed now. Others didn't. He hoped she was okay.

Though dwarfed by the massive blue of the ocean, there was an intricate city hugging the shoreline. The city sprawled far bigger and more elaborate than any city he'd seen in the colonies. He saw a massive roadway network, with ground cars and trucks traveling along them like ore along a dozen conveyor belts, headed in every direction. What looked like a large starport was near the city's edge.

He was several thousand meters up now, and Dayton seemed to be headed for a towering structure at the center of many similar buildings. Closer and closer, it came until a gust of wind carried him for what seemed kilometers. He passed by a number of other buildings, more of those artery-like roadways, and rows and rows of small, rectangular dwellings. The further he went, the more people he saw—thousands of them—standing out in the side streets, all looking up and pointing.

FOUR

Dayton zoomed at a sharp angle and narrowly missed the stainless-steel point atop another tall structure. The simple controls on his chute let him negotiate around the next glass-and-steel building. He tugged up, gaining some altitude. There was a flurry of vehicles below, on the streets. Thousands of cars were stopped on the roads and elevated highways, with spectators clamoring out of them and gawking skyward. He didn't relish the thought of trying to land in that mess.

A dirt-and-grass hill rose from the city sprawl. There were some communications arrays on it, but other than that, it looked deserted enough. If he could stay away from those radar dishes, he might land safely on that elevated ground. Dayton tugged hard to his left and held on tight as the elliptical chute changed direction.

Too late, he was coming down too fast to make a safe landing. CLUMP! He hit, the bottoms of his boots grinding into the dirt and plowing two rows as he was dragged along. The canopy locked into some heavy crosswinds and pulled him off the hill. WHOOSH! His boots left the ground again as he shot off the other side of the hilltop.

"Grrr," Dayton pulled down on the steering toggles, hoping in vain that his canopy would head down those last few, and seemingly unobtainable, meters. It didn't work. Turbulence bumped him along, with the spectators now clearly visible below.

A rush of air pushed the canopy upward and Dayton along with it. Again, he ascended into the sky, this time just missing an unmanned advertising blimp. He almost crashed into the air balloon—the side sported some dancing, animated digital screen proclaiming the benefits of foundationless makeup.

He pulled the toggles right and left as the blimp plodded along beneath him, oblivious to the near collision. Then, as if on cue, the blimp went into a dive, its propulsor jets filling Dayton's canopy and shooting him skyward.

"Ahhhhhhh!!!" Sound escaped his lungs as Dayton pulled hard on the toggles, only to find he overcompensated and began spiraling down.

He tumbled toward a sprawling structure with several glass domes dotting its roof. That roof came up fast, with his feet leading the way. He grabbed hold of the chute's controls and made one last attempt to steady his tumbling descent.

No go.

His heart raced, his blood pumping through his veins so fast his head throbbed. He crashed headfirst into one of the glass domes. He was no longer a plaything for the winds, but Dayton had no time to celebrate. He plunged and somersaulted into the building.

He was in a sprawling shopping structure, about four stories up, with open levels on all sides of him, headed for the ground floor. Dayton thrashed about as the fall seemed to take on a slow-motion effect. His lungs ached as he realized he hadn't taken a breath in some time. He exhaled and drew in the stale, dry air of the suit's life support system.

Crash! His feet smashed through a surprisingly flimsy skylight, and yank! He bounced to an abrupt halt. He dangled in mid-air, hanging by the chute cords.

Maybe it was seconds, minutes, or hours later, but after a blank spot, Dayton perked up and looked around. Below him was a crowd standing at the edges of the pile of broken glass. Shouts of "Are you okay?" reached him. Most of them held their wrists up, getting images and videos of the event on their personal comm links.

"Help me," Dayton called back. Looking up, he saw his chute was stuck, caught in the twisted metal frames at the base of the roof dome. Activating his wrist-mounted rangefinder, Dayton pointed it down to see just how far off the ground he was. The readout came back at 18.288 meters.

For a moment, he simply stared at the people. They looked much rougher than he was used to seeing. Perhaps the result of living on the surface of the planet with solar radiation and the elements beating down on them. Despite this, their clothing looked incredibly thin and was a blend of many colors. The clothes didn't appear to completely cover them either, which, in Dayton's mind, defeated the purpose of clothing.

They didn't know exactly what to do either. Dayton certainly didn't. A few uniformed individuals, either security or law enforcement—he wasn't sure which because at most colonies, there wasn't much of a difference—held the crowd back.

A figure shot from the crowd, waving at him. It was a girl, perhaps no older than Dayton. She was a waifish figure, with smooth white skin and jet-black hair that cascaded down past her shoulders in curly waves. Her eyes looked pleadingly up at Dayton.

He didn't know how long he stared at her, but he couldn't look away. He locked eyes with her, though she probably couldn't see that through his visor. To her, he was some weird guy in a spacesuit dangling from a failing harness. But to Dayton, well, his mind rushed through possibilities.

The girl pulled up her comm wrist and began talking into it. She showed authority, directing some people and motioning others back. Dayton didn't know if this girl held any special rank out here. She wore a flowery print blouse under a dark red blazer, with light blue jeans and black boots. She certainly wasn't wearing a uniform. But she acted like it.

She came to stand directly below Dayton and shouted at him. He held up his index finger, hoping she would recognize that as the sign for "wait a minute." She seemed to, and Dayton slid the quick-connect ring on his helmet. He felt a rush of cool air as it detached from the suit.

He lost his grip on the helmet, and it fell to the tiled floor with a resounding crash. The girl ducked out of the way in time, and the helmet bounced away and skidded into a central fountain.

"S-So-Sorry," Dayton called down. "Did I hit you? I mean, I didn't want to — try to."

"No," she said. "Clean miss. Are you okay? What is going on up there? You fell out of the sky!"

"Well," Dayton thought about it for a few seconds. "I think I'm okay. I'm not bleeding or anything."

"You crashed hard. Hold on. I called nine-one-one. Someone should be here soon to get you out of this mess."

"Nine-one-one?" Dayton repeated. "What is that?"

Dayton checked the instrument cluster on his right arm. The air pressure around him was higher than he was used to aboard *Venture*. His lungs didn't have to work as hard, and he was getting light-headed because of it.

He felt the straps slacken, and he fell a couple of dozen centimeters. "Uhh," Dayton said. His voice sounded a little more terrified than he wanted to let on. "I don't think this roof is going to hold."

"Hold on," the girl said again. "My name is Allyson. The fire department crews will be here in a minute or two. The fire department, or maybe a unit from the spaceport."

"Fire department?" Dayton looked around from his position. "You mean the guys with the big red trucks and mobile ladders?"

"Those are the ones," Allyson said. "Be just like getting a cat out of a tree. You'll see."

Well, they had ladders. That would certainly come in handy right about now.

There were numerous glass domes atop the ceiling, affording Dayton a glimpse of the sky. It was blue, dotted with white clouds that looked just as impressive as the ones he'd seen in videos. It was also filled with white vertical trails.

Dayton could see that his escape pod hadn't been the only one. In fact, from the way the ship had emerged from the tunnel, there possibly were hundreds of pieces that had broken off and fallen to Earth. He dropped down another centimeter or two, but it was enough to increase his already fast heartbeat, which he felt powerfully in his head, just behind his eyes. That painful air pressure.

People poured out of the storefronts to look. They stood there with their necks craned to the sky, their wrist comms taking videos. It was a disaster for Dayton, but to these people, it must have seemed like a giant show in the skies above their city. To everyone but Allyson, that was.

Dayton said, "I don't know the size of your fire department, but there are pieces of *Venture* coming down all over the place. They might be a little busy right now. This chute isn't going to hold me much longer. Help?"

As if on cue, one of the cords snapped with a loud crack, and Dayton's right side dropped below his left. The crowd, which had now reached hundreds, let out a collective gasp.

He fumbled with the buttons on his harness. His training took over. "I'll need to hit the release and deploy the airbags in the re-entry kit."

Allyson retrieved the helmet and looked up at Dayton. "Even if I could get this up to you, the release ring has been bent," she said. "It won't re-attach." She regarded Dayton's astonished face. "My dad's a space engineer," she said by way of explanation. "He tells a lot to me. Can you swing up to the third-level railing? We could get in position and catch you."

"I don't know if the chute straps will support that kind of maneuver." He took a deep breath. "I can drop without the helmet."

"You can't," Allyson said. "Those airbags ... Isn't that what those are? You'll suffocate."

"Assuming a high-altitude reentry," Dayton called down. "I can hold my breath for the few seconds it'll take for this drop. Then, I'll bounce along for a few more seconds. Once I come to rest, the bags will deflate. Just be ready to pry me loose."

Okay, Dayton thought, *this is going to be difficult.* Hit the release on his harness, then activate the airbags. And he would have perhaps two seconds to do that.

"Ready?" Allyson asked, pulling in several volunteers to help her out.

"No," Dayton replied. He ventilated, loading his lungs with as much oxygen as he could.

Time slowed to a standstill. He steadied himself, swaying slightly. People down below had spread out in a wide circle. Allyson backed up, never taking her eyes off him.

Click.

Dayton plummeted. He pulled the airbag release. In a flash, he was surrounded by white Mylar, then felt a cushioned blow as he landed. He had no control whatsoever now and couldn't even breathe as he bounced along end-over-end like he was caught in some giant, opaque rubber ball.

Dayton bounced once under his feet, then again under his head. Occasionally, he felt some resistance to the bags, as if they crashed against or through something. Then he slammed up against something solid with a resounding thud. What it was, he had no idea. But he had definitely stopped.

Instinctively, he tried to breathe, but his mouth only sucked in airbag material. He tried to force it out, only to find his nose filled with Mylar. Reaching, he tried to pull the suffocating material out, but his arms were constricted by the deflating balloons and couldn't reach his mouth. He flayed about, only to feel more trapped with each movement.

He knew he should hold his breath, but he tried to force the membrane out to let some air in. Only his starving lungs never got the air so desperately needed. He only got more airbag material. Was this how it ended? Shooting billions of miles through the vacuum of space just to die of suffocation in an Earth shopping district? His mind shot through all the possibilities he might not live to see. Becoming a Recon pilot. Eventually getting his own command. What had happened to Zara, his father, and the rest? Would they survive?

A team of hands was tugging on his Mylar tomb. His head grew faint, but at last, he felt a tug on the infernal piece of airbag that was stuck to his face. It came off with a loud pop, and suddenly, Dayton could gulp down precious air.

Dayton was up against the tumbled remains of a store display in a small sea of deflated airbags. Hundreds of identical yellow boxes labeled "*Grav Caddy v 5.0.*" The smashed store window and scattered merchandise told Dayton he must have crashed through the glass on his way in. A number of rectangular, floating signs flashed a colorful *"As Seen on the Net! Back to School Sale!"*

Spectators crowded in front of the store entrance and the broken window. They burst into applause and cheers when they saw Dayton was free.

"Who are you?" a man in an emergency rescue vest asked. "Are you doing okay?"

"I'm Dayton Murdock, by the way, of the Fourth Surveyor Wing, Alpha Group."

Over the man's shoulder, Dayton could see Allyson peering at him. Her eyes were large and green. She waved. He tried to smile back.

"What happened?" the man asked, checking Dayton's suit, untangling straps and buckles.

"The ship was falling apart. Zara and I took an escape capsule."

"Who's Zara?" Allyson interrupted and asked. "What ship?"

"*Venture,*" Dayton responded. "I need to find out about my dad and every—"

"Just take it easy, son."

Everyone and everything he knew in his life had been aboard that ship. Now, it seemed it was literally falling apart, and there was nothing he could do about it. He could feel a team of hands pulling and tugging his legs free. The first thing he noticed was the air. It was warmer than he was used to and carried all kinds of smells. On *Venture,* the air was conditioned and recycled. It had a metallic tinge to it, a condition some of the older crewmembers likened to the air on a passenger jet.

The remaining security pushed the crowd back, making a path. Dayton was carried to a bench in the central courtyard. "Something must have really gone wrong up there," a voice said. "We've got reports coming in from all over about pods and junk falling from the sky."

This wasn't exactly comforting news to Dayton, and his mind flashed back to his dad, Zara, and Turco. "Are any landing close by?"

The man focused on the eyepiece on his comm unit. "Yeah, a few crashed in the desert. Most are splashing down in the ocean right offshore here by the city."

"What city is this?"

"Los Angeles, California."

Dayton collapsed on the bench. He had heard the oxygen content on Earth was thicker and that the gravity was somewhat lighter. Not that it made any difference to him now. For him, the gravity worked just fine here.

Dayton's head was swimming, but he sat up and undid the ring locks on his suit. The warm air settled on his face, and the suit was starting to heat up. The man must have read his mind, because he helped Dayton remove the mid-section.

"I'll be." the man's eyes went wide with surprise as he noticed Dayton's squadron patch, a multicolor affair that showcased his Survey Team. It had a modded-out surveyor with flames down the side and shark's teeth exaggerated in the nose. "You really are a surveyor pilot. That's the only way to earn a patch like that. Incredible. You must be, what, eighteen?"

"Sixteen," Dayton replied. "And yes, I got this patch with my Class Two rating."

"Absolutely amazing," William said. "You know, the neighbor's kid just got his driver's license."

"For what?"

"To drive an automobile."

That seemed a little late in life to be getting a license to operate much of anything, Dayton thought. Maybe the neighbor's kid didn't do well on the qualifying tests. But to ask about it would be rude, so Dayton kept it to himself. Ratings were always an immense source of pride, or humiliation, on *Venture*, depending on how you did.

"Who are you?" Dayton asked.

"William," the man answered. "That was my daughter, Allyson, who radioed for help."

"Here's your helmet," a young voice said. Dayton looked to see two boys, perhaps no older than nine or so, present Dayton with his suit helmet.

"Thank you," Dayton said. Based on appearances, the boys were probably William's sons.

Dayton felt a surge of energy and climbed to his feet. Despite his shaky balance, he could remove the space suit leggings. He felt more comfortable now that he was completely out of the thing. He tossed the gloves in the helmet, then folded the various suit parts into a bulky pile.

"I guess that's everything, minus the chute," Dayton said. He looked at the roof he'd fallen through. The chute was hanging like a set of broken tow cables from the ceiling. That fire department was going to have one hell of a time removing it, Dayton thought. "So, what do I do now? If the emergency services firemen are busy, I will need to report to the Agency on my own."

"Then that's where we need to go," William said. "My grav van is just over in the parking lot. We'll take you there."

William led Dayton out of the mall and into a giant parking structure. After piling Dayton's suit in the back of his grav van, William, Dayton, and the two boys headed out.

"What about Allyson?" Dayton spat out as soon as he thought it.

"Allyson visuatexted me," William pointed to his left eye.

"I told her we're taking you to the spaceport. She had to go to work. She does promotions mostly right here at the mall."

Despite the fall from orbit. Despite his friends being in danger. Despite it all, one thought raged through Dayton's head.

Bummer.

FIVE

"Where's my dad? Where's Zara?" He'd been taken to a medical center, and it seemed like the people examining him were deaf. In a sterile room better described as a tank, Dayton was sitting in a giant vial of clear water. Technicians scanned him and went over readouts.

Before that, he'd sat on an examination table as medtechs probed him and drained his blood into sample tubes. He could hear and see other *Venture* crewmen being brought into the facility. Zara or his dad could be in the place right now, but he couldn't go to them. He was trapped. How long had it been? He couldn't really tell. They had taken his chronometer to download the mission data.

The water was room temp but gave him a wonderful sensation. He could touch the bottom of the tank with his feet, so there was no fear of drowning. He was naked, and that was the strangest sensation of all. Dayton couldn't recall any time in his life he was without the minimal shipboard clothing. He reminded himself he wasn't in space and that this was a normal thing for the people of Earth. Still, it felt so strange.

He looked at his hands and saw they were getting wrinkled. Did excessive exposure to water cause your skin to deform? Not for the first time, his heart sped.

"Excuse me," Dayton shouted through a hoarse throat. "I don't know what's happening, but I don't think it's a good idea to leave me in here. Are you done?"

"Yeah, we're done here," a voice came over a speaker mounted directly over the tank. "You can get out now. Please put on the garments on the table to your left.

Dayton did that. The garb he was given was light, made of some kind of plastic, and without any undergarments.

The guard, who was probably only two or three years older than Dayton, shrugged and led him down the hall to the converted cafeteria. A hand-written sign that read "STAGING AREA" hung over it. Inside, Dayton found himself among his fellow *Venture* crewmen. Some were lying on makeshift cots, being tended to by medical teams. Others were huddled in blankets, nervously talking to themselves and each other as they sipped liquid from bottles and cups. They wore the same plastic examination gowns.

"Dayton," a familiar voice called to him. Turning around, he could see his old friend Turco waving to him, along with several others from the surveyor wing.

"I see you got dressed for the party," Turco chuckled, tweaking his own plastic exam gown.

"Turco. Oh, thank God." Dayton crossed his arms in front of his face in the traditional off-world greeting and got a bear hug from each man in turn. "You guys are safe. Is my father okay? Has anyone seen Zara?"

"You mean she wasn't with you?" Turco's eyes went wide. "I thought you guys were in the forward Crab bay."

"We were. We jettisoned in the escape pod and got separated when the thing's chute mortars didn't fire."

"Zara's a survivor," Turco said. The other pilots nodded in agreement. "She'll make it. Don't worry. Your father was in the central habitat module when this whole mess started. He probably rode the whole thing out in style. You'll see."

"How did you all get here?" Dayton asked, changing the subject. "What in wolf's moons happened up there?"

Turco's mouth pulled down at the corners. "You know we can't talk about that right now. Just know it wasn't a Survey issue."

"Sir," the young guard said behind Dayton. "Please come with me."

"What?" Dayton looked at the stone-jawed guard.

The guard didn't flinch. "You need to be escorted to the minor holding area."

"Leave the kid alone." Turco rushed to the front, squaring off with the guard. "He doesn't belong in any juvenile detention facility. He belongs here, with us."

"I have my orders, sir." The guard looked past Turco and straight at Dayton. "We are to take all minors to the minor holding area."

"That is messed up," Turco said. "This young man here is every inch the pilot we are. In a matter of hours, he'll be a Recon pilot. You know what that means? You have no right to take him away from his own kind."

"I have my orders, sir," the guard repeated. "Mister Murdoch, if you'll follow me?"

"Go away." Dayton crossed his arms and leaned against the bench. He tried to look tough, but he knew that in his examination gown, that was a tall order. "These are my brothers. This is where I'm staying."

"I can always call in more guards," the grim-featured guard said. "Or you can come peacefully with me."

"Oh, it's on." Turco's bright eyes shot lasers into the guard. The other survey pilots struggled up and braced themselves. They weren't in the best shape to fight, especially since most of them were in gowns just like the one Dayton wore.

Dayton knew that the pilots looked out for each other. "You go after one of us, you go after all of us. We are the Alpha Group." The other pilots grunted in support.

The guard pressed his comm device at his hip, and six more guards filed into the room, each holding a stun club. Turco and the others stood across from them, weak and unkempt but willing to fight.

It didn't take long for Dayton to figure out what would happen to his fellow pilots if it came to a fight. The guards were fit and rested, with stun clubs no less. Dayton knew there was more than one way to watch the backs of his fellow pilots.

"No." Dayton held up his hand. "Let's not make any new enemies. It's not worth it. I'll go."

Turco backed away from the guard slowly, his fierce eyes never leaving his grim, emotionless face. Dayton motioned for the guard to leave first, which he did, backing away as if expecting to be jumped.

The guard handed Dayton a clear plastic bag containing his clothing.

He led Dayton down the hall, stopping at a double door. One door was slightly ajar, while the other sported a hand-written sign that read "MINOR HOLDING AREA" with an arrow that pointed to the open door.

"Please go in, *sir*." The guard held the door and motioned for Dayton to enter.

Dayton walked in to find a hastily converted multipurpose room containing several couches, several folding metallic chairs, and a giant table strewn with backpacks and utility belts. The room was crowded with young *Venture* crewmen, most of whom Dayton recognized.

Several of the kids greeted him, flocking like steel slivers to a magnet.

"Hey, glad you guys are okay." Dayton shook hands with several of the older children and hugged the rest. "Does anyone know what happened to *Venture*? Has anyone seen Zara?"

"You're the first ranking officer we've seen," one of the boys said. He was a sixteen-year-old named Trenton Overshaw, a heavy-worlder possessed of a squat, muscular form. *Venture* had picked him up several years ago from the high-G world of Aponos Four. "Most of us were working in the access corridors when it happened. The ship was buckling like crazy when we re-entered normal space. We hit the escape pods."

"Have you met anyone for debriefing or anything like that?" Dayton asked.

"None of us, I'm pretty sure," Trenton said.

Using the gown to hide his privates, Dayton struggled on his flight suit and shirt. The jacket probably wasn't necessary, but he needed to look the part. He discarded the gown with extreme prejudice.

"All right," Dayton continued. "Trenton, you're the second-most senior guy here. Let's get everyone lined up and accounted for."

Trenton bolted to round up the rest of the kids just as the door swung open and five men entered the room. The one Dayton guessed was in charge was a tall man in a dark suit and tie, with graying temples and a bald pate. His eyes locked onto Dayton. A pair of assistants and two security guards followed him.

The man extended his hand. Dayton grabbed it but found it lacking as a handshake. "I'm Doctor Weiss. I was sent here to help you and the other *Venture* children through this trying time. Taking the initiative, I see?" He eyed the kids lined up. "A word in my office. That okay?" The doctor motioned to follow.

Dayton shrugged. He nodded to Trenton on the way out.

Down the hall, Weiss opened the door. "My office," he said, leading Dayton in.

Weird. There was no other way to call it. The office walls were pastel yellow with holowindows showing images of a forest glade. Chipmunks, squirrels, and other small furry animals darted across bright green grass. The office had a brightly-colored table and chairs sized for a three-year-old. Though he'd never seen them before, Dayton recognized two bean bag chairs in the corner, next to what was obviously Doctor Weiss' desk. Toys and board games were everywhere.

"This is an office?" Dayton asked as he took it all in.

"I work from here, yes," the Doctor said. "Please sit down." He motioned to the bean bag chairs. Dayton hesitated but sat. He released his weight and sunk into the bag as an air bubble seemed to form around his hindquarters. The bag hissed as it settled into Dayton's weight. The whole experience left him disoriented, and Dayton felt as though he couldn't stand up again without falling over.

"Comfy?" Doctor Weiss asked.

"Yeah," Dayton said, though he was disoriented as he spoke.

"I admire you," Doctor Weiss said. "In fact, the men in Acquisitions at first thought you were a member of *Venture's* crew."

"Well, I am a member of the crew," Dayton said.

"In times of emergency, we sometimes imagine things," Doctor Weiss said.

"Huh?" Dayton said. "We were in the forward Crab bay when we went to Emergency Jump Protocol Niner-Alpha. We jettisoned when the ship started falling apart."

"And what were you doing in the forward bay? Were you playing in there? I know we all seek a private place, away from others, when we get scared."

What was Weiss getting at? "Playing? The Bay Master sent me there to fix Crabs."

"You know," Doctor Weiss clapped his hands in front of him. "I think that being scared of something like your ship falling apart makes you assume to be someone you're not. Where did you get the jacket? Did you find it? Does it belong to someone else?"

"Okay, you know what," Dayton struggled to sit up, an effort that proved futile, "I don't know your angle here, but I earned this jacket. If you check Duty Roster 654A-E, you'll find—"

"Actually, we're still sorting the file work," Doctor Weiss said.

His tone was disturbing and more than a little condescending.

Weiss continued, "We could probably check things out faster if you let me have the jacket. Just for now."

"That's not happening," Dayton said. He struggled in the bean bag chair but found he had no leverage. "Get me out of this thing. Look, let's go back to the big room. Turco can vouch for me—"

Doctor Weiss pressed a button under his desk. Silently,

Dayton felt a sharp prick on his underside from deep within the bean bag chair.

It was the last he remembered as everything went black.

45

SIX

Dayton awoke on a metal bunk, seeing only blurry images around him. One image was familiar—colors were rotating, fading from ice blue to bright red, to neon green, then back again. He concentrated on it and realized it was Zara's hair, the stripe in her bangs. Gradually, her face came into focus.

"Zara?" Dayton rubbed his eyes. They appeared to be in some kind of locked cell similar to the brig on *Venture*. There wasn't much there: just two beds, a stainless-steel sink, a toilet, and a chair. Zara's right arm was in a cast, a tube of gray plastic that covered her forearm.

"You're injured?" Dayton struggled to say.

"Oh, this," Zara hefted the cast in front of her. "I tumbled down, then the auto-chute deployed, and next thing I was floating in a ton of water. Got a little banged up on the way down."

"Is your arm broken?"

"No."

"Does it hurt?"

"Naw."

"I saw a lot of water," Dayton said. "What do they call it? An ocean? Lake? Sea? Something like that."

"What they don't tell you is that it's deep," Zara said. "I was flailing around there, then this water jet thingy zipped by and scooped me up. They took me here."

"Thank God you're okay. What are we doing here?"

"This is where they put the bad kids," Zara said. She glanced out of the small square of a window in the top center of the door. "Apparently, we're just children here and not allowed to wear our uniforms," Zara continued. Dayton felt cold and realized his jacket was gone. Zara was without her flight jacket as well.

"Is that what it was all about?" Dayton propped himself up on the bed. "I think I've been drugged or something."

"Or something, yeah," Zara laughed. "Welcome to Earth." She said it so loudly that it echoed down the hall outside. She plopped herself on the narrow bed and turned away from Dayton. "I hope you know this is the way they treat us. Get used to that. And I checked the chronometers. We're still sixteen, which means we made that tunnel from the Outer Rim to Earth in five days."

Dayton rubbed the back of his head, only to find his hair sweaty and matted. "I saw Trenton. What about our parents?"

"I ask and ask. They say they're okay and they'll be here soon."

Dayton let out a big exhalation of relief. When he opened his mouth to ask Zara more, she was asleep. There was no way he wanted to be part of this planet. Treated like a kid? No. This wouldn't do. Once they realized his service record, they'd restore him to duty.

Once he got new training, he could sail through the remaining time to get to Recon. Just fourteen hours. That was it. Then he could wrangle a new assignment, someplace far from this place and its judgmental inhabitants.

Dayton rolled over and faced the duracrete wall. He'd just plummeted to Earth, nearly died in a shopping mall, and been stripped and examined, wrestled, and then drugged, and to top it all off, he wasn't twenty.

Things were not off to a good start.

***

Time for another meal. Dayton heard the electronic click of the lock, and the thick metal door swung inward.

And there stood his father.

"Dad?" Dayton leaped to his feet as Zara stirred.

For his part, his father managed a weak smile, but it was all the invitation Dayton needed. He was across the cell and pulling his dad in for a bear hug as soon as the thought crossed his mind. "Is it you?" Dayton said, not entirely believing his senses. "You're okay? You're good?"

His hug was returned in equal measure. "Thank God you're okay," his father said and nudged Dayton to forearm's length. He extended a hand to Zara, who clasped it.

Dayton had always relied on his father. Whenever things didn't make sense—and they often didn't—Dad would be able to explain it in a way he understood. In a lot of ways, Dad was his user manual on life. And right now, he needed that manual.

"I have been running every database update on the planet looking for records of you. Both of you! I've been in this facility all day."

"What happened up there?" Dayton asked. "The whole ship was falling apart."

"It was the pressure seals," Dad said. "They were simply too weak after two decades of exposure. We came out of grade seven or better. We were scheduled to pick some up on our run through System 08-157. But our emergency entry into the tunnel skipped us right past that."

"But why did we enter the tunnel?" Zara asked.

"Micrometeors," Dad answered. "They were completely radiated. We think all that radiation gave us a boost, which is how we covered so much distance so fast."

Dayton figured his dad probably knew very well what had happened to the ship, but was under a security order not to talk about it. Radioactive micrometeors? The effect of radiation on faster-than-light travel through the quantum tunnel still wasn't fully understood. It was possible but didn't seem very likely.

"Anyway, it happened. I made it to the five-thousand-habitat module with Toki and his family," his dad added quickly, moving the conversation on. "We rode it out."

"See?" Zara said, trying to lighten the mood. "I told you

your dad was going to be okay."

"But, Dad," Dayton said after catching his breath. "Did anyone die?"

"No one died," Dayton's father said in a reassuring voice. "*Venture*'s still largely intact. Most of what fell to Earth was escape pods and outer sensor arrays and stabilizers. No reports of fatalities. Seems the safety equipment did its work today."

"And my mom and dad?" Zara's voice rose as she spoke. "They were doing some mapping in a shuttle."

"The shuttle came through the quantum tunnel with *Venture*. It got caught in the bubble. Your parents are safe; they'll be here soon enough for you."

Zara relaxed for the first time since Dayton could recall.

"I didn't know what to think," Dayton said as he held his emotions back. He was so panicked. So anxious. So not in control.

"Come on." Dad motioned. "Let's go."

Dayton got three feet into the stark hallway when he looked around. "Dad? How come there are no guards following you around?"

"Because I'm an adult."

"What does that have to do with anything?"

"There's a great deal I need to explain to you. For now, let's just get the heck out of here."

"Anyplace is better than here," Dayton said.

The three of them plodded down the hall.

Before long, they were met by two men in black suits with ID cards hung prominently from their breast pockets. *What now*, Dayton thought.

"Agent McCourt," one of the men, a dark-complexioned fellow with close-cropped black hair, stood and shook Dayton's hand. He gestured to his partner. "This is Agent Takenaka."

"And where is this young man's mother to also sign the release form before you go?" the other man said.

Zara put a hand over her mouth. There was an awkward pause.

"Deceased," said Dad quietly.

McCourt and his partner looked uneasy.

Dayton filled in the space. "Mom died when I was two. We can talk about it. It's okay." McCourt made a note on his datapad as Dayton moved closer to the men.

"Do you guys have the retraining schedules?"

"Well, yes," Agent McCourt said. "Right here. I don't know why you would want to look at that."

"Well, can I see it?" Dayton said. "Of course I want to look at it."

"Okay." Agent McCourt handed over the data tablet.

Dayton flipped through the spiraling lists until he came to his surveyor wing. They were to begin flight retraining in two weeks at the Agency Orbital Facility 39. All the names seemed to be there, along with the correct flight codes, registrations, and call numbers. He went down the alphabetic list.

"Where's my name?" He hit refresh. Still, his name did not appear.

The agents looked at each other, then quizzically at Dayton's father.

"There have been some reorganizations made," Dad said. "I'll explain it to you later."

"Okay," Dayton said. "Reorg is fine. But my name should still be on this list."

"Let me see that." Zara snatched the tablet and swiped through it. "Hey, what gives? I'm not even in here."

The agents unceremoniously took the tablet from Zara and abruptly changed the subject.

"First things first," Agent McCourt said. "How about a visit to your new quarters?"

The other agent pulled out a jingling chain. "And a car. It's right outside in the lot. Look for this license plate," he said, indicating a number on the fob.

Dad took it. "Let's go, Zara," he said. "You can come home with us until your parents arrive."

"We can't allow that," Agent McCourt said rather loudly.

Dad's mouth fell open and then shut firmly. "And why not?"

"I'm sorry, sir," McCourt said. "She can't leave with an arm injury. I can only release her to her own parents."

"What?" Dayton cried. "How long—"

"Her parents were aboard a mapping shuttle," Agent McCourt continued. "It got caught up in the same quantum tunnel as the *Venture*. They were with you the whole ride. Unfortunately, they came down in Siberia. They'll be back here in another twenty-four hours."

Zara's eyes went misty. Dad enveloped her in a hug, and Dayton threw his arms around both of them. "See? Good news. They rode out the tunnel with us the whole time. Everything's going to be fine."

Even though she wasn't his child, Dad still looked out for her. The man had a very paternal way about him for everyone, it seemed. Not just for Dayton. It made Dad kind of a sage for the younger crew. A person they could all turn to. Dayton was proud of that.

Zara wriggled out of their embrace. "I'll be okay. Mom and Dad will be here soon." She looked sad but was refusing to cry.

Dayton could tell she was being her bravest.

Agent McCourt shut his tablet with a dying whirr. "Dayton, you and your father are due at the school registry. After that, you can go to your new home."

Dayton put his hand on Zara's shoulder. "Bye. See you soon, okay?"

He and Dad gave her another hug before walking for the exit. At the big doors, Dayton turned around to wave. Zara looked so small in her hospital gown between the two huge agents. She gave a little wave just before the doors shut with a clang.

*****

Outside, the air was moving around in a way that Dayton had never experienced before. Unlike the partially terraformed planets he'd been to, this air moved gently. His father took great lungsful and said, "Now this ... this is fresh air."

On *Venture*, there had been processed and recirculated air hissing through vents. Dayton mimicked his dad and drew the air in, smelling it as it came past his nostrils. The air was sweet, laced with sunshine and what he figured were subtle smells of grass, plants, and warm asphalt. Unlike *Venture*'s air, it wasn't tinged with that metallic odor.

It smelled clean and fresh and tinged with unfamiliar scents. He kept pulling in great breaths of it as Dad led him down rows and rows of parked vehicles with their hoods and bumpers gleaming in the sunshine. Every so often, little birds would swoop down from where they were gathered on tall light standards. They chirped, as though they were curious. It was all new and different, and yet Dad seemed as though it were nothing special—nothing he hadn't seen before. Because he *had* seen it before. Unlike Dayton, he had been born here.

"There," Dad said. "That's our car."

Dayton gawked. He'd seen cargo pods with thicker metal.

"Don't look at it like that," Dad said. "It's economical."

It was red. It was small. It had wheels made for a hanger tool cart. The name badge across the front of the hood said "TATA."

"C'mon," Dad said. "Let's go."

"In that? Seriously?" Dayton said. He stood his ground, not venturing closer.

Dad opened the vibrating door with a telltale squeak.

"Look," Dad said. "You need to get used to things. Everything around here is not built to space specs."

Dad squeezed in, and the tiny motor in the imported Indian Tata turned over with a pathetic grind and shook to life. Dayton gingerly followed and closed the door, which locked with a feeble click.

The body was so flimsy Dayton felt as if he would be crushed if another car, or worse, a heavy-duty truck, slammed into them. He could have sworn the pathetic vehicle flexed whenever an exceptionally strong wind kicked up.

A small navigation screen showed where they were going, and Dayton passed the time by reading the digital billboards and ad blimps that floated over the roads.

It was night by the time they arrived at the habitation dwelling. Dayton saw it had a large patch of green in front and a couple of light poles. He didn't see much else. By now, his head was fogged. The exhaustion of the past cycle caught up with him in an enveloping, overpowering wave, and it proved more than he could take.

Sure, he'd pulled serious time in the pilot's chair. But there was something about this situation. The freefall from orbit, the processing, the near-fight experience. And most of all, the lack of control over any of this.

They entered the dwelling. The place came furnished with basic chairs, tables, and other items, but all Dayton wanted was a sleep capsule.

"Down the hall and to the right," Dad said, as usual, picking up on Dayton's thoughts.

"Sleep capsule's down here?" Dayton staggard down the hall, lumbering towards his goal.

"No sleep capsule," Dad explained. "Here, just simple beds. It'll be fine. You'll get used to it."

Dayton entered his room. It was small, not that much larger than his room aboard *Venture*. It had a desk, drawers, and a closet.

And a bed.

Dayton did not like beds. He was used to being in the secure embrace of a sleep capsule. Living a lifetime with the possibility of explosive decompression tended to do that to someone.

At the moment, however, it was all he had. And he didn't

have the energy to complain anymore.

He fell onto the bed. It had no sheets, but it was soft, and he relaxed into it.

That was about all he remembered.

The Tata puttered into the high school parking lot. In front of them lay an expansive array of duracrete-and-glass buildings, all blue in color with golden numbers stenciled across them. The front walkway was preceded by a sign that was easily the size of the Tata. It proclaimed the place "Chuck Yeager High School."

Dad tooled around the parking lot, which was huge—large enough to land a shuttlecraft. It had hundreds of spaces, all marked out in angled white paint over a gray plasticrete surface. It was largely empty, save for a few other ground cars that looked infinitely less embarrassing than the Tata.

"Dad," Dayton said. "What are we doing here? This is a civilian educational facility."

"Son, I need you to come with me," Dad said. "Let's go inside and talk to the principal about some things, okay?"

"You have been very quiet on my current record status," Dayton said. "Everyone has. What is going on here?"

"Let's just go inside," Dad said. "I promise we will explain everything to you."

"For the record, I don't like this one bit," Dayton said.

"I know," Dad said. "This hasn't been easy on me, either. Just promise me you'll keep an open mind to all this."

"To all what?"

Dad didn't answer. His look said it all.

"Right," Dayton said. "Inside the building. All my answers are inside the building."

His dad never had problems explaining things before. Of course, before was on *Venture*, when everything made sense. Now? Who could tell now? Whatever was going on, Dayton knew two things: Dad couldn't easily explain it, and Dayton didn't like it.

"Hey," Dad said as they passed another sign. "Look at that." He pointed to a white plastic sign with black removable letters. It said:

"Get ready.

The Back to School Dance is coming.

This time, the gals ask the guys."

Dad pulled into a space and cut the tiny engine.

Dayton pushed the unwilling car door open, and it obeyed with a stiff groan.

"Ready?" Dad said with a smile.

"How could I be ready? I've never been here before," he answered.

"C'mon, we'll do a little datawork, meet the principal."

***

"This will be a wonderful opportunity for you," the principal said. "It will be a pleasure to have you at Chuck Yeager High School."

"Thank you, Mister Ramirez," Dayton shook hands with the man. A good, solid handshake. "I doubt I'll be here that long."

Principal Ramirez ignored that and addressed his father. "I think he'll find this school will offer far more in terms of social integration and experience."

"Well, that's my hope," Father said. "I really want him to fit in around here."

"I've had the opportunity to review your records," Ramirez continued. "You began your education and on-the-job training at an early age. You have mastered basic sciences, physics, and math."

"Well, yeah," Dayton said. "I'm really not supposed to be here. I'm supposed to be twenty when we got here, right?"

The principal handed Dayton a message pad. "That is the mystery everyone's talking about," he said. "But the fact is, you are sixteen and belong in school."

"It won't be so bad," his father said. "You'll see. Just give it time."

Dayton read off the classes. "English One, American Government, American Literature, Physical Education Two, History One, and Calculus AP." His head was swimming. This was not the right course. He was supposed to be in training now. Fourteen lousy hours! That was all that stood between him and that Recon patch. Didn't these guys get that?

"Not that you need Calculus," Ramirez said. "But I didn't want your schedule to be entirely intimidating. You see, most of those classes will educate you on the basics of what it takes to fit into our society."

"Wait-wait-wait-wait," Dayton said as his head rose above the assault of information. "I'm not going to be here long enough for this. This is not what I'm doing. I need to be back in training at the start of the next cycle."

Principal Ramirez exchanged glances with his dad. A silence held the room for what could have been hours from the way Dayton felt. Why weren't these two men getting it? School didn't apply to him. He was getting his certs, and then bam! Back out in space.

Father turned to his son. "You won't be going back into training."

"What? No. No! I'm fourteen hours away from Recon cert."

Principal Ramirez looked over his glasses. "You're not old enough to become a Recon pilot. Son, you're only sixteen."

"That didn't stop me from becoming a Survey pilot on *Venture*," Dayton felt himself shaking. This couldn't be happening.

"On *Venture*, we had no choice," the father said. "It was either train our children or return to Earth. Here, we have laws. And those laws say you're still a minor."

"But they can make an exception for me," Dayton argued, pleaded, perhaps bargained. "You said I'm the exception. Just talk to the Agency. They'll waive my transfer."

"That's not going to happen," Dad said, closing his eyes and shaking his head. "You can apply for pilot training when you complete your education here. Until then, this is where you'll be."

"Okay," Dayton stood up and glanced around, as if that would help him somehow. "All right in the meantime. How long can that be?"

"Two years."

Dayton stumbled at the words from Principal Ramirez. At first, he didn't think he heard the man correctly. Two years? Why not a lifetime? What in the name of the Space Kraken was he going to do, stuck on Earth for two years? He had only fourteen hours to go. Fourteen. He could do that in an extended orbital loop. He wouldn't even have to leave the planet.

"This—this isn't right." Dayton threw his hands up, pacing in front of the principal's desk. "I'm not a student. No way. I've done all the training I ever needed to do."

"I'm sorry," Principal Ramirez said.

"This can't be happening," Dayton said, under his breath and more to himself. "What do you expect me to do for two years?"

"There's a lot you can do," Dad said. "You'll see. Life doesn't have to be all certifications and flight hours. This is a wonderful planet, full of experiences. Just give it some time. You'll see."

Principal Ramirez handed him a pad. "Maybe you could give our physics team a boost while you're at it."

Dayton looked at it. "I don't need all this. Government? Literature? And what is this Driver's Ed? What the hell is Driver's Ed?"

"It's where you learn how to drive a ground car," Principal Ramirez said.

"I already know how to drive a ground car."

"Yes," his father jumped in. "But here, you need a license. You need to learn the rules governing the roads and fly lanes around here."

"Oh, for crying out loud." Dayton shook with pent-up anger. "I can drive an ore crawler across half the Expanse on five different planets, but I have to learn to drive a pitiful ground car? Those things we passed on the road on the way over here? This is a joke!"

"I know this isn't what you wanted, but it has to be," Dad said.

"You could stop this."

"No. I can't."

"I hate you!" Dayton erupted and stormed out of the office. He stomped down in the hall and sat back against the lockers. *This* was where he was going to be for two years?

There had to be a way out of this.

There just had to be.

SEVEN

Micrometeorites slammed against the Old 21 surveyor. Dayton grimaced as Old 21 bucked and shimmied as he tried to slow the vehicle down. Even though the canopy held, just seeing the meteorite storm outside was enough to stop his heart. Rogue asteroid fields. Fist-sized, white projectiles sounded like steel ball bearings hammering metal.

Another spinning rock, this one easily twice Old 21's size, barreled down on him. Dayton jerked the joystick left, though not in time. The ball of minerals crashed against Old 21's undercarriage and shook Dayton to his bones. The tell-tale "beep-beep-beep" of the emergency horn filled his cramped cockpit.

But it did slow the spinning, if just enough for Dayton to recover his stomach, and he tried the stabilizers.

No go.

He clamped both gloved hands on the stick and heaved. Old 21 didn't even out. If anything, it got worse. More micros. More ball bearings shattered on the metal. What was it they called it on Earth? Hail stones? The sound was deafening, enveloping.

"Mayday! Turk! I've lost lateral control," Dayton shouted into his mouthpiece over the din of hail and alarms. "I need a Class Five tow. Unhook your cable. I repeat. Unhook your cable."

"He can't hear you," a voice crackled over the comms. The cockpit flashed with green light as a palm-sized hologram of Milly materialized on the dashboard holopad. "You don't belong here anymore."

The miniature Milly visage laughed uncontrollably, an evil, cold cackle that seemed to be everywhere in the cockpit.

Dayton's arms burst with pain and stiffness. He pulled hard on the inflexible joystick, but the vehicle kept speeding and threatening to spin out. Old 21 fishtailed and shuddered.

"You're no pilot." Milly's laughter cascaded all through Old 21. It was all around Dayton, even through him, chilling his bones like the vacuum of space could never do.

The sarcastic simper came again. "Your time out here is over."

Dayton felt a shiver through his sweat. "No, it's not," he yelled, both into the mouthpiece and at the tiny green hologram. "I belong here. This is my life." He leaned forward, his flight straps fighting him every millimeter of the way. He tried to put his weight behind pulling the joystick, but again, the stick would not budge. Earth now consumed his entire view. And he traveled right toward it. Turco was little more than a spark in the depths, off in deep space. Dayton glanced at the readouts. Gauges, some analog, some digital, spun wildly, reflecting this just wasn't right.

"You're a child," Milly's form said. "You never had any business being out here."

Dayton and his surveyor fell backward, deeper into Earth's atmosphere. The warning klaxon beeped as Old 21 began to spin and tumble. He felt sick. He felt heavy, weighted down as his world became a storm around him. There was a tug on his right shoulder. His survey patch, the blue one that he so prized, came off his shoulder as the stitches popped one after another, pulled out by sheer centrifugal force. The patch landed with a splat against the canopy. Like a rag stuck to the side of a spinning laundry chamber, sheer inertia held it faster than any quartermaster's tailoring ever could.

"That means nothing here!" Milly's holograph howled in amusement, pointing at the patch pinned to the canopy. "Soon, you'll be stripped of everything you ever were."

All around Dayton, pieces of Old 21 fell off, flung away from the spinning Old 21. Groans. Squeaks. Pops. Grinding.

And shaking. Oh! That eternal shaking.

"Enjoy your stay!" Milly said as the entire cockpit split into dozens of small pieces. Suddenly, his cocoon was spread wide open. Dayton now twisted and tumbled with hundreds of chunks of metal that were once his precious Old 21. He spun, tumbled, and rolled in the chaos, his sore limbs flailing in all directions, grasping for some security that simply wasn't there.

Dayton forced his stiff and sore hand to reach for his parachute. He reached his shoulder, where the pull ring was supposed to be.

There was nothing there. Dayton's heart leaped into his throat as he found he couldn't breathe, and even his flight helmet shot up off his head, now deluging all his senses as wind blasted over his face, peeling back his eyelids and slapping his cheeks, roaring and howling.

Suddenly, it stopped.

Dayton bolted to a sitting position in his bed, wet sheets sticking to his frame. Sweat poured in miniature rivers down his forehead, and his arms were slick with the stuff. His heart was pounding out of his chest, and every breath was labored. It was quiet. It was night. The only sounds were crickets outside, here at Father's new house. A gentle breeze blew into the room, at last, a welcome sensation.

He reached over the side of the bed, searching for the comfort of his flight jacket. But his hand felt only carpet. His flight jacket was usually never far from him, and he missed it. What was it that Father called it, a security blanket? But the jacket was still back at that awful medical facility. So, this is what it had come to: nightmares about being trapped on this planet? Even his subconscious was out to get him now.

Oh God. And I told Dad I hated him.

Dayton fished his comm badge from the nightstand. He scrolled through the contacts until he found his father's frequency. He hesitated, his hands shaking, and then he opened the comm channel. It beeped in the darkness.

"Day?" Father's voice came through when he answered his own comm.

"Yeah, me. I'm sorry. About today. Look, I know it's been kind of awkward since the school. But I don't hate you."

Silence.

"I know, bud," Father's voice was calming, the first calm he'd felt in what seemed forever. "Is that why you're calling me all the way from your room?"

"Yes."

"Well, I'm glad you did."

"Okay," Dayton said. "I'll see you at breakfast in a few hours."

"You will at that. Get some sleep, okay?"

"Yeah," Dayton said, and the comm went off.

Dayton fell back into the bed; wet sheets slapped his body as he landed.

He lay there, listening to the crickets. He didn't want to sleep.

He didn't want to dream.

***

The next time his eyes opened, Dayton could see it was light outside. The clock on his desk now read 1100 hours. Sitting up, he worked the stiffness out of his muscles. He didn't feel very rested.

Getting out of bed, he put on his gray padded shirt and steel-colored cargo pants. Despite the roominess of his new quarters, his pressure-tested clothing made everywhere seem so crowded. He was constantly bumping a hip or his arm into tables and chairs. His pants caught on the drapes when he walked by the living room windows. Maybe the locals were onto something with their light, unobtrusive clothing. Dayton knew he didn't have to worry about emergency decompression every minute of every day, but he was just used to this clothing next to his skin. It was a small, comforting reminder of space.

"I just finished installing the uplink," his father said. "The entertainment center is up and running. Soon, I'll have it in your room next. You'll have a virtual hologram projector in no time."

"All right." Dayton was about to unpack his container full of flight gear, but that could wait. Really, he didn't see the big deal. Entertainment centers sounded a lot like the comm centers they had aboard ships. The comm centers were used for video conferencing, status reports, project updates, and mission monitoring.

"Come on, come on," Dad said and motioned his son along. "You need to see this."

Dayton trudged into the main room of their new house. He didn't care for most of the changes in this house so far, and this new thing wasn't likely to change things. *Don't be negative*, he cautioned himself.

Dad pressed a button on a remote control, and the large, flat holo screen in the middle of the equipment blinked on. It showed a beautiful, bikini-clad woman standing on a large patio with hundreds of screaming teenagers behind her. She was talking about a summer beach house and the marvels of some place called Cancun. The crowd around her all yelled and held up glasses filled with various colored liquids. Dayton was not used to seeing near-naked women, and the sight of this very shapely woman made his jaw drop.

Dad flicked the remote, and another image replaced that one, a movie showing a chase between two grav vehicles through the crowded skies over a city. The men in both vehicles exchanged blue and red fire-blasts at one another.

"Isn't it wonderful?" Dad was all smiles. "We have over eight hundred channels, including off-world and international. I missed this."

"Fine. Have fun with it." Dayton started back for his room.

Only twenty channels on the comm centers back aboard the ship had been reserved for entertainment. Movies, interviews with the crew, and news from major spaceports were the primary content. But here, the majority of channels were devoted to this kind of material. Dayton guessed you had to get used to it. As he went back to his room, he could hear his dad chortling with amusement.

"Hello?" The digitized voice of Zara buzzed from under a pile of clothes in his room. It was followed by a beeping Dayton knew all too well. He tossed clothing aside till he found the comm unit.

"Go," he spoke into the device.

"I'm bored." Zara's voice said through the speaker on the comm unit, which was many times larger than the ones the Earthers used, less streamlined, and blasted by the elements. "I've got this entire house to myself, and I'm going to go crazy if I don't do something now."

"Yeah, me too. What about the parents?"

"Oh, they got called in for some more interviews. They asked me to go along, but I am not going back to that place."

"How's the arm?"

"Oh, all better," Zara said. "Those fusion casts knit your wounds so fast you don't even feel it."

Back aboard the ship, there was plenty to do. Here, there didn't seem to be a lot going on for the average person of their age.

"Maybe we should go explore the area."

"Okay, where?"

"I don't know."

"There's a shopping complex less than five klicks away from our houses," Zara said. "We could go there."

"Yeah, I've already been there," Dayton said as he recalled hanging by the chute straps from the ceiling of that place. "Do I have to buy anything?"

"Probably," Zara said. "That's why that place is there. Why

would they let people in if they didn't buy anything?"

This made sense. His father had bought something at every store they'd been to. He didn't know much about how things worked on Earth, but he did know that selling and buying things was the foundation of existence here.

"I'll see you there at fourteen-hundred hours," Zara said. "We can meet at the front entrance to the theaters. I'm sending you the coordinates."

The small screen on the comm unit blipped as it received the data and called up the location on a small map. It was only a short distance from the house. It was called the Ascension Marketplace, but how would he get there?

His father was still engrossed in front of the entertainment center; the giant flat holo-emitter was now split into five windows, each showing a different program.

"Dad," Dayton hesitated, "Can you drive me to the mall?"

"Sure."

That was easy.

EIGHT

A few minutes later, he and his father stepped outside. It was a clear day, with only a few white puffs of clouds in an otherwise blue sky. The sun warmed Dayton's face, something he really liked. It was a large, yellow sun, not one of those intense red fireballs that made every breeze feel like a blast furnace wave. And there was a distinct smell that wafted across the flower garden in the neighbor's yard.

The Tata puttered into the parking lot in front of the main entrance, below a sign that read "Ascension Mall" in big flashing letters. Signs all over Earth seemed to call attention to themselves and whatever they advertised. It was a big change from *Venture*, where signs were simply for information.

Dayton noticed a large group of girls milling about in front of the entrance of a coffee seller. His dad slowed until he finally came to a squeaking halt directly in front of the girls.

"Thanks." Dayton suddenly felt embarrassed. His breath grew short, and his palms began to sweat as his vision narrowed. He was concerned about only two things at that moment: the girls and how close his father came to them in that pitiful embarrassment of a vehicle.

"What are you going to do here?" Dayton's father asked. "Get school supplies?"

"I don't know." Dayton already had the flimsy door open and had scrambled halfway out. "I'll see you later." Out of the corner of his eye, he could see the girls were looking at him.

"Dayton," his father bellowed from behind him.

Dog it, he thought; his father hadn't moved on.

"Yeah?" He turned and saw his father sticking his head out of the window and over the top of the little Tata.

"When should I pick you up?"

"I'll just walk home with Zara or take the travel tube. I'll be fine."

"Are you sure?"

"Yes, I'll see you later."

"We should probably buy you a comm unit. The ones they have here are so much smaller and lighter. Do you want me to get you one now?"

"No! I'll worry about it later."

"Will you be home in time for dinner?"

"I don't know. Bye."

"Should I leave something for you in the fridge?"

"No!" Dayton said with more emphasis than he'd have liked to. That car was a true embarrassment, and he felt pressured. He felt it even more intensely as a new-looking flyer landed close to them. "Don't worry about it. Just … go!"

His father finally ducked back into the small car and puttered off. The girls were still there, having heard the whole embarrassing exchange. They looked at Dayton and giggled.

"Nice car." One of the girls, a tall blonde with sharp features and high cheekbones, wearing a green digital graphic shirt and white shorts, laughed at Dayton. "Still has a gas engine. Hope you don't blow up."

The other girls fell into a fit of laughter. Dayton didn't really know what to say. His heart was racing, and to further his self-conscious state, he felt a trickle of sweat run down the left side of his forehead. Did these females go to Chuck Yeager High School, where he was going? Would they be at the dances, in those hallways? Did they know Allyson? He shut off that line of thought before he worked himself into a fit.

Coffee. Yes, coffee would work well right now. Dayton entered the coffee vendor's shop, outfitted in teakwood and brass. Wooden tables lined the glass walls, and the back of the bar was overflowing with coffee items. Patrons sat at the tables, with their attentions split almost evenly between their portable datapads and their hot and cold beverages.

"Can I help you?" A tattooed girl with a lip ring asked from behind the counter.

Dayton knew he must've looked perplexed. He'd never known so many different types of coffee existed. Columbia, Sumatra, Kona ... the list was endless.

"Yeah, um," he struggled for words. "I, I'm kind of new here. I need a strong coffee."

The girl at the counter ran through a list of the dark blends, as she called them. Finally, Dayton settled on the Sumatra blend. It was dark, and one thing Turco had always taught him about coffee was to go with the dark stuff if it's available.

Five guys and two girls came into the place after Dayton had paid for his cup and moved off. They were laughing and talking, but all that came to an abrupt stop the second they spotted Dayton.

Each of them gave him a sideways glance, some looking him up and down. Dayton just stood there; he was as interested in them as they appeared to be in him.

As a group, they wore loose-fitting t-shirts and wrinkled shorts that looked like thin cut-offs made from cargo dock pants. Two of them had woven shoes— "sneakers" was what he'd heard them called in videos back on *Venture*. The other three wore sandals.

Their toes. Their feet. I can see their feet. Dayton only saw someone else's feet when they were in the locker room, and even then, it was uncommon. These Earthers, they walked around like that? In the open? All day long?

Dayton wondered how someone could feel secure wearing such flimsy clothing, which starkly contrasted with his shipboard outfit and its heavy, pressure-resistant fibers.

There was an opening from the coffee vendor to the mall, so Dayton rushed down one of the main corridors. The walkway was laid out in mosaic tiles, with shops on each side. He followed the kiosk information and soon found himself at the large glass-and-steel theater. The marquee showed thirty-six movies. Neon lights covered the sides of the marquee, and digital signs hung all over the inside of the lobby, dominated by a large food stand in the middle.

"They really go for the flashy," Zara said, walking up. Her cast was off already, and she shook her arm in the air.

"Hey. Congrats." Dayton felt a little embarrassed that he hadn't seen his friend approaching. But there was so much going on that his senses were overwhelmed. "Bet you're glad to have that gone, huh?"

"No big," she said.

The two friends stood in the middle of the courtyard, looking around. Dayton looked up. The dome he had crashed through had been replaced by shiny new glass. The chute strings, the shattered glass front of the hardware store, and the mess were gone.

"So, what do we do?" Zara sat down on a bench shaped like an antique roll of film unfurling.

"I don't know," Dayton said. "Did you bring your smart card?"

"Yes." Zara pulled her card, which held her disposable income, up for Dayton to see.

"Okay. Let's go buy something, then."

"What?" Zara looked around. "Where do we start?"

"Nice clothes, Outworlder." A female voice shot across the courtyard at them. "Where'd you get that jacket, Astronauts-R-Us?" A chorus of girls howled in laughter behind her.

"Maybe we should get new clothes?" Dayton offered. "We do kind of stand out."

"What? Into the garbage disposal with them." Zara said, loud enough for the other girls to hear. "Like I want to look like some atmosphere-spoiled bitch with flimsy clothing on? I don't think so."

"Okay," Dayton maneuvered Zara further down the promenade, away from the stares her rant had generated. "I get it.

Can we just move on?"

"Oh, but you like that kind of thing with girls, don't you?" Zara said. "Is that what you want? You want to be attractive to them? Your pressure suit and surveyor's badge aren't going to be attractive anymore?"

"What is it with you?" Dayton pivoted Zara to face him. "You *like* making a nav beacon out of yourself? Knock it off."

"Oh yeah," Zara looked around. "Yeah, I really care what all these Earthers think. I don't and neither should you."

"It'd be nice to walk around without getting stared at," Dayton said.

"So, what?"

"We look different."

"We *are* different."

"We're not that different."

"*They* think so."

"I'm going to buy clothing," Dayton said. "You can come with me or not."

"Each store has something different," Zara said. "How are you going to know what is right? Since only *they* can tell you!"

"I think the stores are all right."

"How can that be?"

"Well, they have to stay in business somehow."

"You look fine as is," Zara took a more consoling tone. "What are all your shipmates gonna say they see you in some of those flimsy clothes? All these Earther clothes do is advertise the brands that made them. Like that matters. They don't tell you what your designation is."

"They don't need to."

"So, you want to go through life with people not knowing what you are?" Zara asked. "What would be the point of earning a surveyor patch, then? You're not going to wear it."

"Uh." Dayton glanced over at the group of girls. He knew Zara was right. He shouldn't care what they thought. Yet, for some reason, he did.

"That's your big comeback? 'Uh' is all you have to say?" Zara looked him up and down.

"Let's just go."

"Like where?"

"Whatever," Dayton moved off but found Zara keeping pace with him.

They observed the first group of boys that walked by. The only problem was that those boys took an equally intense interest in their appearance, glaring at them from head to toe. The same thing happened with the second group and then the third.

"Those last guys looked like they wanted to fight," Zara said. "Maybe staring at them isn't such a good idea. You remember what they did if they stared at you on Zeta Reticuli? Well, here I heard it's worse."

"Yeah," Dayton said. "The food court is over there; let's get something to eat."

"I can't believe we're stuck here for two years." Zara rehashed the same talk they'd been having since Dayton's trip to Chuck Yeager High School. Zara had pretty much the same experience when she got there, too. In other words, they were shafted.

"Two years," Dayton echoed. "Two years of them making fun of us. I just don't like being a joke."

"Just do what I do," Zara said. "Make fun of them."

Dayton's quest for learning what to wear vanished when he saw a familiar squat figure seated at one of the food court tables. Despite his small stature, Trenton was hard to miss. He was compact, almost stubby, with the body of a lifelong weight trainer. This was due to him being born and raised on the third planet orbiting Alpha Centauri. The gravity of that world was so much heavier, and all the colonists born of the original settlers developed squat but powerful physiques. Dayton could see that Trenton was getting far more stares than he and Zara were.

Trenton was from a developed world, which also meant

he learned more about social interactions in his sixteen years than Dayton or Zara had. If he was bothered by the stares, he didn't show it. In fact, in all the years Dayton had known Trenton, he had never seen the guy upset or angry in any way. *There was something to be said about that*, Dayton thought.

Trenton was seated by himself, apparently enjoying some food wrapped in foil. He smiled and waved to them, inviting them to sit.

"There's the man." Zara crossed her arms in front of her face, and Trenton did the same back. "Haven't seen you since the holding area. How'd you make out?"

"In style, naturally." Trenton bowed his head in mock recognition of an imaginary award.

"So, lay it out for us." She looked across the food court. "What's the data dump on the life forms around here?"

"Textbook," Trenton said, though Dayton was sure if there was a textbook written on teenage herds, he would have found it by now. "Over at those benches, you got the 'Skaters.' Their whole lives are based on hoverboarding. Eating at the tables by the trash cans are the 'Neuros.' They're self-absorbed and think the whole world hates them. The jocks and the popular students, or 'Pops,' are at those tables over there. They think they're better than the rest of us. Those guys in the black are the 'Griefers;' they exist to suffer in this world and talk about how much they hate everything."

"What about them?" Dayton pointed at a group of boisterous kids.

"Wannabes," Trenton said. "They try to be like the Pops in the hope they'll be accepted by them. They act like they're friends with all the Pops, even though most of them aren't."

"What's the info dump on the loud ones?" Zara said as she motioned toward a group of girls wearing identical outfits with the letters "CYHS" emblazoned across the fronts of their tops.

"Oh, yeah." Trenton cut into his sauce-covered food with

a plastic spork. "Cheerleaders. They are their own little group. Basically, they rank somewhere between the Wannabes and Pops."

"What about the guys with the gear?" Dayton looked off at a gathering of rather clumsy-looking boys with unkempt hair and ill-fitting clothing. They were playing around with their comm units, portable 3D projectors, heads-up displays, and HandComps. In total, everyone was half engaged in their own personal digital gear, but these awkward kids had way more than their share.

"Technos," Trenton said. "Your basic nerd types who hide behind technology. Here, you have a good cross-section of the people we will be going to school with soon."

Things seemed a lot more complicated than they had a few minutes before. And that was saying something. Dayton wondered where he fit in. He certainly wasn't a Griefer. Those kids looked like something out of one of those old dark horror videos he'd seen back on the ship. The Neuros, whatever those were, didn't really look all that different from the Griefers. Dayton doubted he fit in there, either. Black clothing covered them almost completely, along with black skulls on their dark clothing. Even black nail polish to go with their surgical steel necklaces and rings, as often as not shaped like skulls.

Then there were the jocks and popular kids.

Well, Dayton certainly didn't look like any of them. He didn't know anyone, so he wasn't popular. He wasn't even sure what all that entailed. Could he be a jock? He did play grav ball. Would grav ball qualify him as a jock? He supposed it might. Then there were the Technos. Dayton feared his life of learning technology and science pre-qualified him to be one of them. He didn't like that prospect.

"So, where are we in this classification?" Zara beat Dayton to the punch. *Oh well,* Dayton thought, *better someone else ask that question.*

"Easy," Trenton smiled. "We're 'Outworlders.' It's funny

because back on Centauri, whenever these kids would arrive, *they'd* be the off-worlders. They'd be all weak and struggling to walk and stuff."

"Outworlders? Good. I don't want to be anything else. They're inferior to us, physically," Zara said. "We have the advantage because of our higher gravity upbringing. Our time working in zero-G honed our balance better than they could hope for, too."

"Does that go for us as well as you?" Dayton asked Trenton. He did feel the gravity was a little lighter here, but he didn't have the squat, muscular frame you could only get from a high-gravity world.

Trenton dipped a stick of fried crunchy food in a reddish sauce. "You guys, too."

"Then why do they look down on us?" Dayton looked at the popular kids. They did seem to be having fun.

"Because we aren't up on the latest media," Trenton said. "We don't get movies and fashions and all that other stuff until years after they do. So, they think we're out of it."

"That's it?" Dayton had thought there was some secret advantage the Earthers held over him. It was kind of a relief to find out otherwise.

"Yeah," Trenton said. "They think that just because Earth is the center of all media, that it makes them better than us. They're just a bunch of snobs. They're arrogant that way. They make fun of us and expect us to make fun of ourselves. Doesn't even dawn on these idiots we might not share their views."

So that was it. Dayton was an Outworlder, and that was how he'd fit into the grand scheme of things. It was nice to know his place, but his place was that of an outsider. This frightened him.

He looked at the popular kids. They seemed to be the only group that wasn't keeping one eye out for other groups. They seemed happy to be who they were. At first glance, he couldn't say that about the others. They were all locked into their own groups, far apart from each other. This was not something he was used to.

Dayton took the whole scene in. He spotted a dark-haired girl with curly locks that came down to her shoulders. Allyson. She was attractive, all right. He held back from these thoughts. Still, he did look at her. She wore a digitized sweater that changed colors from dark blue to red and a form-fitting pair of black pants that accentuated her impressive figure. She was with the Pops.

Dayton stared at Allyson, but she didn't return the gaze. Either she didn't see him or *pretended* she didn't see him. He kept waiting, hoping with each passing second that Allyson would turn her head in his direction.

No such luck.

He glanced to Allyson's left. There, a dark-haired kid with textbook good looks glared at him. While still holding Dayton's gaze, he motioned to Allyson, who gave him a peck on the cheek.

It was a small, almost subtle sign of affection, but now the boy smirked in satisfaction at Dayton. His message was clear: she's mine. Dayton continued to watch, and the boy threw his arm around Allyson, even kissing the side of her head.

"What are you so entranced with over there?" Zara's voice brought Dayton back to reality. He shot a glance instantly at Zara, breaking off the show.

"No," he fumbled to say. "No. Nothing. I was just thinking about how all our other crew is getting on with this, you know, situation."

"Probably as miserable and hating it as much as we are," Zara said. "This whole place is so scattered looking."

Sure, he knew that people naturally congregated into their own groups. Aboard *Venture*, the groups were usually based on jobs and departments, but even then, people all seemed to share a single purpose.

As a pilot in Alpha Group, he'd always felt a little superior to cargo-shuttle pilots and a little inferior to Recon pilots. They would sit with Survey pilots, eat with other Survey pilots, and generally hang around other Survey pilots. Recon and Cargo pilots had their own groups as well. There were times when the walls came down, such as mission briefings and, of course, poker games. There was joking and kidding around, but it was all in jest.

Here, did the walls come down? Most likely, they all took classes together, but what about the rest of the time? Was it always like this?

Dayton excused himself from the table and went to a Chinese food stand in the court. Of all the food he saw—and there were a lot of different types—he recognized the Chinese. He'd had it on several visits to Chinese mining outposts. He didn't always like it, but it was familiar.

With a tray filled with noodles and vegetables, Dayton turned and faced the food court. His eyes went straight to Allyson. She was sitting by herself. Her Pop friend had left. Why, Dayton didn't know, but without that Pop around, he might just have a chance to talk to her.

"Hey, Dayton," Zara called out.

Dayton turned to see both she and Trenton were waving him over. He hesitated, halfway between Allyson and his friends. Halfway between "two worlds." What if he went over to Allyson? Would she talk to him? She didn't seem to recognize him, but then again, he was across the food court from her.

"Would you get over here?" Zara said, raising her voice.

It took all his effort, but Dayton forced one foot toward his friends' table. The steps over there were not any easier.

"You were going to talk to that Earther, weren't you?" Zara asked as she let out a derisive laugh.

"Whatever," Dayton wanted to shrink at that point. Instead, all he could do was wave Zara's question away. The three settled into their food, none of them talking.

NINE

Dayton's dad pulled the puttering Tata into the high school drop-off area, driving toward where several students hung around one of the old stone benches. Dad approached the curb and just kept drifting toward them.

"Okay," Dayton said. "You-you can stop here." But no, his father kept creeping toward that group, slowly and painfully. "Dad, you can stop here."

The embarrassingly small, primitive vehicle creaked to a halt directly in front of the group. As he had feared, they watched with amusement.

"Have a good day," his father said. "You be okay walking home?"

"Fine," Dayton pulled the handle on the door, and it obediently creaked open, "I'll see you tonight."

When he looked toward the students again, thankfully, they weren't paying any more attention to him. They seemed immersed in their own conversation or their personal comms, playing away on their HUD glasses and comm-linking with others. Dayton had gotten no farther than two meters when he heard his father call to him.

"Dayton," his father's voice boomed.

Dawgs. Why did his father always remember to say something to him after he left the vehicle? Why couldn't he say everything he needed to say before they arrived at the school? They had a whole voyage over here in that stupid toy car. Why didn't he talk then?

Before he could turn around to address his dad, the man pressed the horn, and it burped out a pathetic beep that seemed more at home on a small service Crab than any kind of passenger vehicle. But it was enough to get the other students' attention.

Dayton looked back, and his heart sank. His father was holding his lunch tube. Dayton rushed over to the Tata's open window.

"Thanks," he said as he snapped up the lunch container. His dad was starting to say something, but Dayton darted into the school, past the outlying buildings and into the campus, putting as much of this world as possible between himself and Dad and that feeble car.

The interior of the campus was a sprawling, grass-covered landscape, broken into neat, tree-lined sections by a plasti-crete walkway that curved in various directions. At the center of this was a large statue of a man in early flight gear, gazing dramatically skyward. The plaque at the bottom read:

Charles E. "Chuck" Yeager
Decorated fighter ace. Legendary test pilot. Leader of men. An
icon for the generations.

Dayton needed no introduction. He didn't know much Earth history, but he knew this man. Every pilot everywhere knew of Chuck Yeager. No pilot started training without being taught something of the men who led the way. It seemed only fitting that he was going to a school named in the man's honor. He agreed with the name of the school, if nothing else.

The park-like setting was ringed on all sides by large, three-story steel-and-glass buildings. Large numbers on their sides easily identified everything. This reminded him of *Venture*, where big numbers made for easy navigation, no matter where on the ship you were. At least that seemed familiar.

Just as he was letting his new surroundings settle in, he could feel the eyes on him. He looked around, spotting students walking alone, in pairs, or in groups around the grounds. Their light, casual garments contrasted with his heavier, shipboard wear.

Here, under the kind sun, things were a lot warmer than

most areas aboard the ship. Clothes didn't do anything but cover up nudity, although in some of the more "fashionable" cases, they seemed to be a form of expression. T-shirts supported graphic patterns that digitally changed colors and swirled about. Shoes had exaggerated traction on their soles and came in a variety of color combinations, from the sedate to the neon loud. Most were secured on the feet with nylon strings that were somehow tied together. Pants came in a variety of colors, fabrics, and lengths, which depended on the wearer's preference, Dayton supposed.

He didn't want to linger and get stared at, so he headed down another path. Allyson went to this school, didn't she? She lived in the area, so probably, yes. What would she think of him now, the boy who fell from the mall skylights?

Dayton's heart raced. What if he ran into her? What would he say? *Hi, thanks for saving my life?* No, too cliché. Still, she did kind of do that.

The path wound through some low-hanging branches and emerged, facing a mess-hall-type area. The sign above the tables read "CAFETERIA." Dayton crossed the sea of tables in an instant. A sense of familiarity passed over him as he recognized other Outworlders and nodded to them.

"We were comparing schedules." Zara held up her digital pad for Dayton to see. "Trenton and I have Metal Shop and a science class together. What do you have?"

Dayton pulled his pad from his backpack.

"Oh, man," Trenton said. "We only share P.E. Sorry."

"At least they could've let you and I share one period," Zara said, holding up her tablet. "Aside from P.E. with Trenton, it's just you and the land creatures all day long."

The electronic chime sounded throughout the grounds. It reminded him of a funeral bell.

***

Dayton sat at the back of the class, but he could see the hologram spin in the center of the darkened classroom. It showed the Earth and all its satellites, both natural and artificial. Mister Yutaka lectured about the various countries, which became highlighted on the hologram as he mentioned them. He was an Asian man with long, graying hair and a weathered face. He wore a sports coat that'd seen better times and was faded and brown. His hands were gnarled, baked in an unforgiving sun, and he wore dark granny specs he occasionally removed, revealing steel gray eyes.

Mister Yutaka pulled the hologram view back so the class could see the entire Earth, complete with thousands of small blue dots circling it. "These dots show the current locations of the various orbital colonies, labs, and factories around the planet," Mister Yutaka said as he zoomed in on the area just above the continental United States. Dayton could make out a long, rectangular object, which the teacher magnified. Dayton could see it was *Venture*, surrounded by scaffolding at the Narinda Orbital Drydock. His stomach lurched.

"As most of you who have followed the news know," Mister Yutaka said, "The first of our Anteros class explorer ships returned a couple of months ago. It was a twenty-year voyage, and it had some unexpected results. Can anyone tell us what some of those were?"

Oh no, Dayton thought. Here he was trying to be incognito, and now his ship, and home for all his life, was now the subject of the teacher's lesson.

"Well," Mister Yutaka said when no one in class answered him. "I see no one watched the news much during the summer. No one knows?"

The class sat still, looking off in one direction or another to avoid eye contact with the teacher.

"Really," Mister Yutaka said. He punched a few keys on his display control panel, and the image of *Venture* in the dock zoomed in so finely that the various worker modules and men in EVA suits could be clearly seen.

"You know," the teacher said. "We have a real piece of history right here in class with us. He's probably a little shy, but maybe he would like to share his views with us. Dayton Murdoch?" The man smiled, but Dayton took no comfort in that.

"Yeah," Dayton said as he glanced around. Sure enough, they were all looking at him. Even those kids in front and behind him suddenly were aware of his presence. So much for being "Guy Incognito."

"Now, Dayton was one of the very occurrences I was talking about. He, and hundreds of others, were born on *Venture* and have lived their whole lives in space. In fact, we have three of these *Venture* children attending our school. Dayton, could you stand up, please?"

Okay, things just went from bad to worse. Not only was he being singled out for being different, but now he had to stand up so everyone could see exactly how different he was.

Dayton slowly stood as his head became lighter. He was never much for making speeches or talking in front of groups, even with the familiarity of his fellow pilots aboard *Venture*, and here he didn't know anyone. He concentrated on the teacher, not on the class.

"Dayton," Mister Yutaka said, "Tell us, what were your first impressions of the Earth when your ship arrived?"

What kind of a question was that? Dayton thought. He was mostly concerned with the ship falling apart around him and then tumbling around in an escape pod to have any "impressions" of much of anything except impending doom. "I didn't have much chance to see the planet," he said. "My circumstances were kind of ... well ... chaotic and scary at that time."

"Of course, of course," Mister Yutaka said. He nodded his head dramatically. "But surely you noticed the Earth is unique among the worlds you visited? This beautiful, blue ball in the depths of space, full of life, must have had a lasting impression on you."

Not when you're tumbling toward it at hundreds of kilometers an hour. "Yes," Dayton said. He could tell that this man was not going to be satisfied until he got the answers he wanted.

"That's really profound," the teacher said. "You know, back in the old days, before they found a way to cut greenhouse emissions, we were in danger of losing our precious planet. The eco-friendly technologies we take for granted today, like wind power and the electrical and hydrogen-powered engines in our cars and flyers, didn't exist like they do now. You are all too young to remember, but at one time, most cars burned gasoline, a petroleum distillate, and this caused ..."

Yutaka droned on and on, finally turning his back as he paced around the front of the class. Dayton took this opportunity to sit back down.

"This doesn't seem very productive," Dayton whispered to the kid behind him.

"That's cool," the kid responded. "The longer he expounds, the less work we have to do. My brother had this dude last year. Just let him talk and eat up class time."

"Richard," Mister Yutaka called to the kid behind Dayton. "Is there something you'd like to share with the class?"

Richard was dumbstruck. Dayton had seen this kind of thing before in mission briefings. He knew what to do. "Actually, sir, he was just asking me about how we maintained our waste extraction and water re-circulating machinery."

"Yeah." Richard eased up in his seat. "Yeah, I wanted to know about that stuff."

"What an excellent question!" Mister Yutaka said. His face beamed.

Yep, Dayton thought, this was what he wanted to hear, all right. These nature types really perked up at the mention of waste extraction.

"Dayton, would you please step up to the front of the class and talk to us about that? This is a perfect opportunity to learn how a self-contained society functions."

As he clambered out of his seat and walked forward, the hologram vanished, and the lights came back on. What mattered was that Richard looked relieved and even a bit grateful. It gave Dayton hope that he might have at least one friend in the class.

***

An hour later, Dayton pulled out his lunch tube and peered inside. The sound of the school cafeteria clattered around him. Just as he thought, his father had thoughtfully placed some nutricubes inside. He and the other off-worlders had gathered at one of the older tables in the back of the cafeteria. They all had trays from the kitchen. Dayton wasn't sure what kind of food it was. All he could see was that it was covered with red sauce similar in appearance and thickness to ketchup and came with bread.

"You should see this trigonometry class," Trenton said between gulps of food. "What a walkthrough."

"I know," Zara said. "These guys are way behind the curve."

"You're taking trig?" Trenton asked with a grin.

"Yes," Zara gritted her teeth as she spoke. "I do know more than just how to read a sensor log, you know."

"Either of you guys have Mister Yutaka?" Dayton chimed in. "That guy sounds more like he wants to indoctrinate everyone to his beliefs than teach."

"Yeah," Zara said. "I have him for the third lecture of the day. The guy kept picking on me as an example of progress."

Dayton felt a little better knowing that Yutaka picked on someone besides him.

SPLAT. The remains of a soggy sandwich landed on the table. Laughter from a few tables away told him where the missile came from. It was a table of guys rolling over themselves.

"It's called food," the ringleader called out. "We eat it here on Earth, space cases."

He was a tall, dark-haired boy with perfectly trimmed hair, wearing a button-down shirt with crimson-silver paisley patterns running up and down it.

Mister Perfect, Dayton thought. He fist-bumped with a blonde-haired kid wearing neon orange netglasses, as if congratulating him on throwing the sandwich.

Dayton and the others looked at each other for a brief, tense moment.

"Just ignore them," Dayton whispered.

"What should we do?" whispered Zara back.

"Just say something. Talk to me like it's nothing."

"You should see the guy I have for English," Zara said, changing the subject. "He's all about 'the art of conversation' and some other junk."

SPLISH. Another missile, a fruit cup, crashed onto the edge of the table. A piece of orange stuck to Dayton's shirt. A French fry covered in ketchup landed on the seat next to Trenton.

"Who were they aiming at?" Trenton said loud enough for the other table to hear. He peered over at the offending table.

"Hard to tell," Zara said, with the same volume. "These groundlings are not very coordinated."

Dayton looked over. Sure enough, Mister Perfect was front and center. It was clear who was running the show.

"Let me give it a shot!" Dayton pointed at a container of apple juice on Zara's tray. Smirking, Zara handed it over.

Trenton looked like he was on a slow boil. Dayton tore the top of the juice box until it was loose. He took a careful assessment of the distance to the target, and then he lobbed the juice box in a high arc. The box tumbled end over end and came down directly on the table. SPLOOSH! It landed with an explosion, peppering Mister Perfect's hair and splattering all over those sitting next to him.

"If you're going to do it, do it right," Dayton shouted across the tables. Zara and Trenton collapsed into giggles, and there were a few *oohs* and *ahhhs* from the rest of the student body.

Beep, beep, beeeeeep. A monitor bot came gliding down the aisles between the benches, alerted by the commotion. It hovered close by, assessing the situation. The bot had seen nothing illegal, Dayton knew, or it probably would start handing out those citations from its front slot, as he'd seen it do to the students sucking on nicotine straws. It could summon some human faculty to dole out the real punishment.

"Next time," Mister Perfect said, eyeing the monitor bot.

"Looking forward to it," Dayton said.

***

Physics class. Dayton wondered about what might happen. That punk who had thrown the sandwich seemed to have a lot of followers. And what about Mister Perfect? That guy seemed to control things from behind the scenes. But Dayton had hit him in the clothing, a move that was sure to anger him.

Dayton only knew two people. What would happen if this guy and his followers jumped him while he was walking alone? For that matter, where did this guy hang out? Did throwing food make someone an enemy?

His heart eased to normal when he spotted Trenton and Zara waiting for him by the entrance after class. At least if a fight came, he wouldn't be alone.

"Either of you run into that group from lunch?" Dayton slung his backpack over his shoulder as they started their walk home.

"Yeah," Zara said. "I saw that guy at the end of fifth period. He didn't do anything."

Trenton waved the incident away. "That neopunk is probably too afraid he'll mess up his pretty clothes. He probably ran home to change outfits when you pasted him at lunch."

Flyers and ground cars interrupted the conversation—scattering in all directions away from the school's parking lot. Lines of other kids were snaking out of the front entrance in a lazy river of people.

"That's what I need." Dayton pointed to an air car soaring overhead. "A flyer or something."

"I know," Trenton said. "For the last few years, we've been allowed to drive just about everything in *Venture*'s inventory. Here, all we get to do is walk."

"At least we got some respect at lunch today," Zara said. "Just about everyone was checking us out after we threw that juice box."

"Did I look okay?" Dayton certainly felt nervous when that confrontation happened. He didn't even think about the crowd surrounding them.

"Oh, look okay?" Zara asked in mockery. "Who cares what you looked like? You showed up these groundlings. That's all you need to know. Man, that's enough."

Well, that was something. Would he have to fight this guy from lunch? He glanced up as a flyer full of students went zipping overhead. Clearly, he had to do something. If he had a flyer, that might help, but all he had was a Tata, and that didn't even belong to him.

Dayton couldn't explain the anxiety he felt. He knew he had a lot to offer and could prove himself to these groundlings. He knew he shouldn't want to, but he seemed to have a need.

"Space cadets," someone yelled from an open window as a four-door Toyota ground car sped past.

"What is their problem?" Dayton asked.

"Get used to that, by the way," Zara said. "I told you; they don't like us here."

"Whatever," Dayton said as they headed down the street. He turned into a corner bodega. "Look, I got to get another Coke. I don't know what's in those things, but they are addictive."

Heading down the refrigerator lane in the back of the store, Dayton came to the Cokes. He waved his hand over the crimson sensor, only the refrigerator door wouldn't slide open.

Dayton went up to the counter, expecting a service bot, but in a rare occurrence, he discovered that there was a live human being instead. He was an older man, very gray, with a protruding belly that thrust his smeared white apron out. His face was stern as his gray eyes looked the three of them up and down.

"Hi," Dayton said. "I'd like to get a Coke, please."

"I don't think so," the old man said.

"Are you having trouble stocking them?"

"No."

"Are they still warm?"

"No."

"Then what's the problem?"

"The problem is you, spacer." The old man's eyes glowered at Dayton as if they were on fire. He pointed to a sign in the window. "You see that sign? That says I can refuse service to anybody at any time for any reason. Right now, that's you."

"What did I do?"

"You and your kind come falling in here from out of the sky. All of you cause traffic accidents, road closures, and anarchy. Look at what your falling junk has done to my neighbor's property."

The old man thrust his finger across the street. Sure enough, there was a building with a partially caved-in roof. "You see that? That was caused by your ineptness. The Agency said they weren't going to pay for it, either. So, what happens to my friend? He's outta luck, and it's all your fault."

"Hey, whoa, we didn't do anything," Zara said. "We didn't plan on the ship falling apart."

"Yeah, right," the old man said. "And now you're here, with your advanced knowledge and more than ten percent of your brains being used. You don't even eat real food. Because of you, my grandson might not get into college because you guys are raising the curve."

"Man, you Earthers got some issues," Trenton said. "Look, all we want is a Coke, okay? We're not keeping your grandson from going to college."

Dayton said. "I'm sorry about your neighbor's roof over there. If you let me speak to the Bureau of Civilian Affairs, I'm sure we can get that taken care of."

"The BCA is a joke, and so are you," the old man said. He crossed his arms in front of his chest, shaking with anger. "Now get out of my store and don't ever come back. And stay away from all the other stores on this grid."

Dayton walked out of the little shop. He could feel the old man's eyes boring into him with every step he took.

"Get back into high orbit!" Some guy, not much older than Dayton, shouted from the window of a passing ground car. "Yeah, that's right. Go back to space."

The whining of the little Mitsubishi Esparza picked up as it barreled down the street. All Dayton could do was watch.

He looked to Zara, who just rolled her eyes and stated, "Like I said, get used to it."

TEN

Dayton pressed the auto-opener to the garage door of his new Earth home and stared inside. The garage had a conventional door and an overhead clamshell door that opened for flyers to land. It was connected by an interior door to the kitchen. Dayton wasn't sure how long he'd been staring into the area, which was large enough to fit four cars along with other stuff.

"Whatcha thinkin'?" his father said in a joking tone from somewhere behind him.

"Well, there's room for a workbench in the front. It has four robot alcoves. And I wouldn't mind a gravity fork in the center. Maybe put some scaffolding along the sides for equipment storage."

"That could be done," his dad said. "You could try the Sub for tech and parts."

"I could?" Dayton knew about "the Sub," the nickname given to Sub Level Containment Bunker 327A, a giant storage room about ten levels underground.

"Sure," Dad said. "I think your pilot's ID still gets you to that level."

His father's comm panel went off. With a quizzical look, he answered the call.

Seconds later, he pointed the comm panel screen at Dayton.

And there it was.

The comm panel screen was black, punctuated by a flashing red "A" Alpha sign. Like colored GPS coordinates and a time/date stamp scrolled across the bottom of the screen.

The Alpha Prerogative.

"I'm called up," Dad said with a note of pain.

"Back to space? That's GREAT."

Dad grunted. "I'm not leaving. No way."

"What? Why not?"

"Leave you? After everything?" Father spread his hands dramatically. "I can't do that."

Dayton steeled himself. He never felt stronger about anything in his life. "No, Dad. You must GO. An Alpha isn't up for debate."

"I know," Dad admitted. "I don't want to go."

"What are you talking about?" Desperation edged Dayton's voice. "At least one of us gets to go back to space. It's our home."

"This is our new home."

"It's not. It's NOT." Now, it was Dayton spreading his hands in a plea. "I don't want you to be Earthbound."

His father looked at him, incredulous.

"Please, Dad, please go."

All the air went out of the man.

"You will need to stay with a guardian. I'm not leaving you alone."

"I don't need that."

"Yeah, well, you do," Dad said. "The law says you must. You're—"

"Too young," Dayton answered for him. "I know. I get that a lot lately."

"We could have you stay with Zara and her parents."

"Uh, no," Dayton said in a raised voice. "Zara gets into my business too much as it is. If I moved in there, there'd be no stopping her."

"How about Trenton?"

"Trenton's parents are thinking about moving to Argentina for some science research project."

Dad looked stumped. Good. He was finally seeing things Dayton's way. Dayton had admired his father, but now he was excited for him as well. And bottom line, he was jealous. Dayton wanted to be the one called up. Why couldn't his father see the gift he'd been given?

"There's always your Aunt Margaret," Dad said slowly. "She will step up for family. Might be good for you to have a woman around the house."

"I have an Aunt Margaret?"

"My sister," Dad said. "She's a bit different, but she's good people."

"Fine," Dayton said. He hesitated before saying anything more. It was best to leave the argument there. *Aunt Margaret, huh? What could go wrong?*

***

"It's like sugar with air," six-year-old Toki said from his bed in the medical center.

"I know, buddy, isn't it great?" Dayton said, looking at the tube of blue raspberry cotton candy Dad had given Toki. "My dad picked up a whole bunch for you guys to bring here today."

The cotton candy tube was just one of the many treats Dad had brought to the *Venture* survivors the past few weeks. Toki, and the other injured children like him, were confined to bulky, off-white beds with annoying side rails and the sterile smell of cleaning fluids.

Sounds of excitement came from down the hall, indicating Dayton's father was well into his rounds. The children loved his visits.

"How're the nanites working out?" Dayton put the view-mag loupe up to his eye and focused on Toki's right leg cast.

"They itch," Toki said.

Dayton saw the nanites, thousands of them, crisscrossing and darting around Toki's leg bones, stitching and suturing, making the young man whole.

"It's a real dance down there," Dayton said, replacing the loupe. "But it looks a lot further along than the other day."

"I go home with Mommy and Daddy next week," Toki said.

"Hey, buddy, that's great." Dayton fished into his bag. "I brought you something." He took out more small toys and a handheld game.

The boy had brilliant, shiny hazel eyes that lit up with delight. Dayton ruffled his hair. "Gotta move along, Toki. See you soon, okay?"

***

The red kidney floated in the green saline water of the tank.

"That's all me in there," Turco said, standing by Dayton's side.

"That's your kidney?"

"It'll soon be ready for transplant. I can finally get rid of this reduced capacity thing I've been stuck with for ages."

The tank glugged as they watched the surface of the green saline ripple.

"So, what are you going to do first?" Dayton asked.

"I'm gonna drink a lot of beer and stay out alllll night," Turco belted out, sweeping the medical lab in a dramatic fashion. A few of the techs looked at him dismissively.

"Be careful," Dayton said. "Your new parts won't last that long if you treat them like that."

"Oh, okay, Мом," Turco said with his eyes bulging out of their sockets, an odd habit the man had whenever he conjured up faux anger. "Seems like I been here for years. Stupid kidney."

The pair moved over to a regen chamber. The large glass cylinder was a meter in diameter and probably double that in width. The inside afforded a view of a naked youth bathed in green suspension fluid. He wore a soft bubble helmet that fed him oxygen that snaked down in a white pressure hose from the top of the chamber. He seemed to stand straight at attention.

His arms still showed the burn marks from *Venture*'s destruction. Dayton knew Brock Temple from around the ship but never took an interest in him till his burnt, barely alive body was brought to the med center.

"Brock's coming along fine," Turco said. "Poor guy was sitting front and center when the lab caught fire."

"A fire that fed on pure oxygen, too," Dayton said. "I can't help but imagine that every time I walk by this tank."

Brock's arms were about halfway done. The automatic regenerator limbs danced with inhuman speed, removing the burnt skin and knitting fresh skin, cell by cell, in a complex whirlwind only an ultra-fast auto doc could manage.

"But you know he'll wake up and be fine in a couple more days," Turco said. "And all I'm in for is a new kidney. Why do you keep coming back here, man? And don't tell me it's to watch your dad hand out goodies to the kids."

"I feel at home here," Dayton said after some pause. "It's tech. A building full of people like us, were once us. That world, this Earth, it's—"

"Scary?" Turco finished the sentence.

"Well ..." Dayton struggled with the words. It was one thing to feel emotion but quite another to express it coherently. "There's a million places to go. And everywhere is like I just don't belong there. I don't belong here on this planet."

"But at least you're with your own age group."

"Only a couple of guys even talk to me. And the teachers. Gosh! They pick on me like I'm a lab rodent. I just want to be ..."

"You want to be left alone." Turco again finished his thought.

There was a moment of silence between the two, with only the bubbling of the air hoses in the solution to break the tension.

Dayton turned away from the tank and faced his mentor. "What do I do, Turc?" Dayton said as his veins pumped with fury. "I'm stuck on this planet for two years. Two years. And the only place I feel like I belong is here. And now my dad is leaving."

"Your father said you were planning on converting the garage to a bay," Turco said.

"That's one small space," Dayton said.

"Sorry, kid," Turco said. "There has to be something you like about this place. I mean, I never fit in around here, either. But there's cool stuff here. You must find it. Like girls?"

Dayton looked away, but he felt a surge of blood to his face. But it was evident he didn't react fast enough.

"That's it, isn't it?" Turco said as his mouth grew into a Cheshire grin. "There's a girl, isn't there? Awwwww ... C'mon now. I know that look."

"Yeah, okay," Dayton admitted. "There might be one, yeah. But girls around here are so hard to understand. I don't even know how to approach her."

"Well, why you been keeping this secret from me, buddy?" Turco turned and walked off, motioning Dayton to follow. "Have I not taught you everything you know?"

"Well, yeah. The cool stuff."

"Please. Step into my office."

The two made their way down the lab floor. It was a center aisle, with the glass of hundreds of vats and tanks on either side. It resembled a fish store his father had dragged him into the other day. A lot of clear containers, tanks, only these tanks were filled with organs and limbs attached to all manner of hoses and clamps. Dayton even thought he saw a spinal column in one of them.

Overhead, there was scaffolding and catwalks. Long I-beam-supported gantry cranes that picked up and placed the vats depending on the growth of their contents. All controlled by the watchful and ever-present computer AI. There were human techs all over the place, too, though they didn't seem at all concerned with visitors. They mostly conversed amongst themselves in groups of twos and threes, consulting their datapads and readouts on the tank monitors.

"Say, Flight Officer Murdoch," a vaguely familiar voice

sounded from directly behind Dayton. Doctor Weiss stood there, clean cut as ever, wearing a dress shirt and slacks, no white doctor's coat.

"Yes," Dayton struggled to sound polite. Even that one word proved difficult.

"I just wanted to see how you were doing," the doctor smiled as if recalling some pleasant memory. "You know I saw you here a couple of times earlier, but you escaped before I could catch up to you."

Escaped. What a word for him to use.

Doctor Weiss said, "Well, I'm glad I caught you this time."

"Is there something I can do for you?" Dayton held for a moment. "Doctor Weiss?"

"I simply wanted to see how you were doing," Doctor Weiss repeated at a distinctly higher octave as he spoke. "We're all friends here, right?"

Dayton kept his face without emotion. "That depends," he said flatly.

"Look," Doctor Weiss said with a flustered voice. The doctor glanced up and down the aisle as if worried there would be an audience for what he was about to say. "I know there was a misunderstanding, but I'm trying to make sure there's no lasting animosity."

Dayton thought quickly. "There is something you could do to make sure of that ..." he said, testing.

Turco looked back and forth from Dayton to Dr. Weiss. Unlike Earth adults, Turco was not about to step in and shut Dayton down.

Doctor Weiss stepped back two feet and cocked his head. "What might that be?" he asked.

"Return my flight jacket. After you drugged me, it was taken from me."

Weiss's face grew pale. "Now see here ..." he stuttered.

"What the kid here is trying to say," Turco started, "is that he knows you jabbed him with something, like you did a lot of the kids I've spoken to, and stole his jacket. So, if you don't return it right now, I'm going to kick your sorry egg-head butt into one of these regen tanks."

Doctor Weiss glanced at the two of them as if expecting an uppercut, punch to the gut, or worse.

"I wouldn't want that, by the way, Dr. Weiss," Dayton said mildly.

"We'll be in my room," Turco said. "Make sure it gets here on the immediate. Got that?"

"I-I-I'll have to make a requisition," Doctor Weiss said. "It's in storage."

"No," Dayton said. "I think you're mistaken." He was guessing but wanted to call Dr. Weiss's bluff. "It's sitting in your office."

Doctor Weiss fumbled with his wrist, fingering his comm unit. "This is ridiculous," he said with conviction, though he backed farther off. "I see that flight jacket means a great deal to you. I'll make arrangements to have it returned."

"Please do that," Dayton said.

"As soon as I can."

Dayton gave the doctor a cold, measured look. "Immediately," he said softly.

"I will ... of course ..." Doctor Weiss said and walked away at a brisk pace, his dress shoes clapping on the duracrete floor.

Dayton and Turco looked at each other.

"Were you really going to kick his butt?" Dayton asked.

"Yes. Were you going to help me?"

"Nah, you looked like you could handle it."

"What if he called the orderlies in and I couldn't?"

"Then I'm there."

"Survey pilots forever," Turco said as they laughed and fist-bumped.

Turco's quarters were part apartment, part hospital room. It had the same cold floor as the rest of the place and a bed done up with shiny metal rails and manilla-and-white bedding. But there was a desk, not unlike those in *Venture*'s staterooms, and an imitation wood dresser, from which Turco's clothing protruded through open drawers.

"My office," Turco sat in the desk's metallic black chair, which squeaked against the floor as he pulled it up. He motioned for Dayton to sit on the bed.

"Now, this girl we were talking about," Turco said. "What is her name?"

"Is that—is that important?"

"Yes."

"I don't see how."

"You want my help or not?"

"Yes."

"Then what's her name?"

Dayton was about to speak when a metallic figure beeped at the open door.

"Excuse me, sir," the shiny robot said through a speaker on its cylindrical head. "I have a possession to return to a Flight Officer Murdoch."

"That's me." Dayton took the jacket when the robot's mechanical arm offered it. Dayton then pressed his thumbprint onto the pad in the robot's other hand, and the bot went on its way.

"He didn't have the guts to deliver it himself," Turco said.

"No, he didn't," Dayton flung his flight jacket on. It felt cool but welcoming. "But that just means I scared him. I'm good knowing that."

"Her name, tough guy?" Turco snapped his fingers, shaking off Dayton's victory.

"Allyson," Dayton felt relief when he said the name. "She goes to my school."

"Okay," Turco steepled his fingers in front of his face as if processing the data. "Do you have any classes with her?"

"No."

"Do you see her at the same time every day? Like, in the halls, or maybe at your locker?"

"No."

"Uh huh," Turco seemed lost in thought. "Do you know any of her friends? Someone you could roll up on when she's talking to them?"

"Well, kind of, but I'm not too sure about that."

"How well do you know her?" Turco asked.

"She kind of helped me when I crashed into the mall."

"What?" Turco laughed. "My young friend, THAT is your in."

"So, what do I do?"

"Just approach her and introduce yourself."

"Does that work? What do I say to her?"

"How about 'thank you for saving my life'?"

"But that's so simple," Dayton said.

"Uh." Turco pinched the ridge of his nose with his thumb and forefinger. "It's not always what you say; it's how you come across saying it. She will be so impressed you had the thrusters to come up and talk to her that what you say won't matter that much. My stars! I thought I had taught you better than that."

"You did; I'm listening," Dayton said. "It worked all through space."

"Ask that father of yours if you can get a cool set of wheels. Earth girls like cars."

"They do?"

"Of course they do. You need to adapt. And stop hanging around this place so much. You're bringing me down."

ELEVEN

"You guys sure you'll be okay?" Dad asked, pulling the Tata over and surveying the bustling crowds outside. "I can meet you at the car in about thirty minutes."

"Make it an hour," Dayton said. Here at the swap meet, he felt a sense of belonging. It reminded him of the bazaars on frontier worlds. Zara and Trenton were in a like mind, smiling and excited to enter the noisy throng of people.

"I'll synch the chronographs with the beacon on the Tata," Dad said.

"Okay, great," Dayton said as he, Trenton, and Zara got out and moved off.

There were inventions, tools, and food to catch their eyes, nearly all of it wrapped in clear plastic bags hanging from pegboard shelves, heaped on insta-tables, or strung up on shiny braided cables across the entrances to the stalls. Customers hustled in and out of the booths, tearing off in every direction. It was confusion. It was a touch of a life they once knew.

In one stall, a sales bot demonstrated a foaming window cleaner that used bio enzymes to wipe up after itself. On an elevated stage, hundreds of micro-robots called Scrubbies, each the size of a quarter, spun and swarmed an old economy ground car. They danced across the weathered car, alternatively cleaning it, waxing it, and buffing it out to the delight of the crowd.

"See, I can handle this," Zara said.

The trio struggled their way through the crowds to where a pair of black duraplastic grav platforms hovered two meters above the ground. They were four meters apart. Connecting them was a white metal beam no more than a hand-span wide.

And on top of the far platform stood a man wearing a

skin-tight neon green latex suit spattered with corporate logos. He held a double-headed staff two meters long and as wide as a flagpole. The man was muscular and toned, and his frame and tattoos shone through his tank top. He wore a zebra-striped cowboy hat that barely contained his bursting blond mane. He stood on a floor of dayglow pink and yellow padding, meaning anyone who fell from the beam wouldn't be seriously injured, if at all.

"You know," Trenton said. "I did not expect to see that here."

"It's a Zhandou arena," Dayton exclaimed.

"Are they serious?" Zara laughed. "Zhandou? Here? I didn't think these Earthers had it in them."

Zhandou. Chinese for *combat*. A martial art that had taken the outer worlds unlike any other spectacle. It was the first thing Dayton transferred his martial arts training to. He liked to think he did well at it.

"So, do I have any challengers?" The man in the green suit played to the crowd. "We have a five-thousand-dollar credit tube to anyone who can knock me off the beam in combat. Who dares challenge me, Daft Zeus?" He brandished his fierce-looking staff, which was made of lightweight foam.

The crowd cheered as one eager volunteer handed his shopping bags off to a friend, grabbed a staff, and mounted the opposing grav platform.

"Are you ready?" Daft Zeus belted out to the audience, flexing his muscles.

"Yes!" shouted the throngs of spectators.

A holographic siren directly overhead blared a klaxon.

The volunteer shuffled forward, one foot leading and the other sliding up behind. He glanced down, more concerned with his footholds than with the green-clad muscle man twirling his combat staff.

By the time the poor guy looked up, Daft Zeus had landed a padded strike to the man's head. He plummeted to the padding below, uninjured except for his pride. The crowd heckled and teased the poor man, and he dusted himself off, returned for his bags, and meekly made his exit.

"Oh!" Daft Zeus shouted. "No five-thousand-dollar credit tube for you. Nice try, though. You lasted twelve seconds. That's ten seconds longer than the last guy. Am I looking at a bunch of weaklings out there? Who thinks they can go the distance with Daft Zeus?"

"Hey," Zara pointed at Daft Zeus. "Do you see that, Dayton? He has a brown belt. You have a brown belt, don't you?"

"Yes," Dayton said. A brown belt ranked just below the series of black belts denoting mastery of the sport.

"All right!" Daft Zeus threw off his zebra cowboy hat and screamed to the skies. "I'm getting really bored with you weaklings! Do I have to take you on two at a time? Because I will."

"Hey," Zara cried out.

Daft Zeus cocked his head.

"I got two guys here who can take you, no problem," Zara continued. "You scared?"

"I'm Daft Zeus," the man pounded his chest to the cheers of the crowd. "I don't fear nothin'."

"What are you doing?" Dayton leaned over and whispered into Zara's ear.

"Having some fun with the Earthers," Zara shot back. To Daft Zeus, she yelled, "You look scared to me."

"Well, what do you think, brothers?" Daft Zeus yelled to the crowd in general, but Dayton and Trenton in particular. "You think you have the guts to face me? Do you each want a five-thousand-dollar credit tube? I bet your mommies don't let you out to play much, do they?"

"Oh, it's on." Dayton grabbed the padded dueling staff.

From below, a third grav platform inserted itself in the middle of the beam, creating a third position midway between the first two. Daft Zeus hopped on the middle platform and flexed his muscles.

"Bolang Posui," Dayton said to Trenton as they headed up

to their respective platforms.

"I agree," Trenton smiled. "Time to let the waves crash."

Dayton had decided on *Bolang Posui*, meaning *waves crashing on rocks*. Like the waves, Zeus would strike at them, but his blows would be ineffective. But unlike the waves, he would tire. Dayton had fought alongside Trenton before. Trenton, being of a squat and heavy frame, was not as agile as those who came from a lower gravity. But what he was, more than anything, was solid. Once Trenton placed his feet firmly in place, it took a grav truck to move him. And the waves would crash.

Dayton hefted and spun the staff. It was a classic *rongyu*, or honor staff. It sported cylinders of foam padding at either end rather than blades. The idea behind the *rongyu* was a fight for honor, not blood or death. It was adequately balanced.

The crowd cheered, many of them calling out bets and electronically sending them to Zara's waiting pad.

The hologram spun red, and the klaxon blared. The crowd erupted in a great crescendo.

Daft Zeus trotted forward, twirling his staff like a fan. He spun to the left, then caught it with his right hand and spun it to the right. "Who do you love?" He shouted into the crowd.

"Daft Zeus!"

"What's my name?"

"Daft Zeus!"

"Who is undefeated?"

"Daft Zeus!"

The colorful clown always went for the feint, Dayton observed. He leaped forward about half a meter, landing squarely on the beam without so much as a balance correction. Zeus' eyes went wide in surprise for a millisecond. He covered it in a near-instant, but Dayton saw. There was a flash of worry.

Yes. It's not going as you planned. You don't know how to handle it.

Provoked, Daft Zeus charged forward, left foot leading. Dayton held his ground, showing his opponent a side stance.

Daft Zeus yelled, thrusting his staff at Dayton's head. Dayton shifted, avoiding each attack.

"What's the matter?" Daft Zeus said, trickles of sweat dripping from his forehead. "You AFRAID to use that little staff you got there? You know it won't make a dent in THIS body." With that, Daft Zeus pounded his chest with one arm while holding his weapon aloft.

Good. Lose your focus. Get angry. Cloud your mind. Fight a two-front war.

"What's the matter, little man?" Daft Zeus shouted at Dayton. "You come all the way up to MY arena and don't even take a swing? What are you, a peace lover? Show me what you got."

Daft Zeus let out another shrieking war cry, then let out a wail and brought his staff down hard on Trenton's shoulder. Trenton just stood there. Another strike, this one at Trenton's mid-section. It failed to register. Another punch to the gut, and still nothing

Daft Zeus sprang back at Dayton, twirling his staff above his head. Fire lit behind his eyes.

Dayton smirked, just to provoke him.

Daft Zeus came in hard, screaming an animated war cry that was a mix of frustration, anger, and insult. He swung again at waist level.

Dayton pulled back. Zeus' pad came within millimeters but didn't connect.

Zeus came out of the swing as overextended and overbalanced.

Dayton shoved him in the small of the back.

Daft Zeus tumbled, screaming, down to the padded pit.

The crowd cheered! Dayton stood on the beam and held his staff over his head in victory. Onlookers roared, holding their fists over their heads, while Zara cheered like an Earth girl.

Dayton hopped down, and he and Trenton shook many hands offered.

The waves had broken on the rocks.

The adoring crowd parted as Daft Zeus marched up to the duo.

Here we go. Another sore loser.

Zeus came to a stop, squarely facing them. The man was big, easily six inches taller, and possessed of a lot more muscle tissue. Daft Zeus looked stern.

Oh boy. This is going to be one ugly scene in a second.

And he stuck out his hand.

Dayton hesitated, then grabbed the offered hand. It was a tight grip. About the third pump, Daft Zeus' face broke out into a smile, and he gave a similar handshake to Trenton.

"A job well done. Head on over to the promo booth and grab your prize."

"Wow," Zara said. "Did not expect that."

"I know," Dayton said, sweat beading on his face. "They like us."

Zara grabbed Trenton and Dayton each by the hand and led them to the promo booth. "You're nothing but a dancing bear to them. Let's get that reward money. I want to see that promo booth."

As they got closer, Dayton spotted a familiar raven-haired beauty working inside the booth.

"Allyson," Dayton said, more to himself in wonder at seeing her there. But she heard him anyway and responded with a smile.

"Oh hey, Mall Jumper and the heavy-world guy," she said. "I saw you two beat Daft."

"Yeah, I get the idea he isn't defeated that often," Dayton said, stuffing his nervousness deep down into his chest.

"You're the first," Allyson said with a smile. She handed the credit tubes to Dayton and Trenton. "He won't forget that."

"Thanks," Dayton said, his smile bursting across his face. Finally, a legitimate reason to talk to her, and Mister Handsome wasn't around, either.

She mirrored an enthusiastic smile back. "You even got a round of cheers from us Earthers."

"Yeah, this time. But trust me, not everyone loves us space kids."

Dayton's heart pounded in his chest, but not from his combat with the dethroned Daft Zeus.

"Do you have an ID ping?" Dayton didn't want to say it that way, but there it was.

Stupid. Stupid. Stupid. Of course she has an ID ping. Everyone who has a comm has one. They always show up whenever a person comms in someone else. Literally billions of people have them. And I ask, "Do you have one?" Ugh.

"I mean, unless you have a boyfriend, or something," Dayton quickly chimed in.

"I'm seeing someone," Allyson said. "But it's not exclusive or anything like that. He always reminds me."

"So …" Dayton said. "Yes? No? What do you think?"

"I like that jacket," Allyson said, grabbing it with her thumb and forefinger. "Kind of like a motorcycle jacket, but way nicer."

"Thanks," Dayton said. "It's the one piece of clothing that you Earthers seem to like."

"Oh, I think a trip to the mall would do wonders for that problem."

"Are you offering?" Dayton barely held his voice from cracking. He almost willed himself not to sweat, though he could blame that on Daft Zeus.

"I don't know," Allyson smiled. "Are you asking?"

"Yes."

"Okay then," Allyson said. "Yeah, sounds like a plan, then. Ping me."

"I will," Dayton brought his voice under control. "Tonight."

"Dayton!" Zara's voice boomed from behind him.

"What?" Dayton spat, irritated. He turned around.

"C'mon," Zara said, walking away. "Say bye-bye to your

'girlfriend' already, and let's go."

Dayton felt the blood leave his face. For a split millisecond, he was panicked. Did Allyson hear that? He turned back, but Allyson was now off helping someone else.

Dayton proceeded with his friends, crestfallen. So close.

Then his comm beeped.

It was Allyson's ID ping, followed by a smiley face.

Mission accomplished.

TWELVE

"Thanks for saving me in Mister Yutaka's class," Richard said from his seat, again behind Dayton.

"Huh?" Dayton asked.

"Remember you covered for me in class when we were caught talking? I didn't want to start in a bad way with that teacher. He can be a real horrorwraith."

"No problem," Dayton answered. "I just wish it hadn't led to me talking for fifteen minutes about waste extraction."

"You really know your crap," Richard said with a laugh. "Hey, I saw you getting into it with Bradford and those desis at lunch, too."

Bradford. So that was his name. "Yeah," Dayton said. "Basically, he can't throw food, and I can. What's his story?"

"Popular, doesn't really do more than look good. You tarnished that image with the food fight."

What was Allyson doing with this guy? "Does he have a lot of friends?"

"Yes, he does." Richard took out his homework pad and called up the literature class on it. "Basically, they're a bunch of desis and cowards. You show them you're up to brawl, and they'll scatter for sure. They like to look good, but if a fight might mess up their precious faces, they find a way out of it."

"I wonder why he started trouble with us." Dayton pulled up his StudentAid 8.0 pad. "What did we do to him?"

"You're new," Richard said. "He probably thought he could scare you, but well, he was wrong, and now the whole school knows it."

"So, a lot of people saw that?" Dayton didn't know the full view on that incident yet. It was hard to keep tabs on such things when your adrenaline was pumping at re-entry speeds.

"Just about the whole school," Richard said. "Everyone loves it when there's drama. Some guys even captured the thing and posted it on the Net. By now, everyone's seen it."

"But there wasn't drama," Dayton flipped through the pages on his pad. "Was there?"

"Oh yeah there was," Richard said. "It made Bradford look like a total gelback, too. Man, it's not often someone shows the desis."

"Desis?" Trenton hadn't mentioned that group when he'd explained the school cliques at the mall. "Who are they?"

"More like another race," Richard said. "*Desi* is short for *designer children*. Mommy and Daddy had the bucks to get their kids' DNA manipulated into the perfect kid. All the best traits, like tall, nice skin with no pimples, perfect eyesight, no bad breath, no plaque, smart. Everything a loving couple could want."

"And they say the off-worlders are taking unfair advantage of the system around here," Dayton said.

"Not even," Richard said. "You guys have a lot of skills and stuff, but you sweat like me. But those desis have all the props."

Mister Segramson entered the class, old-style books in hand. He glanced quickly at the attendance board, the device that biometrically read each student as they sat in their assigned seats. He checked to see that everyone was accounted for.

The lecture, a multimedia display of holograms and charts, began with the teacher's voice droning over them. Most of the class looked bored, which Dayton found happened all too often.

"Pssst," Richard whispered. "Have you seen this?" He held out a picture on his comm of a cavernous cement bunker filled to the ceiling with barely-organized used equipment. These were parts of *Venture*, and they sat in an underground storage area almost as big as the ship itself.

Dayton glanced. To him, it looked like recon heaven.

"Yeah," Dayton said. "That's the Sub."

"Sub?"

"Short name for the Sub Level Containment Bunker Three-Two-Seven-Alpha," Dayton said. "It's the place they put all the *Venture* spares now. Place is like ten levels underground."

"I'd love to run free in there."

"My pilot's ID gets me in."

"You think we could go?" Richard scrolled his comm. "It also says *Venture* crew gets first dibs on anything in there."

"Show me that picture again?" Dayton said.

Richard swiped the comm. "You wanna go? I'll take you." He didn't even try to disguise his eagerness.

But Dayton didn't answer. His eyes were glued to the screen where endless piles of parts and wreckage glistened under the artificial lights and gantry crane beams of the bunker warehouse. In his imagination, he was looking at his next set of wheels, and it was going to be a lot better than an ordinary set of Earth wheels. He was going to score a flyer. A flyer to take Allyson up in.

At the front of the class, Mister Segramson cleared his throat, and Richard sat back in his seat, taking the comm with him.

***

The Tata squeaked to a halt just short of the house. A UMoveIt van was out in front, its clamshell doors open, with a metallic, ribbed ramp lowered from the back. A bushy-haired woman stood out in the yard, hands on her hips. Wearing a generous, flowing geometric print dress and leather sandals that showed her bare feet, she looked to Dayton like that depiction of Mother Nature he'd seen on the fuselage art on the Recon ships.

But unlike that artwork, this woman was real. She had brown eyes and black hair that tousled all down her shoulders, held in place by a bandana sporting red and yellow colors.

"Your Aunt Margaret," Dad said as the Tata bumped into the driveway.

"THAT'S Aunt Margaret?" Dayton's jaw hung open.

"Oh yes. My gosh. She's early. Come on."

His dad was over to the woman before Dayton shut the door of the car. He approached the two as they shared an intense hug. They finally pulled away, all smiles, and Dad motioned him over.

"This is your nephew, Margaret," his father said. "Dayton, your Aunt Margaret."

He extended his hand, and Margaret grabbed it and pulled him in. Despite her diminutive size, her arms surrounded him. She held the hug longer than he would have liked, finally releasing him and holding him at arm's length with foggy eyes.

"Oh, my Maker," she said, stifling a tear. "You look like your mother; may the Maker bless and keep her. We have so much to catch up on."

"Well, I tell you what," Dad said. "Let's get you all moved in."

"Uh yeah, that sounds good," Dayton said. He looked around for the moving robots that came with each rental truck.

He didn't see them.

***

"That's the last of it," Dad said as he dropped an overstuffed chair on the living room floor. It joined two dozen other items of furniture, knickknacks, clothing, boxes, and other belongings.

"Wouldn't this be easier with a bot?" Dayton asked.

"I don't believe in bots," a female voice said. Dayton turned and saw the woman, who had appeared from the kitchen. "They make people weak and lazy."

Easy for her to say, Dayton thought. They had just moved

all her stuff in, and she'd hardly lifted a box. Margaret had an almost serene smile about her as she moved off to the kitchen. She was shorter than Dayton, barely coming up to his chest, with wild black hair and brown eyes. Margaret seemed to prefer long, flowing dresses and fibrous sandals that looked as if they were constructed by hand. While he considered the calf-high, pressure-sensitive, and buckled boots standard necessities, he wondered how those sandals could save her feet from anything.

"Robert, you bought some meat dishes." Margaret held up a shiny plastic pouch labeled Chicken Parmesan. "I'm going to toss them. You really have backslid in the past twenty years."

As a child born aboard a spaceship, Dayton had the pleasure of meat perhaps ten or so times in his entire life. Even then, the meat was from freeze-dried packets. Meat was considered rare and valuable. But now, having had fresh meat, it was as if something had awakened his taste buds to a whole new reality. How could she simply throw it away? Margaret seemed to feel there was something significant about this fact, however. Dayton thought to ask her but then thought again. He really didn't want to know.

"You know what?" Dayton moved to the recyclobin and retrieved the packets before the top loader closed. "I really like this stuff. I am going to put it back."

"Do you know what meat does to your digestive system?"

"Fills it up?"

"Ruins it with unhealthy ingredients."

Dayton looked at the packets. The ingredients were printed prominently on the back. "They appear to have a lot of my nutritional needs."

"I think what Margaret is referring to is how the food is made." Dad came to a stop between them.

"Well, that's easy to determine." Dayton replaced the packets in the freezer. "A simple chemical scan will tell us everything we need to know."

"You can't trust those things," Margaret said.

"Can't trust them?" Dayton felt the blood rush to his face and his muscles tighten.

"Son, I think what she means is—"

"No, it's okay." Dayton held up a hand. "I got this one. Margaret, I have used chemical analyzers my whole life. From checking for coolant leaks below decks to fissure cracks in the middle of ore fields, each time, they have saved my life. How many times have you used them?"

"This is not some space emergency." Margaret's face went pale. "This is a simple matter of diet. You need to know the difference."

"Until the chemical analysis is done," Dayton said. "The meat stays with us."

"Let's have a look at the rest of the house." Dad put his arm around Margaret and tried to steer her into another room of the house. The woman chose instead to stay right where she was, in front of Dayton.

"There is also a washer and dryer in the back." Margaret smiled. "I will contact the real estate company and have those removed."

"Better we have an electrostatic machine," Dayton said.

"Oh, no," Margaret acted as if she'd been insulted. "We'll wash them by hand. Believe me, your skin will thank you for it. We need to do something about those clothes you have on. What are they, nylon polymers?"

"Yes," Dayton said. "Among other things."

"Well, I have got to take you down to the Mother Earth Store." Margaret ducked into the refrigerator once again, this time coming out with a container of milk. "It has all our life-style needs, including some good hand-woven clothes for you. This milk is not organic."

"Actually," Dayton snatched the milk from her and replaced it in the fridge. "I really like this milk."

"But it's not organic."

"It comes from cows."

"Yes, I know."

"How much more organic can milk get?"

"There's a lot you don't know," Margaret repeated as she unplugged the convection unit and turned it around. "Once you are educated, you'll see how bad these things are for you."

"Once again, a chemical analyzer will tell us everything we need to know." Dayton turned and walked out of the kitchen and made his way to the living room. Dad soon joined him.

"I really don't like the idea of giving away our technology," Dayton said to his father. "She doesn't like anything."

"Be patient." Dad set his hand on Dayton's shoulder. "Margaret is a member of NLM, or the Nature Lover's Movement. Her ideas on modern living contrast with what we're used to. Just give it some time. We'll strike a balance."

"There doesn't seem to be much balance," Dayton said. "The water that comes out of the faucet was bad for us. We shouldn't eat McDonald's because the company gets their beef from some slaughterhouse in Argentina. I thought the idea when we arrived was to fit in, not reject everything. Now, the house technology? Where does it end?"

"I know. I know. It's been twenty years for me. She has become a bit more zealous, it seems, in the past two decades. It will be all right," Dad said. "You guys may bump heads a little, but that will smooth out. You'll see."

Dayton wondered about that. In the few hours he'd spent in her company, Margaret named about a thousand things wrong with modern society. It was times like those Dayton was glad he'd developed the ability to make his mind wander when Milly was lecturing to him in the craft bay.

"Wow. I am exhausted after moving all those boxes." Margaret spun out of the kitchen, and Dayton could hear her sitting down in the stuffy chair he'd lugged in earlier. "You guys get out the Areca Leaf plates," she called from the other room. "I will be making you both my famous spinach mushroom quiche tonight."

"Actually, you two have fun." Dayton had never eaten such a thing, but it didn't sound very appetizing. "I'm heading over to Zara's tonight."

"Dayton," Dad said. "This is Margaret's first night with us, and she wants to thank us by making us a gourmet meal. It would only be polite if you stayed and ate."

"So, after moving her stuff all day, I have to do her yet another favor?" Dayton collapsed on the couch. "How about you do me a favor for once? Let me go to Zara's."

Dad pressed his point. "Just give it a shot," he said. "Cooking meals is considered a huge compliment among people. The whole concept of dinner is an important social custom that brings families ... umm ... people together. Meals are not just nutrition cubes to be taken at a moment's notice."

"I don't know, Dad. The first place I ever ate here was at a McDonald's, and they seemed to be designed to be eaten quickly."

"That's fast food," his father rolled his eyes at the thought. "Yes, some food is designed to be eaten quickly, but that's not what we're talking about here."

"Well, is it okay if I invite Zara over?" As soon as he said it, he could have kicked himself. He wanted to ping Allyson tonight. Of course, he didn't know what he would say to her. He had to prepare something. *Okay*, he thought, *I'll get to that later*. First, get through dinner.

"Sure," Dad said. "Give Zara a call. Margaret, can you make food for one more?"

***

Zara and Dayton sat in his bedroom, flipping through the many channels Dad's holographic entertainment center now had. Dayton glanced at his comm unit again. He'd set an alert earlier, and Allyson's name, with trademark smiley face, flashed on the screen. He only needed to press the screen to contact her. But his thumb wouldn't move.

"You expecting a newsflash?" Zara glanced at Dayton with a scowl. Her eyes darted to his comm unit. "You keep looking at that thing. What, is the captain gonna ping you?"

"No," Dayton tilted the comm unit's screen toward him, away from Zara's prying eyes. "It's just ... don't worry about it."

"Sheesh. Sorry." Zara turned her attention back to the entertainment holoscreen.

"You'd think with this many channels, there'd be something interesting on," Zara remarked as the channels scanned past. "So far, it's all just entertainment."

"Like your favorites on the ship's netcast?" Dayton smirked.

"Hardy, har har," Zara said. "No, I mean, look at all this brain-dead matter. Half the channels show people arguing. Others show people crying and losing their tempers in front of an audience for no reason other than their own immaturity. Even their news programs just talk about the 'social consequences of *Venture* and its people' till you're dead in the ears from hearing about it."

"It seems like a lot of wasted bandwidth. These broadcasts could be put to much better use."

"Wait," Zara held up her hand.

The channel popped on the screen and showed a man standing in a launch prep area talking about new propulsion systems for extravehicular craft.

"Yeah, that channel."

"This could be good," Dayton said. Zara merely grunted in agreement. "We've got about twenty years of catching up to do."

Dad appeared in the bedroom doorway. "Guys, dinner is ready."

***

"So, Dayton," Margaret took another glass of wine. "How do you like being back on Earth? Pretty exciting, I bet."

Dayton shrugged. "To be honest, I find it very constricting. Of course, this is the first time I've been here."

"What I think Margaret means is how do you like Earth?" Dad said.

"Yeah, but she assumed I've been here before. I haven't."

"Okay, well, you can perceive the general meaning," his father said. "You don't need to analyze every word."

"Sorry," Dayton said to Margaret. "But I'm trying to make communication here as clear as possible. To answer your question, it's very restrictive."

"It's nice to breathe without a filter mask," Zara said, trying to make things light. "The gravity isn't so heavy. Makes walking everywhere a lot easier."

"I see," Margaret said, though her tone betrayed that she really didn't understand. "Well, then, do you like school? I understand Yeager has a brilliant academic program."

"Yeah," Dayton said, as a memory of Allyson in the halls sparked in his mind. Dawgs! Why were there so many people around right now? Why dinner like this? How could he let things get like this when what he really needed was some time alone in his room?

Time alone to ping Allyson.

He could text her. No, that would come off as cowardly. If he was to contact Allyson, it had to be live, person-to-person. He congratulated himself again on getting her ID. He was in rare form, as good—no better—than when he was in space. But all that might come to nothing if he let too much time slip by. The pressure was building. He had to do something tonight.

"No," Zara declared, and so loud it brought him out of his reverie.

"This is a major first for you." Margaret held up a fork full of food, apparently to illustrate her point. "This food is all organic. It has no processing, no pesticides, no aeroponics, genetic engineering, or anything else. I shiver when I think of all the processed and freeze-dried foods you three have survived on. The toxin levels in your systems must be high as a kite."

"Kites don't go that high," Dayton said.

"It's just an expression," Dad said.

"Well, it's not a very accurate one."

"Actually, the food we had was scientifically designed to meet our bodies' every nutritional need," Zara said. "Every blood test I ever took reflects that."

"There are things your doctor won't tell you, Zara." Margaret took another bite. "You need to be careful about that. You know, I can recommend a holistic healing specialist. Lord only knows what exotic chemicals you could have in your system."

"Thanks," Dayton said. He didn't really mean it, though. He'd been given a complete physical after he'd crash-landed, and they didn't find anything wrong with him. If he had any exotic elements, toxins or otherwise, he had no doubt the doctors would've found them.

"It's the best time to become aware," Margaret said. "You're only sixteen, after all."

I'm constantly being reminded of that fact every day that I'm here, Dayton thought.

"I am sorry I won't be around for, well, everything," Dayton's father said. "No telling how long I'll be gone."

"Zara." Margaret scooped another helping onto her plate. Dayton noticed she was the only one who had done so. "I understand you might still go to the new IT school they're setting up."

"Oh yeah," Zara pushed the food on her plate around. "My parents said I should give public school a chance."

"They're right," Dad said.

"I guess they want me nice and normal, whatever that is," Zara said and elbowed Dayton.

Margaret smiled. "We will be sharing the house for a while. Did your dad explain your chores?"

"Yeah, I'll take care of them," Dayton said.

"You'll find I'm not such a bad person," Margaret said.

"I didn't think you were," Dayton said, eyes wide with surprise.

"Well," Margaret looked equally surprised. "I just didn't want to be known as the wicked auntie." Margaret laughed nervously, a habit Dayton noticed she had.

"I don't understand," Dayton said.

"So, uh, Zara," Margaret switched subjects. "How do you find your new school?"

"Sucks. Recomposited refuse," Zara said, without looking up from her meal. It was clear she didn't want to continue this line of questioning.

"Are you done, Dayton?" Margaret got up from the table and collected Dad's plate. She then leaned over.

"Yeah," Dayton pushed his plate forward.

Margaret glanced at his plate; her face contorted with contempt. "Well," she said, "You filled up pretty quick, I see."

"Yeah," he said. "I have to take this Earth food kind of slowly. Digestive issues." His father opened his mouth to say something, but Dayton jumped ahead. "My stomach is playing grav ball down there."

"In time," Margaret said. "I have a lot of different dishes."

She carried the dishes back to the kitchen while Dad looked at the table and shook his head. Dayton and Zara shot from the dinner table.

They'd both made it as far as the end of the driveway when Dayton spoke.

"Where to?" He fingered the ID pad to the fragile Tata.

"Are you stealing your dad's car now?" Zara asked.

"No," Dayton said. "I have my Agency Operator's License. Until they revoke it, it clears me to drive around Earth for now, anyway. Where to?"

Zara looked him directly in the eye. "Anywhere," she said.

THIRTEEN

It was called the Rust Pile. A bunch of rusting maglev rails were stacked in a miserable pile; five open-topped fuel drums were crackling away as makeshift fire pits. A weathered stone maintenance shed had seen better days. And all of it was sitting on a combination of ancient disintegrating concrete, gravel, and loose stones. It probably looked even worse in the daylight. Trenton was with them; it had only taken a quick message to get him out of the house. The place was a local hang-out. Zara was okay with it so far.

A sprawling crowd was gathered, encircling a massive bonfire nearly three stories high and at least a third as wide.

"Look at all these Earth losers," Zara said with attitude.

Dayton made a face. "Can we live without the commentary for five minutes?"

"I call it like I see it," Zara said. "And right now, I see losers."

"You don't know them."

"I don't *want* to know them."

"Would you two knock it off?" Trenton said. "It took me all day to find out this is where everyone hangs out."

"What is the purpose of this gathering?" Dayton asked his heavy-worlder friend as Trenton took in the sights.

"It's a relwake. A relationship wake," Trenton said. "It's like the beginning of the school year, which is the breakup season, for some reason."

"Really?" Dayton was all earphones now. *The breakup season? Does that mean* EVERYONE *breaks up with their significant others and is free? This has potential.*

"Oh, give me a break." Zara rolled her eyes.

"Shhh," Dayton hushed her. "They're doing something."

A blonde girl, perhaps no taller than Allyson but sporting

a similar figure, stepped forward with a cardboard shoe box. She flung the top off and into the fire.

"I am here," the girl announced to the largely hushed crowd. "To rid myself of Joey Martinez. He is a jerk. And now I toss all my memories of this cheating king. I declare myself a free agent."

One after the other, the girl pulled bracelets, pictures, teddy bears, permaroses, and necklaces from the box. Each time, she cast the item into the raging bonfire. And each time, the crowd erupted into cheers. With nothing left in the box, she threw that, too, in the fire. The girl took a series of bows and blew kisses to the crowd.

Dayton's comm unit lived in his hands now. And much of the time, Allyson's ping ID was loaded and ready to go. Could he call her from here? Yeah, that might work. Show her he was someplace everyone wanted to be. Without much prompting, he selected the send icon and brought the comm up to his ear.

Then Dayton saw her. Allyson. She was standing at the far end of the crowd. That model-looking guy wasn't with her, either. Could she be here for her own relwake? Would she be next?

This went on for several more kids, both sexes, who declared their relationships over for all to see. The crowd grew more unruly with each caster. Each time, Dayton looked to Allyson. She shifted occasionally in the crowd, and each time, Dayton's adrenaline pumped. But in the end, she never went to the front, nor did she cast anything into the bonfire.

"And now," a grungy-looking boy, perhaps Dayton's age, scrambled to the front and center of the crowd. From the dismissive reactions of the crowd, the boy didn't seem too popular. "My girlfriend Jenda thinks she can just leave me in the dust with her new flyer her daddy bought her. Well, not without these."

The boy held up a power cell in each hand. The cells were white in color and far more streamlined than he was used to, but Dayton knew a cell when he saw one. He also knew they didn't react well to heat.

"Is that idiot going to toss those in the bonfire?" Zara started backing away.

"I think so," Trenton said, following suit.

Dayton glanced over. Allyson was walking away with her friends.

The grungy kid tossed both fuel cells into the fire.

"Run," Dayton screamed.

In a human wave, everyone stampeded away. Nothing organized, but Dayton's call had the intended effect. He found himself faster than the Earthers and had gained the most distance from the bonfire when it happened.

Boom! Boom!

Dayton turned around in time to see the bonfire had erupted, spewing flaming garbage high into the air and creating nothing so much as a whirlwind of fiery objects raining down as far as he could make out.

In the distance, the high squeak of a police siren blared out. Across the garden of flame, Dayton could see several light bars going off in alternating blue, white, and red.

Enforcers.

Attention. You are all in violation of Municipal Code 73345.1 and are subject to arrest by order of the City of Neubayern. Proceed with all due order toward the officers.

And what the firestorm started, the enforcers only made worse. It seemed like hundreds of kids all scattered in every direction. Every direction away from the enforcers, that was.

Dayton headed into a flat area filled with stacked shipping containers. The panicked crowd had disappeared in this makeshift maze, so Dayton followed suit. The enforcers' lights were making their way after the throngs of teens. They were at least two meters off the ground, so he knew they were enforcement skimmers. Those disc-shaped robots meant there weren't a lot of enforcers there. Probably just one or two human enforcers directing the robots.

If these officers were anything like their cousins in the mining colonies, they probably let the skimmers do all the work. And, if the skimmers used sensor packages similar to the ones on the colonies, then they could be fooled.

Dayton darted through the maze of shipping containers, stacked three or four high with only a meter between them. Over the raucous noise of kids shouting to one another, the same electronic voice repeated the "Attention" message. Rounding a sharp corner, he saw a door was hanging open. He gave it no thought as he darted into the container.

He whirled around to catch his breath and was relieved Trenton and Zara were still with him. Seven others were there as well, all laboring to catch their collective breath.

"Shut-shut the door," Dayton said to Zara between gulps of air.

Zara gripped the door and pulled on it. The door came to a handhold's distance from closing and stopped dead cold. "Stupid thing," Zara grumbled as she pulled harder. The door would not close.

Trenton joined in, as did two of the other kids. Even with their combined effort, the door remained JUST open. "It won't give," Trenton said, releasing the door. Zara and the others did the same. "Any of those bots will detect us anyway, so I don't know what good hiding in here will do."

Dayton pulled out his hand scanner, a matte black device no larger than a small entertainment center remote control. "You remember the feedback trick we used on those urban pacification bots on Echo-Alpha-Two-Two-Eight?"

Trenton's face went wide with surprise and hope. "Oh yeah," he said. "That was a cool trick."

The other kids looked on, wondering what the outworlders were talking about. But the three of them knew. By changing the scanner to a "white noise" feedback, it could block the bot sensors. Urban pacification bots were hulking giants that packed all manner of smoke, tear gas, and net guns. They stomped around on two giant mechanical legs. So, if *their* sensors could be fooled, the pitiful skimmers wouldn't stand a chance.

He hoped.

Dayton scanned the frequencies as the sounds of fleeing teenagers dissipated in the background. No luck.

"Why can't we just make a run for it?" Zara gave the door one last, useless pull before slamming it with her fist.

"Nowhere to go," one of the teens said. "That whole area backs up onto the mag rail yard. There's a huge duracrete wall. They'll be cornered."

"It's okay." Dayton held up his free hand while manipulating the scanner with the other. "Almost there ..." *Or maybe not.* He wasn't going to say it out loud. The frequency was out there. It *had* to be. The tiny digital windshield wiper swished back and forth, looking for the enforcer bots.

The ghostly hum of antigravity pods mixed with the whirring of automated limbs and cameras assaulted Dayton's ears. And the noise was getting louder. A few select profanities told him other bonfire-goers had been found.

What if he was caught? It probably wouldn't be much punishment, he hoped. But Margaret would surely make a giant deal out of it and tell Dad, and Dayton'd never hear the end of it. On the other hand, how would an arrest affect his chances of ever re-entering the Service? Dawgs! The sensor frequency had to be out there someplace.

Zara said as a light shone outside the shipping container, "Hurry up with that."

Everyone scattered to the back of the container. Dayton stayed put. As far as he could tell, fleeing further inside this container wasn't going to help. Not with enforcer sensors. Just as the hushed positioning jets came clear, his sensor registered the scanner frequency. He set it on feedback and got the result he needed.

Just as the skimmer appeared at the door crack.

The skimmer floated there, its spotlight sweeping around the area. The light flashed inside the container for a millisecond, lighting everyone up. The skimmer stayed in place, just outside of the door, as if wondering what to do. Had the feedback worked? Could the skimmer detect them?

Then it moved on.

Dayton let out a long sigh of relief, and he wasn't the only one. Sweat poured down Dayton's cheeks as his body returned from fight or flight mode.

"Did it see us?" one of the others asked.

"No," Zara answered. "It would have gone into arrest mode if it detected us. But it just moved off. It didn't see us. We can leave now." She moved to the door and was about to push it open when Trenton stopped her. Zara glared at him as Trenton motioned her to step back.

"Uh, no," Trenton said. "They're still out there."

"He's right," Dayton said, just as Zara was getting ready for a comeback. "We stay here; we have our very own shielded hotspot."

To his surprise, Zara didn't have any witty retort. She moved toward the back of the container, sat down, and put her head in her hands. Dayton couldn't blame her. He felt exhausted, too, but if the yelling mixed with the cacophony of police sirens was any indication, things were falling apart out there for anyone stuck *out there.*

Not in the shipping container.

Trenton and the others settled down on the steel floor of the container. Dayton preferred to stand. The adrenaline might be gone, but the nervousness remained. What if the skimmers didn't spot them but reported an anomaly and sent for the human enforcers to check it out? What then? Was Allyson arrested? Would it impress her if he wasn't caught? What would he say to her now?

The sounds and dancing lights faded gradually until they were gone. Dayton now heard crickets, which was a good sign.

His dad had told him crickets chirped only when no one was around.

"Is it clear?" Zara moved to the door. "Let's go."

"Not yet," Trenton said.

"Why not?"

"They might be out there watching from a thermal optics."

"Night-vision equipment-stuff? Seriously? Oh, you are so paranoid."

"Maybe, but I'm not—"

"Shush." At first, Dayton didn't know if he had heard something or not. Then he heard it again. A distinct, feminine voice. One he'd heard before.

"Hello? Are you guys still there?" The voice. He knew it was Allyson. Blast, he hadn't pinged her.

"Uh yeah," Trenton answered when Dayton hesitated. "Is it clear?"

"Yeah," Allyson came to stand in the doorway. "The cops left. You guys were lucky they didn't spot you." Her eyes traveled over Dayton and then to Zara right beside him.

"Luck," Trenton said, winking at Dayton. "It was luck. Yeah, let's go with that."

Allyson laughed, smiled at Dayton, and moved off, calling out to other possible survivors.

And through the whole exchange, Dayton had just stood there. Like an idiot. With Zara beside him. He hadn't pinged Allyson, and here he was out with Zara. Sure, she was just a friend, but Allyson didn't know that. He had to get hold of her and tell her why he was delayed. He really did want that shopping trip, and Zara was just a friend. Period.

The whole walk home, Dayton could not get that brief exchange out of his head. It was what he secretly feared every time he launched on a mission. Like the time he was twelve and he was sent into the upper maintenance tubes to root out some pests. He had found a whole nest, and they swarmed him when he shone the light on them in that dark passage.

He had bug spray on him but didn't spray one bit. He was too overwhelmed with all those nasty insects.

He had choked.

Dayton approached his new house only to find the lights were on in the living room. It was past the time he said he'd be back, but Dad wouldn't mind. He touched the keypad with his right thumb, and the door clicked open.

There was a humming. And not a mechanical or electronic hum, either. Dayton ventured into the living room. The first thing he noticed was the couch had been moved to the far wall.

Margaret, clad in a flowing flower-print dress, sat cross-legged in the middle of the floor. She rested on a reed mat depicting a wide-mouthed fish and held her hands palm-up in front of her, emitting a hum from her mouth that didn't skip a beat. Surrounding her burned five black-and-white candles that gave off an unpleasant, stinging scent.

"Oh, hello." Margaret opened her brown eyes and serenely smiled at him. "I'm glad you're here."

"Uh," Dayton fumbled for the right words. "You're busy. I'll just go to my room." He hoped nothing about his appearance gave away the Rust Pile craziness.

"No, no, no," Margaret waved him over to the mat. "Please, I need someone to meditate with me. Your dad's asleep."

"You know, that's really not my thing. I really should be getting to bed."

"Nonsense," Margaret patted the mat and moved two of the candles off to the side. "Look at you, all huffing and puffing. You need to align your consciousness."

Well, Dayton thought, he was having problems concentrating. "I don't know ..."

"It'll help you sleep," Margaret said.

"Is that anything like my old martial arts warmup?"

"Better."

"Better?"

"Better!"

Dayton hesitated, but he had to admit he was worked up, even somewhat disappointed in himself. His mind kept going back to Allyson, try as he might to think of something, anything else. How was he supposed to contact her now? He had seen her this very night and let Trenton do all the talking. What would he say?

He sat next to Margaret and did what she did.

But his mind wasn't in it. His heart wasn't in it. He would see Allyson tomorrow. What would he say to her? His mind spun with conversation starters, each one worse and more cheesy than the last.

He slept no better that night.

FOURTEEN

The day at school seemed to have no end. Even then, in sixth period, the clock refused to move. Dayton should know. He looked at it enough. Today, he'd said "hello" to Allyson, but the embarrassment of the Rust Pile kept his ego out of the picture. Without confidence, what could he do?

She was always with her friends. That complicated things to no end. Whenever she saw him, she smiled and waved. That was a good sign.

"Am I boring you, Mister Murdoch?" The teacher, Mister Blackwell, stood expectantly with his hands on his hips. His graying black hair was closely shaved, and he wore glasses so thick that Dayton, at first, thought they were lab loupes.

"No," Dayton said sheepishly.

"Very good then." Mister Blackwell turned his skeletal head back to the holo presenter. "It always shows. If you don't do well on this next test, I'll know your mind is elsewhere. You'll never get to the university. You are going to at least a university, aren't you?"

"Well ... I don't know," Dayton said, caught off guard.

"You don't KNOW?" Mister Blackwell stood over Dayton, admonishing him. "Well, I can see you have about as much motivation as some of these other desk pupils. And motivation is the key. If you have none, you really have to ask yourself what you're doing here. What are you doing here?"

Dayton felt a pulse from his comm unit. It was the special 3-2-2 vibrate setting for Allyson. She'd contacted him!

"Well ... I suppose I'm ..." he fumbled. He had seen Blackwell do this to students before. Now, it was his turn. And right when Allyson pinged him. For that split-second, he was trapped between looking at the ping message and keeping his pretend focus on Mister Blackwell.

"Well-well-well-well," Mister Blackwell said, every word dripping with sarcasm. "I'll let you figure that one out for yourself. Did you see that education tablet I brought in from Australia? Over THERE, kids know how to study. And at a much higher level. This whole education system over here is mediocre at best. My eyes are open. Mister Murdoch, yours are closed."

Mister Blackwell walked closer as the comm unit buzzed again and then again.

Dayton maneuvered his hand close to his front flight jacket pocket. It was there. Allyson was trying to communicate with him.

Thankfully, Mister Blackwell padded past, going on about the class and their test scores. Dayton reached into his pocket, feeling the lingering cold of his comm unit. It shook again. His pilot tactics kicked in. He knew as soon as Mister Blackwell rounded the back of the class, he would be out of his line of sight. The teacher stopped just short of the back of the class, apparently giving one student another "motivational" lecture.

But his back was to him. Dayton fished the comm device out and swiped open the screen.

Hey, you! So, today I have time if you want to go to the mall. Are you busy?

The klaxon sounded, ending the school day. The class turned into confusion and chaos as students scrambled out of the desks and out the door. Dayton was among the first to leave, but he managed a quick return ping:

Yes. Let's go.

The walk from campus kept Dayton on air. As Allyson came into view, she was wearing skin-tight black pants and a halter top that danced with animated graphics. Her hair was curly, like she'd just had it done, and she wore a pair of shiny crystal earrings that sounded like tiny chimes as she walked. He and Allyson, for all this world to see, heading somewhere together.

"About the Rust Pile," Dayton said. "I know I didn't say much to you then."

"No worries," Allyson waved the incident away, "I heard from the others you used some kind of tech to fool the cop bots?"

"Yeah," Dayton felt as though a pallet of industrial metals had been lifted from his chest. She didn't care. "It was simple, just a basic function, really."

"You did good," Allyson said. "I heard there were like ten arrests that night. Could've been more, I guess, huh?"

He extended his hand, and she took it willingly, even squeezing it lightly. It was all Dayton could do to maintain his composure. Outside, he hoped he looked relaxed; inside, his heart pounded at speeds that even evading a micrometeorite storm couldn't equal. Okay, Dayton thought, maybe I don't need to mention Zara. What was it Turco used to say? Let sleeping frozen passengers lie ...

Allyson dragged him by the hand into the mall and down the promenade. The Mall Service ButlerBot detached from a rack and fell in line behind them. "Come on, let's go to the stylist. We need to get that mop of yours worked on."

Dayton had to be honest. His hair really didn't have a style. Aboard *Venture*, there was no one dedicated to hair. It just wasn't an essential occupation. So, hair was shaved off every few months, or the individual crewmen just let it grow out till the next time they broke out the electric razors again. In zero-G, hair never stayed in place anyway. It just floated, and when you hit gravity, you just tied it out of the way.

Allyson was headed to a flashy steel and mirrored place on the third level. There, they were met by Javier, a flamboyant guy with bright red colored hair and a necklace of chunky, medical-grade steel around his neck.

"Please," Javier bowed and swept with his left arm toward the chair. "Any friend of Allyson is a friend of mine. Be seated, and I shall work my magic on you." *Great.*

Dayton had many doubts, but he buried them deep and plopped into the chair. Javier fitted him with a cover and began teasing his hair.

"My word," Javier sighed. "I have never felt hair with this texture before. How do you wash it?"

"Well," Dayton thought back. "Usually, we just use sonic waves."

"Well, you will stop that," the dramatic stylist stood in front of Dayton, hands on his hips. "I have got some shampoo and conditioner that will work wonders on this wild hair of yours."

Javier got to work, and Dayton felt trapped and powerless. The stylist cut and cut, and Dayton was worried that he was losing too much hair to the man's clippers.

Finally, Javier spun the chair around so Dayton could see the transformation. Dayton's hair was closely cut on the sides, with the top of his head longer and tousled forward. He had to admit that it looked pretty good, but he could now feel the cool air on his ears, and there was no feeling at all on the back of his neck anymore.

Dayton looked over at Allyson, who stood a short distance away, smiling. She gave it a thumbs up and mouthed, "Looks good."

Dayton felt the air conditioning on the back of his neck. The air was exceptionally cool and much stronger than he remembered going in. It was the first time he noticed the mall was teaming with shoppers, many of them with their mall-provided robot pursers in tow. Some sat at the cushy chairs that interrupted the walkway, while others stood in line at that coffee house he had visited before. Everyone chattered amongst themselves, drowning each other out in a mess of humanity Dayton now found himself a part of.

They walked three doors down to L-PLC, a self-described clothing store.

As they entered, several red beams scanned Dayton from

his boots up to his freshly cut head. A simple beep came from a kiosk directly in front of him, followed by a thin strip of white paper.

"Go ahead," Allyson said. "Take it."

Dayton grabbed the receipt-like paper and looked at it. There, in simple black text, he saw all his measurements: his shoe size, his inseam, shirt size, and hat size. It all looked correct, as much as he kept track of those kinds of things.

"Okay," Allyson said with a smile. "We got your vitals. Time to select."

"Hello, customers. My name is Billy Odd Nine. May I be of service?" A very obvious android approached them. It was white, like so much of the store, with a black trim and animated face.

"Uh yes," Allyson grabbed the ticket from Dayton and inserted it into the android. "We'd like to see Carter Hill, Temp Four-Fifty-One, and Rendezvous River in these sizes. Keep the colors to blues, grays, blacks, and greens."

"Very well," the Billy said in its electronic voice. And it was off.

"What are those, brands?" Dayton asked.

"You'll see," Allyson smirked as she spoke. "I think those'll work really well on you."

The android returned carrying two armfuls of clothing. It presented them in grand fashion to Dayton, who took them with some confusion. Allyson, seeming to enjoy the whole spectacle, motioned Dayton to the dressing rooms in the back.

In the changeroom, he selected the faded forest green digital-print tee, along with a pair of blue-white jeans, a black belt, and a pair of black shoes.

He fastened the belt and looked at the full-length mirror. What stared back at him was an Earth kid. The only hint that he grew up anywhere else was the insecurity on his face. To look at him, who would know he didn't grow up down the block?

But the pants did puff out a bit. It was the underpadding from his shipboard clothing. This made him look fat, like he possessed a middle-aged belly and thick thighs. This padding had to go. "Billy?"

No answer.

"Allyson?"

"I'm right here." Allyson's soothing voice came from behind the stall door.

"I need something to go on under my pants," Dayton said, and not without hesitation. "Do you know anything about undergarments?"

"Absolutely," her voice came back. "I see displays for Makers Run, El Scape, and Skorpian."

"Uh, okay," Dayton said. "I'll try the Skorpian."

"I think you'll like those," Allyson said. "Did you want boxers, briefs, or boxer briefs?"

More choices.

"Bring me one of each type." Dayton wasn't sure what any of this meant. He didn't know why he cared so much about underwear, but it felt like he was being judged.

"Oh wow," Allyson laughed. "Brave man. Most guys stick with one of the three."

"I can't settle till I've tried them on," Dayton said.

Seconds later, three sealed plastic packs of underwear shot through the clothing chute in the door.

He settled on the lime green boxer briefs.

"Uh, Allyson?" Dayton called out through the door. He didn't know if she heard him over all the music that was constantly blaring in the background. He grabbed his comm unit and wrote a simple text asking her to come to the door.

There was a gentle knock at the door a few seconds later. "Dayton?" Allyson's muffled voice came from the other side. "Is everything okay?"

Dayton opened the door just enough for her to squeeze through. "What's going on?" Allyson looked Dayton over.

"Wow. You really look modded out. Let's go out and show you off."

"Not yet." Dayton held up the black shoes. "I don't know how these work," he said as he held the shoelaces out to her. "I know they go through the holes, but that is about it."

Allyson laughed. Again, not mocking, demeaning laughter. She seemed amused, but not at his expense. As she grabbed the laces and one of the shoes, she said, "Here, I'll show you."

***

"Let's go to the Galaxy's Edge Gift Shop," Allyson tugged him in the direction of the store, near the center bridge overlooking the first-floor fountain.

"Are you really sure I need new clothes now that I have new hair?" Dayton asked. "I mean, do you think we chose the right stuff?"

"You really are fresh to this, aren't you?" Allyson laughed. Not a demeaning, caustic laugh, but one of pure joy. "Come on, I bet you haven't seen anything like what they have here."

Allyson dragged him by the hand into the gift shop. "Oh, I like this." Allyson picked up a 3D lava lamp and turned it over. "So, you're not going to use your mind powers to take over my mind?"

"No, I think I'll spare you any mind probes today." Dayton gave her a playful tap.

Allyson giggled. "I heard you guys trained to do work from age three or something," she said. "So now you're like a master pilot, right?"

"I wish," Dayton said. "No, I was trained as a survey pilot and servo/grav technician."

"So, you could fix almost anything." Allyson set the lamp aside and looked directly into Dayton's eyes. "Just don't get any grease on those new clothes."

"You know what I think," Dayton grabbed both her hands

in his. "I think you wanted me to get all those jackets and hoodies so you could keep wearing my flight jacket."

"I would not." Allyson pretended it was an insult but couldn't keep the smile from her face as he took the jacket off and handed it to her. She slipped it on. "This fits great. How is it that this jacket can be so heavy but not be hot?"

"What it's made out of mostly." Dayton released her as his eyes wandered to a black-light picture of dogs playing poker. It looked just like the one in the rec room aboard *Venture*. "I thought as much. I'm never going to see that jacket again, am I?"

"Sure, you will," she said. "On me."

Dayton, Allyson, and the robot butler walked out of the store and found a bench near the planters in the center aisle of the mall. "I need to ask you something," he said. "About that guy ..."

"Bradford," she said helpfully.

"Yeah."

"It's an off-and-on kind of thing."

"So, is it off right now or on?"

Allyson shifted her gaze to look right into his eyes. "I was at the Rust Pile the other night for breakup season."

"The relwake? From Bradford?"

"Yes."

Relief washed over him. Should he explain to Zara now that Bradford was sorted out? "So, tell me," Dayton said as the ButlerBot extended his right arm full of bags to him. He dug through the largest of the bags. "Which shirt and pants should I wear to school first? I don't want to get the looks wrong."

"Why don't we try the new stuff out at my house and see how you look?"

"Huh?"

"You could come for dinner. I already asked Mom."

The Zara talk would have to wait.

***

Dayton and Allyson came to the front door of her house. Dayton lugged eight shopping bags full of clothes. The sliding, break-in-resistant polymer door wasn't exactly welcoming, but compared to everything else about this planet, it was about what he expected.

Dayton stepped on the aqua and teal sensor pad that read "WELCOME," and the door chime sounded. The distant sounds of barking, muddled with growls, grew louder from within the house. Soon, the animal—Dayton assumed it was a dog—was just on the other side of the front door.

The door slid open on Allyson's retinal scan, revealing William, Allyson's dad, dressed in a button-down dress shirt, slacks, and shiny black shoes. The man's face lit up, putting Dayton's nerves at ease, if only slightly.

"Hey," William said. "It's the Mall Jumper himself. How're you doing?"

"Oh, very well, thanks." Dayton shook the man's hand. He only hoped he managed to keep his palms dry enough. "It's good to see you again."

"I'll be right back," Allyson whispered. She skipped down the hallway.

Dayton felt a sudden poke in his crotch. He looked down to see a large, yellow dog thrusting its nose into him. Dayton threw his hands up and nudged away, but the dog pressed his probing.

"Lysander," William said, pulling the dog back by his collar. "Lysander, stop!"

"Is he okay?" Dayton asked.

"I'm sorry about him," William said, pulling Lysander aside to let Dayton enter the home. "He's just very curious about new people."

"So, is it all right?" Dayton asked.

"Oh, fine," William said. "He's just getting familiar with you."

Dayton had no pets aboard *Venture*. They were considered

non-essential consumers. But here, everyone did. It was a little jarring at first, but in time, maybe he could get used to having an animal around. He wondered what Margaret thought of animals. Lysander seemed to bring energy to the household, as well as a warmth and friendliness that seemed so genuine.

"Allyson, you're back," William announced.

"I made my dad get rid of my little brothers for the night," Allyson said.

"Uh, in a good way," William said. "They're at the Nakasones' house for a sleepover. I thought it should be just us adults tonight."

They entered the living room. There, sitting on a gravity-well chair, was an older woman, perhaps William's age, with features similar to Allyson's. The woman snapped up and was over to Dayton between blinks, wearing a wide smile.

"My wife, Sonia," William said by way of introductions. "Sonia, this is Dayton Murdoch."

"I heard a lot about you," Sonia said. "All good. You don't forget meeting someone who literally fell to Earth."

"Your daughter and husband got me out of a bad situation." Dayton took her hand when she offered it. It was soft, like Allyson's, but firm and confident.

"Hey, these two still have some uses," Allyson's mother laughed, then studied Dayton's face. "Hungry, aren't you?"

"The growling of my stomach should tell you that," Dayton said. "But yes, dinner smells wonderful."

Dayton took a seat directly across from Allyson. He figured that would allow him to be close to her yet not look too eager or, how did they say it? Presumptuous. Sonia and William sat at either end of the table as the butler bot began serving them.

"So, Dayton," William said, "I assume life has been a little better since your big fall from orbit?"

"I would say so, yes," Dayton said, keeping in the light-hearted tone of the question. "I'm learning a lot of new things."

"Like what?" Sonia asked.

William and Allyson shared a knowing glance, then looked apologetically at Dayton.

"Oh boy," Dayton said. "Where to begin? It's literally everything."

Sonia sipped from a water glass. "There is enormous potential in you. I read you as a creative, an analytic, and a leader. You're extraordinarily strong with those."

"Thanks," Dayton said. It was one of the most condensed compliments he'd ever had, but he'd take it. "Right now, all I get is a lot of low-level hostility. Except from Allyson, of course."

"You're the type that intimidates the other alphas," Allyson's mother said. "Most promising young men do."

"Yeah," Dayton said. "I'm tired of that. What can I do about it?"

"Nothing," William spoke up. "Just be who you are, and don't let anyone drag you down. You, young man, will soar given the right encouragement."

"Dad," Allyson said. "Don't make him nervous. You're gonna wreck all that confidence we made at the mall today."

"That's not going to happen," William looked at Dayton. "It'll take more than a few turkeys to keep this eagle from flying."

"Pretty good for a non-empath, William," Sonia said. "You are right on center with that assessment."

She winked at Dayton.

"I'm guessing art and literature are new to you," Sonia said. "Am I right?"

"Correct," Dayton said.

"You know, I'm a holographic artist," Sonia said. "But now I assess personalities for an insurance company, so I do this for a living. And with you, I see an appreciation of the creative. It intrigues you."

"Correct again," Dayton said.

"She's good," William said. "A real pro at finding someone's worth."

"That's why we're married, darling," Sonia quipped. "But Dayton, I sense that you're put upon, assaulted. Don't let it get you down. You have enormous potential. Be strong."

"Well, thanks for the pep talk, Mom," Allyson said. "Now Dayton has got to be feeling weird."

"No," Dayton was quick to say. "No, not at all. I could listen to this kind of talk all night."

Up until now, only other *Venture* crew could lift his spirits. But here, sitting across from him at the dinner table, were three people who seemed to believe in him, and one of those was an empath.

As the night went on, Dayton enjoyed the best meal of his life.

And it wasn't just the food.

After dinner, Dayton was invited into the study, where he was shown a number of holo art pieces, as well as Sonia's collection of printed books. She read passages to him. It was unlike anything he'd encountered before. It was a new way to think. Not the direct, instructional ways of manuals and training media. Those were written in and could only be taken one way. But in this book, everyone who read literature or witnessed art saw something different in it. It meant something different to each mind. Training manuals couldn't offer that.

Much sooner than he wanted, the evening came to an end, much to Dayton's dismay. He and Allyson walked out to the waiting AutoTaxi, briefly holding hands.

Allyson nodded back to the house. "You made a spectacular impression. My mom sure couldn't get enough of you."

"Yeah, sorry about that," Dayton said. "Your dad wanted to talk to me about how *Venture* used those thrusters he worked on as an intern. Your mom kind of monopolized me."

"That's okay," Allyson said. "I think seeing my mom this happy made all of that worthwhile."

"So, see you tomorrow?" Dayton asked.

Allyson laughed. "Of course," she said as she took his

hands in hers. "Now get out of here before my dad comes looking for me and blows all that goodwill we worked so hard on tonight."

And with that, Allyson leaned over and kissed him. Dayton's heart clicked up several tempos, blood rushed in his veins, and the sweat he'd been holding back all night now gushed forth, dousing his armpits and making his hands clammy.

"You okay?" Allyson asked.

"Yeah," Dayton said, flustered. "Yeah, no. I'm fine. It's just ... thanks."

"Pleasure's all mine," Allyson said with a smile.

"Allyson," William's voice came from back in the house.

"Time to go." Allyson released their hands. "Now get out of here. Go work on your servos or grav plates or whatever it is you do."

Dayton climbed into the AutoTaxi; its electronic driver beeped in recognition. At the last second, he stashed the shopping bags beside him in the back seat. Allyson beat a path back to the house, turning around exactly three times to wave goodbye.

And yes. Dayton counted.

FIFTEEN

Once he got used to the lighter clothing, Dayton didn't feel naked anymore. This morning, when he'd ventured outside, a wind hit him. He thought his clothes were going to fly off, leaving him naked. But after a few hours, he had adjusted. The worst was over, and the fear of clothing-flight was now a minor distraction. He'd decided to go with the gray long-sleeved animated-graphics shirt and black jeans. He must've dressed and redressed five times before deciding on that combination.

But here he was in class, and the day was crawling along at school. He scribbled Allyson's name in his notebook for entertainment. It was hard to concentrate. More and more posters were appearing around the school for an upcoming dance, whatever that was, but he knew it was a prized social event. He had the courage to ask Allyson and even figured she'd say yes, but apparently, Earth guys were supposed to pick up their dates and drive them to the dance. But in the Tata? The thought made his skin crawl. Turco's voice kept ringing in his ears from their visit to the medical center: *Earth girls like cars.*

The school klaxon rang out and put an end to his worry for now.

In the hall, he reunited with Trenton and Zara for the final march home among the waves of students all heading out the entrance. He'd started walking to school since it was a lot less embarrassing than driving in the Tata. Somehow, Zara and Trenton decided they'd do it, too. Now came the real test of his new clothing. Neither said much, though their eyes took Dayton all in. Trenton smirked and nodded slightly, as if approving of the new look but not going far enough to say it. As a heavy-worlder, Trenton had a lot of trouble finding clothes on Earth, and he'd scored an oversized neon green t-shirt with a fake self-destruct code on the front.

Dayton liked Trenton's new look and wanted to compliment him but held back. The less time spent on the subject of clothing, the better.

Zara didn't say anything. She didn't have to. Her disapproving sneer said it loud and clear. To Dayton's non-surprise, she still wore her cargo pants with the utility harness. It might have been normal in space, but on Earth, she resembled one of those highway workers on the grav beacons in the skyways. All she was missing was the white helmet.

They weren't even clear of the parking lot when a couple of desis zoomed overhead in a new Flyer Series, just like the ones Dayton saw in video advertising. Messenger companions were ringing with flash clothing sales at the mall, which always came in just as school let out.

Then it dawned on him.

He needed credibility, and walking home, or worse, being driven home in that ridiculous Tata, was not the way to get it. No, he needed a flyer. If he was stuck here for two years, he might as well be respected. Acceptance or not, he didn't want to be made fun of.

Dayton's communications link buzzed, and he answered it. Margaret's voice came over his earpiece. "Do you need me to pick you up?"

"No thanks," he replied. "We're walking home."

"It's no trouble," Margaret persisted. "I can be there in ten minutes."

"Thank you, no," Dayton said. "We're fine."

"Are you sure?"

"Very."

"Wouldn't it be easier to drive you?"

"No. It's fine. I want to walk home."

"Is there something wrong?"

"No."

"Are you sure?"

"I'm pretty sure."

"All right," Margaret finally relented. "I'll see you when you get home. When will that be?"

"I don't know."

"There is a riot at the City Center," Margaret said. "You need to get off the streets."

"A riot?" Dayton asked. "Well, we're nowhere near the City Center."

"You need to come home," Margaret said.

"Okay, I'll come home, on my own." He clicked off his earpiece. Aboard *Venture*, you only needed to say something once. You didn't tell someone something you didn't mean. How the hell did these people on Earth communicate? God, if they were all like Margaret, it'd be anarchy.

"That woman bugging you again?" Zara walked next to Dayton. "It sounded like a really big argument this time."

Dayton called up his "NewsFeed" and selected "Local." A video sprang to life on his weathered hand comp screen. In it was a scene of pure carnage. Hundreds of demonstrators smashed windows, threw bottles, and set piles of garbage on fire. Smoke was so thick Dayton barely made out some of the rioters in the background as the videocam danced around. An announcer gave a voiceover.

"It seems that the protesters have gathered in a show of unity against *Venture* children entering our public schools, and their perceived detrimental effect on our society, beginning here."

The reporter cut to a group of witnesses, who complained that their properties were damaged by falling *Venture* debris and that they were out sizable amounts of money. Another woman interrupted and claimed that the *Venture* crew hadn't been on Earth for twenty years and thus did not deserve the same social services as those that had remained on Earth all that time.

The emotions were fierce as yet another man muscled to

the front of the crowd and seized the microphone. "And now they just come back," the man screamed. "How do we know what possible space bacteria they bring back with them? We will not have any immunity to that, and the government says they're fine? I heard some kid landed in a mall full of people. Who knows who he might have infected?"

"You see?" Zara asked. "They don't want us here. We're probably going to be separated, and you know what? I'm fine with that."

This is not good, Dayton thought. Just as he was starting to figure out how things worked on this planet, suddenly they were talking about taking him out of school. He caught himself. Since when would that be a bad thing? Now he worried.

The trio made their way down the suburban streets until they heard a commotion coming from an alleyway. It was Bradford and his group from the food fight in the cafeteria. Only this time, they were ganging up on Richard from Lit class. They surrounded Richard, dumping the contents of an old disposal bag on his head.

"Yeah, you were laughing at me at lunch, weren't you?" Bradford said, with the support of his followers. "You ain't laughing now, are you? Go ahead, normie, laugh now."

"Oh, we gotta stop this," Dayton said. "That's the fleshpod that started a food fight with us."

"I'm up for it," Trenton smacked his right fist into his left palm.

"No, no, no, no," Dayton said. He motioned both friends back around the corner. "We do this. We do this right. Bradford likes to pour garbage on people. So, we give him something he'll appreciate."

Dayton pulled his remote controller from his belt. It was a device used commonly to take control of cargo and mining bots to maneuver them around the maintenance and deployment bays. Dayton had also heard Turco talking about how, with a little frequency modulation, they could be used to take control of common, everyday civilian robots. Right now, Dayton was eyeing the garbage bot lying against the back of a building next to some grimy yellow disposal bins.

"Let me see," Dayton said. He worked his controller's frequency until he found the one the bot would take commands on. "Got it."

"Don't those bots have security features or something?" Zara asked as she watched the event unfold.

"Pssh!" Dayton said. "They might as well control them with cables for all the protection it gives them. Military and Agency bots are a problem. Civilians, not so much."

The readout on Dayton's controller read "READY TO ACCEPT INSTRUCTIONS" and displayed a brief pull-down menu of the garbage bot's commands. Dayton selected standby.

The bot's servos whirred and hummed as it reactivated and stood at attention. This interrupted Bradford and his taunting friends, but only for a second. One of them even commented, "Oh. It's just a trash man."

Dayton punched up the arm controls and set them into a maintenance spin. He then set the bot's legs to step up and down in place. This got everyone's attention.

Finally, he punched in the audio command, instructed it to say "*Kill all humans,*" and set the audio on an endless loop, to be repeated on maximum volume. He then instructed the bot to begin high-stepping toward Craig and his crew.

Kill all humans.

Kill all humans.

Kill all humans.

Bradford's face went white as he and his terrified friends stumbled back down the alley. "Amok bot," Bradford cried, as if not truly realizing what he saw. "Amok bot!" The others repeated this, shouting it the whole way down the alley, looking back with flushed faces to see if they were being pursued. All that was left was Richard, terrified, and four backpacks.

Dayton shut the robot down, and he, Trenton, and Zara

stumbled into the alley, their faces wide with laughter.

"You?" Richard said sheepishly.

"Me," Dayton said. He held up the controller to show it to Richard. "With a little help from this baby."

"Thanks. But what about their backpacks? Should we toss them?"

"I got a better idea," Dayton said. Fiddling with the controls, Dayton brought the trash-bot back to life. He then picked up the four packs and handed them to the robot, who took them by the straps in his left arm.

Dayton maneuvered the robot back to its original position in the alley, only now it held the backpacks in an outstretched arm.

"He has them now," Dayton said, motioning to the robot. "If they want them back, they'll have to come get them."

"God, that guy never leaves me alone," Richard said, grabbing his own pack.

"No worries with Bradford," Trenton looked in the direction Bradford and his horde went. "If they ever come after you again, just call us."

"Definitely," Zara reached out and shook Richard's hand. "I'm Zara."

"Let's give you some escort," Dayton said.

"Normally, I drive," Richard said. "I use the family's car, but Bradford and his followers keep throwing garbage on it in the parking lot and hassling me every time I get into it. I thought by walking, maybe they'd leave me alone, but they didn't."

"I can relate," Dayton recalled his father dropping him off in that embarrassing little gas-powered throwback. "Where did they go?"

"Back to stare into some mirrors, I bet," Richard said.

"I'll keep that in mind," Dayton said as his comm unit beeped. "Hang on, I got a message coming through."

"Hey," Richard said. "You guys want to come over and

play a Sony 3D? I just got the console."

"Sounds up top," Trenton said. "Dayton, you in?"

Dayton held up the screen of his comm unit to the others. "I just found something I need to check out. This says that according to UN Charter 57901.3, *Venture* crew gets first dibs on discarded *Venture* salvage. I just got my clearance to go to the Sub."

"Oh, we are so there," Zara said.

"We gotta go," Trenton joined in.

"Can I come along?" Richard seemed to be excited by the news.

"Sure," Dayton said. "Can you drive us?"

Richard's face lifted with a wide smile. "I can do that."

***

Richard had never been to the spaceport before, but Dayton figured Richard had probably watched the shuttles fly in and out. That was about it. When they passed the freeway sign that read "Los Angeles Spaceport Next Exit," Dayton saw his new friend get excited. Richard's car, a clean Chrysler CX, glided its way along the freeway, its quiet, electric engine drowned out by the noisy growls of the more common hydrogen-powered vehicles it shared the road with. It did come with a nice entertainment console, and the HD Radio blasted out Red Zone's rendition of the Paramore classic "All I Wanted" through the milli-thin SurroundSpeakers. Dayton could see why Richard was so self-conscious about the ground car. It was an old man's car. Guys at his age simply didn't drive cars like this.

"I have never seen *Venture* up close," Richard said as he changed lanes. "I mean, I've read about it, but that's about it."

"Don't get too excited," Dayton said. "The Agency calls it junk. It's going to be recycled."

"Easy for you to say," Richard said. "You grew up on that ship. This is like really new to me."

Gate Number 23 had a lot of vehicles that were leaving for the day, but not much was going in. A guard sat in a small shack by the entrance; only he seemed more engrossed in his 3D portaconsole than in checking the people who entered.

"Excuse me," Dayton yelled from the front passenger seat.

The guard shifted his head to face Richard and glared at him as if the guard was being interrupted.

"Yes?" The guard didn't even get up and, instead, merely shifted forward in his cushy chair.

"Dayton Murdoch, Class Three Survey Pilot, registration number Five-Four-Seven-Niner-Two-Zero-One, here to visit Surplus Warehouse Fifty-Seven-Alpha?"

Dayton extended his ID across Richard to the man. After a couple of seconds, the guard took a heavy breath and expended considerable effort to move his bulk and take the ID. He swiped it on a console below the console, which beeped in recognition.

"Okay," the guard half tossed, half pitched, the ID back into the car. "You're clear. Go ahead."

"Don't you want to check the rest of us?" Dayton said. He didn't really care much for security types or enforcers, but he knew when someone wasn't doing his job.

"I said you're fine," the guard said, indicating the conversation was over. He returned his attention to his 3D projection of some action show. "Go on in, sheesh."

Richard's car was dwarfed by a few rocket engines and thruster assemblies that occupied the open ground. Soon, they reached the rows of immense, kilometer-long warehouses. Dayton instructed Richard to stop in front of the one labeled 57-A. The huge double doors were open, and Dayton could make out a junkyard full of equipment piles that seemed to extend into the horizon.

Dayton was out of the car and up to the inventory console before Richard turned off the ignition. The status of the warehouse contents scrolled by until Dayton stopped his search and bolted into the piles of discarded technology. It was here, his friend, Old 21. It had been cast aside, but with luck, Dayton knew he could catch it.

"This way," he called out as he ran down the aisle.

Dayton bobbed and weaved through the piles and piles of metal and plastic. He stopped in front of a line of surveyors, all positioned side by side in various stages of cannibalization.

"Over here," Dayton zeroed in. She was there, the third one from the last, Old 21. The well-used Planetary Survey Vehicle still looked like a vintage Lamborghini with anti-gravity plates so it could fly.

"What did you find?" Zara said as she and Trenton suddenly appeared next to him.

"It's here, Zara." Dayton pulled junk off the vehicle until he could make out the mostly eroded tail number ending in "21."

"Old Twenty-One. I can't believe it," Zara said as she pulled a coil of fiber optic cable off the rear panel. "It's been stripped."

"It's not that bad," Dayton said. "All the major components seem to be intact."

"No propulsors, though," Trenton ran his hand over some burn marks on the vehicle's rear top panel. Two sets of large, circular holes were evident. "You're going to have a heck of a time getting around without those."

"I'll find more propulsors." Dayton reached down and pulled the gull-wing door open. "I can't believe they'd just throw it away. Old Twenty-One was still functional. We just took it through a complete maintenance overhaul a week before the crash."

"You still need propulsors." Zara picked up a piece of reducer coupling and threw it high in the air. It landed with a bang somewhere over the junk pile.

"Can you guys look for Section Green-Fifty-Nine? I think we passed it on the way in. It looked like they dropped all the used propulsors over there."

"Yeah, sure," Zara said. "But I want to look for some stuff for me, too. They have grav cycles down near pile Blue-Three. And one of those would be a heck of a lot easier to revive than this thing."

"You served with me in this thing for almost two years," Dayton said. "You could be a little more supportive here."

"I liked Old Twenty-One," Zara said, "but it was always yours. I was just along for the ride. Now, if you don't mind, I'm gonna look for your stuff."

"Yeah, I think I saw some comm gear by the north wall." Trenton marched off, his thick feet churning up debris as he walked. "If I can assemble enough of it, I might be able to send messages back home."

"No problem." Dayton climbed into the seat and began plugging in a test comp, which he never took off his web belt. "Tell you what. You guys just go look for whatever you want. Richard and I can find what we need."

"Are you planning on taking this?" Richard peered inside the vehicle.

"You got that right," Dayton punched up command codes on the console. A small screen on the dashboard lit up and began ticking down a list on the flight check computer. "They can strip her, but I can put her back together again."

"Well, that would take weeks," Richard looked over the vehicle. "It's a long way from working, even I can tell that."

"You see junk," Dayton's eyes lit up as he spoke, "but like that Ozzy guy in the story, there's more to it than that."

Richard took a long look at the salvaged vehicle. "Like what?"

"Like it's logged hundreds of thousands of kilometers on planets, in space, asteroid fields, you name it." Dayton lovingly moved his hand over the worn and oxidized body of the vehicle, his eyes glistening. "This thing can fly higher and faster than anything anyone at Chuck Yeager has ever seen."

"You plan on driving this thing to school?"

"School and everywhere else," Dayton said. "Think about it. Who is going to laugh at us in this thing? Who is going to throw junk on the hood?"

"Well, I admit it's no old man's car." Richard looked around. "In fact, I'm really not sure what it is. But it does look kind of cool."

"Yeah, it does," Dayton said. "I've always liked the looks of this surveyor. It beats anything anyone else has. Even that new BMW. We can put this together." Dayton pulled a multitool and began removing an access panel. "I just need your help."

"You think I can help you?" Richard seemed surprised.

"Well, sure," Dayton looked surprised. "Why not? Let me beam you the list of parts I need. Each item will be listed with a description and a schematic, so you should have no trouble finding them."

Richard glanced at his hand computer's readout. "I see each item on the list has a destination."

"Great," Dayton's face lit up. "If you find anything you want, just pick it up, and I'll get it for you."

"What are we going to use to carry all this stuff?"

"Sit tight." Dayton bolted from the seat and made his way toward the front of the warehouse. "There's gotta be a grav carrier around here somewhere."

SIXTEEN

The grav carrier was a little more vehicle than Dayton was used to, but it still felt good to be at the controls of something so big and solid again. It was a hulking cargo carrier the size of an old public transportation bus, rectangular in shape and roughly twenty meters long. Crablike cargo claws were mounted underneath its grav propulsors. The dull gray paint was dented and dinged, and it rumbled and growled like a monster before lifting creakily into the air.

The lights of the city twinkled below as Dayton and his passengers hovered over their first stop of the night.

"Is it all secured?" Dayton called back to the cargo hold.

Trenton finished strapping himself, and his crates of equipment, to the cargo arm. He gave the thumbs-up sign.

"Here we go," Zara said as she manipulated the control panel for the cargo arm. At treetop level, the arm swung out from the middle of the grav carrier and lowered Trenton and his gear into Trenton's backyard.

"You sure you don't want a vehicle?" Dayton asked Trenton through the communications link. "There looked like there were a couple of good units still left."

"I like what I got." Trenton hit the release on the grav lock, and Zara brought the cable back in. "Thanks for the lift. See you in school."

"Next stop, my house," Dayton said. He smiled over at Richard, who sat nervously in one of the passenger seats.

"Just relax," Dayton said when he noticed Richard's nervousness. "I've been operating flyers for years and have had the best training available. Zara, you sure we don't need to drop you off at your place?"

"Nah, I'm good." Zara knelt at a tied-down grav cycle,

making adjustments with pliers from a large tool kit she had set on the cargo deck. "I practically have this thing running. Just head to your house." She had really gotten lucky with that thing. It had somehow been missed by gear cannibals and needed only a new battery and some minor adjustments to its gyrostabilizers.

Below, Dayton's house came into view. He hit the remote, and his garage door opened, revealing a new, relatively untouched, and empty garage bay ready for a fill-up.

The carrier would have a hard time backing up at ground level, so Dayton kept it at tree height and backed in over the driveway. The characteristic "*beep-beep-beep*" accompanied him as he executed this maneuver, but eventually, he landed and positioned the back of it even with his garage, even though the front end of the huge carrier stuck out in the middle of the street.

Dayton glanced out the side window and saw several neighbors standing on their front lawns staring at him. Some of them held netphones to their ears.

"All right." Dayton activated the cargo ramp at the back of the carrier and climbed out of the cockpit. "We're poking into the street here, so let's unload this puppy before we create a traffic jam."

Dayton activated the grav plates, and he, Richard, and Zara pushed Old 21 off the cargo truck and into the garage. Then, they started the offload of several crates of diagnostic equipment, scanners, a fusion power plant, and the nearly functional grav cycle.

"Are we done yet?" Richard wiped the sweat off his brow. "I need to get home."

"We're almost there." Dayton pushed the grav pallet jack back up the ramp. Richard's car had been loaded in first, and it sat just behind the pair of tarp-covered maintenance robots. "Let's get the bots out of there, then I'll take the carrier down the street to that empty lot, and you can just drive out."

"Dayton!" Margaret's voice filtered in from the interior garage door. "What are you doing out here?"

"We picked up some surplus equipment from the Sub." Dayton pulled the tarp off, revealing the two bots.

"I still think these don't look very human," Richard said. "Did you see the new Honda models?"

"I never cared for bots that look human," Dayton said. "Besides, these were refurbed at the machine shop on the ship. They should be good for another ten years at least."

Dayton positioned the grav jack under one of the bots, and he brought it into the garage. Margaret now stood at the foot of the ramp, hands on her hips. "Where have you been? You were supposed to be coming straight home."

Zara jumped in to deflect. "We're sorry. It was my fault. I wanted—"

Margaret waved her away and kept her attention lasered on Dayton. "Where are you going to put all this?"

"Right here in the garage."

"What if I want to park here?"

"You always park on the street."

"But what if I wanted to?"

"You never do."

"Is that a car?" Margaret pointed at Old 21.

"It will be." Dayton maneuvered the first bot into the bot alcoves of the garage. To his surprise, it fit perfectly.

"Can we activate these bots?" Zara said. She pulled off the access panel on the front of one of them.

"Their batteries are drained," Dayton said. He headed back for the second robot. "We need to pick up some new power cells at HomeSource or Constructors, something."

"Where did you get these things?" Margaret said as her face grew red. Her words came out amid clenched teeth.

"I told you," Dayton said as he unloaded the second robot. "At the Sub."

"I told you I don't believe in robots."

"Well, I do." Dayton found the other robot fit perfectly in the opposite alcove. "You don't have to use them if you don't want to."

"Are you going to have them work around the house?" Margaret practically spit the words out.

"One of them, yes," Dayton said. "The other I am going to program to help me rebuild the surveyor."

"What would your father say about all this?" Margaret said. Without waiting for an answer, she huffed back into the house.

An electronic honking and single siren wail echoed in the garage. Turning, Dayton saw a flashing red-blue-and-white light.

"Cops!" Richard exclaimed from the front of the garage.

"Enforcers." Zara threw a loose tarp over her grav cycle. "That's just wonderful. I wonder if *they're* going to call your dad."

Dayton grunted in frustration as he walked to the driveway. There, landing just in front of the mailbox, was a police flyer. "Who's piloting this thing?" One of the officers climbed out of the cruiser and jerked a thumb at the enormous carrier blocking almost half the street.

"I was, officer," Dayton said.

"Son, you need a Class Two license or higher to operate a rig like this."

"I'm a Class Three." Dayton produced his operator license and handed it to the enforcer. "I've been certified at that level for over a year now."

The officer's eyes went wide when he saw the license. "You must be one of *Venture*'s children. I heard a lot of you guys had some serious ratings at a very young age."

"That's us," Dayton said. "A bunch of real freaks."

"Oh no," the officer said. "You guys should be proud of what you've accomplished. I served with the Agency myself before becoming a cop. What was your assignment?"

"Surveyor Pilot," Dayton said proudly.

"No kidding?" The officer handed Dayton back his license. "I piloted the big cargo ships from the asteroid field to the processing station above Luna."

"I always admired you guys." Dayton knew of the same type of pilots aboard *Venture*. Frankly, he always thought that line of piloting was mind-numbingly boring. He wasn't going to say that now, though.

"It really starts to drain you," the officer said. "The pay is good, but the job bored the hell out of me."

"That's what I hear," Dayton said. "Anyway, I'm really sorry about this. I was just taking some stuff from the Sub. I wasn't planning on keeping this here all night."

"I can see that," the officer said. "You know you can't fly over residential areas with a grav vehicle, don't you?"

"I do now." Dayton had spent some time reading the rules concerning driving here on Earth. Frankly, he was amazed that you could do much of anything burdened by so many laws.

"Okay, here's what I'm going to do." The officer looked the carrier up and down. "Go ahead and move it out of here now and get it back to the spaceport."

"I have to take everything back? I can't keep the flyer?"

"The flyer's fine as long as you keep it in the garage. But the carrier you brought it in on has to go back."

"Okay." Dayton smiled with relief. Behind the officer, Zara and Trenton relaxed, too.

"I could cite you for several things," the officer continued, "but as a former pilot, I know you *Venture* arrivals are having a tough time adjusting to life here. You made it this far; you can certainly have this carrier removed in the next two minutes."

"Thank you." Dayton was glad he got a break. He shook hands with the officer and headed back down the driveway. All he needed to do was pull up the cargo ramp and get the carrier back to the Sub.

"Dayton," Margaret called from the front porch. "Hurry

now. Your father's been called up early. He's leaving on his mission."

"What? When?"

"Right now."

***

Dayton rolled his father's luggage pod along the enduro-crete floor of the L.A. International Spaceport. The "miracle concrete" was durable yet easy to walk on. The pod weighed exactly 23 kilograms, which was the limit set by the Alpha Prerogative. Back at home, Margaret had made her tearful goodbye because they all knew a civilian would never get past security. Dayton wasn't even sure he would. Each security measure was different with an Alpha.

As they trundled along, he could hardly believe the coordinates. He'd checked and rechecked on his armcomp, and this was the place. Turned out the Alpha rendezvous was a lobby at the Spaceport. Commercial, not Agency. As they progressed down the halls, the crowds grew less and less until, finally, only Dayton and his father trudged along the corridor.

When they next saw another human, it was in the form of a private security guard at a checkpoint. The man checked their IDs and let them both pass. Dayton grew a little concerned at this. The man looked Dayton's ID over, studying it.

Never had Dayton known a private guard to take this much interest in an ID. He'd encountered private security guards at just about every mining town or waystation he'd been to. But then again, the man here at the Spaceport probably wasn't all he appeared to be.

The corridor came to an end, emptying out into a cavernous, circular lobby filled with metal-backed chairs lined up in neat rows. There were five ticket booths and boarding gates, but only one was staffed, again by private security guards.

The windows opening to the tarmac were tinted black.

Still, Dayton could make out the form of an orbital shuttle. This could mean the call-ups, meaning his dad, were headed to an orbital station or a larger interplanetary vessel that would take them where they needed to go somewhere in space. Then again, they could be using the shuttle to ferry from one terrestrial location to another.

Dayton fixated on the shuttle silhouette, focusing his eyes. He couldn't make out much. It had a V-shaped tail assembly and a large, bulbous front. Okay, so it was a Class-G shuttle, most likely. And with a big front end like that, it was self-piloted. So, wherever the call-ups were headed, it wasn't any place dangerous. For sticky situations, they still relied on human pilots.

Dozens of people milled about the lobby, most saying goodbye to their loved ones, some crying, others hugging. Dayton noted his father avoided eye contact with him, which meant the man was at his emotional limit.

"Not a big group," Dayton said. "I figured with an Alpha, they'd have a hundred or more in here."

"I don't know," was all his father said, again looking away. "I don't even recognize most of these people. Not a lot of *Venture* vets here."

"Yeah, but there's a few." Dayton turned to see Turco making his way down the concourse. He threw his arms wide and somehow enveloped both Dayton and his father in an enormous hug. "How you doing, my brothers in space? I see they called you up, too."

"Only me," Dad said. "Dayton escaped the Alpha net."

"Oh," Turco clutched his heart in mock mourning. "That's right. You got kicked down to high school. Too bad, kid. I don't know what this is about, but we can always use a future Recon pilot on our team."

"You don't sound too bummed out about being here," Dayton said, observing his mentor.

"I'm not," Turco's light brown eyes beamed with pure

intensity. "Since I got back, I been wondering what I'm gonna do. Now, I got a job opportunity given over, and I didn't even have to apply for it. It'll be great. Excuse me."

Turco headed, rucksack on his shoulder, over to the baggage area.

"Well, I'm glad someone's happy about all this," Dayton said.

"It's Turco," Dad said by way of explanation. "Man won't be happy till he's in a ship surrounded by billions of klicks of sheer vacuum."

A pit was forming in Dayton's stomach. Suddenly, his situation didn't seem too bad after all. All Dayton had to do was attend a high school. Dad, though … What would Dad face? Dayton had no way of knowing, but if he was being called up so fast, it was bound to be important. Alphas weren't used lightly.

"I am sorry about this," his father said after a long pause. "I'm leaving you when you need me the most."

"Dad," Dayton held the man's gaze. Dad's eyes were misting up. "You're not leaving me. You always taught me we have a duty. We knew it was coming eventually."

"I know," Dad said. "I just thought my role at the Agency was done now, that they were letting us be. Someone up there has to know I'm a single father with an underage son. I told them over and over."

"It doesn't matter. When you're called up, you're called up."

"Yeah, I know, buddy." Dad looked down at the enduro-crete floor. Somewhere in the background, Turco was chatting it up with some of the other call-ups. At least he seemed happy about deployment. The ones without families always were.

Nothing about life was fair, and this wasn't, either. Dad had been so happy to be back on Earth. Now, after no time at all, he was being called back to service. More than likely, the decision was made by some statistic-crunching AI units.

Dayton was the one who didn't want to be here on Earth. Why not take him? He would have relished the opportunity. All he needed was just a few more hours at the controls of something—anything—that flew. It could be a simple orbital ferry. Even one of those old worker pods around the shipyards would do the trick. Fourteen hours. Might as well be fourteen hundred hours, for all the difference it made.

"I'll forward Margaret my comm numbers," Dad offered. "I mean, I don't know where they'll be sending us."

"We don't know," Dayton said as unemotionally as he could make it.

"We don't know," Dad repeated.

"Boarding call, Flight Two-Thirty-Four," the electronic voice echoed in the lobby.

"I'm guessing that's me," Dad said. Behind them, the others were lining up at the boarding gate.

"What was it you always said to me in the deployment bay?" Dayton asked. " 'May the wind always be at your back' was a favorite of yours."

"Whenever you left, I had some small consolation that Turco was going with you," Dad said.

"Yeah," Dayton forced a chuckle. "And now he's going with you. You'll be fine."

"I will be fine," Dad reiterated. "And so will you."

Dayton hugged his father and held the motion for a few moments. Neither seemed willing to break it off. Dayton knew this might be the last time he'd be able to do this for a long, long time.

"Hey, come on, guys." Turco barged in on the moment. "The flight's gonna leave. You need to be on it, right?"

Father and son broke apart, semi-embarrassed. Dayton was surprised he was already crying. His dad hadn't been able to hold back the tears either.

"Hey, man." Turco squared Dayton's shoulders and held him at arm's distance. "You're gonna do great here, okay? And do not worry about the old man. I'm keeping him close to me at all times. Ain't nothing going to happen to him. You got my word on that, okay?"

Dayton grasped Turco's forearm, and the two locked. His eyes square on his father, though. "You two," Dayton said. "Look out for each other. Now, go on. Get out."

Dayton wanted to break off, head back the way he came. But he was locked in place, as if some force field kept him from moving. Instead, he watched the two most influential men in his life get in the line.

It was a matter of minutes, but the next thing Dayton realized, he was staring at a closed boarding gate. The line had gone in.

"Sir," the not-a-security guard said from behind him. "Sir, we need you to leave."

"Y-Yeah," Dayton said as he regained his bearings. He turned to go.

There was nothing to see here anymore.

SEVENTEEN

"Try it now," Zara called out to Dayton, who was seated in the driver's seat of Old 21. The gull-wing doors folded down smoothly, thanks to a good lubing, and latched with a satisfying click. Dayton fired up the engine, and Old 21 lifted off the ground. He stabilized the old vehicle at one meter, keeping it from rising further and hitting the garage ceiling. "All right," he said with pleasure. "That's half the battle. Now all we need is the forward grav plates, and we're set."

"Uh, I hate to remind you of this." Trenton peered over the workbench. He was wrestling with an old propulsor unit and had the thing half disassembled. "Without these units on the back of that surveyor, you aren't gonna be doing anything but floating in the breeze."

Dayton recognized his friend's frustration when he heard it. "We have a way to go on those?"

"I only got one working," Trenton said. Despite his bulky, squat body, his hands were as skilled as a surgeon. Only thing was that the surgery didn't seem to be going so well. "I had to take parts from two other propulsors to make that one work. Now, this one." He motioned with a wrench to the part on the workbench. "This one must have been used on a floater before it got cast off."

Dayton brought the vehicle back down to the ground and headed over to the garage's other workbench. He knew what "being on a floater" meant. "Floaters" were surveyors that were used as backups for survey squadrons, pulled from wherever they were parked, used, and then dropped off again to wait for somebody else. The only problem was that floaters didn't belong to anyone, so no one took care of them.

"I'm sorry." Richard stopped his work soldering a circuit

board. "I must've picked up the wrong ones at the Sub."

"Eh, don't worry about it." Zara waved her hand in the air in dismissal. "They were probably all like that."

"She's right," Trenton said. "All the good ones were probably kept and stored someplace. Who knows why; they're twenty years old, but somebody kept the good ones."

"That's item number two million on the list." Dayton looked at the wiring harness on the workbench. "These directional controls are way out of sync. I don't even know where to begin."

Zara slid on the creeper to just under the front driver's side grav module. "What did they do to your baby? Those guys are butchers."

"No arguments." Dayton checked his chronometer. Here it was nearly 9 p.m. on a Friday, and they were all stuck trying to bring old parts back to life. There had to be something more to do tonight. "I wonder what the desis are doing tonight."

Zara snorted.

"There's also Trumball," Richard said. "That's the entertainment complex near the freeway."

"Let's go check it out."

"I don't know," Richard said. "Bradford and those guys hang out at Trumball sometimes."

"So, what?" Zara slid out from under the surveyor and stood up. "Those punks aren't going to do anything."

"No, nothing," Trenton joined in. "I got you covered."

"We all do," Dayton said. He didn't want trouble, but no way was he going to back off from those useless punks. "We want you to come with us."

"Besides," Zara said, "you're the only one with a working vehicle. We can't exactly fly over there with all of us on my bike, can we?"

"Well," Richard sounded hesitant, jarred.

"Is that the place where we beat Daft Zeus?" Zara said eagerly.

"No, he's at the swap meet," Richard answered.

"How do we get to this Trumball place?" Dayton said. "No way the surveyor is going to be ready tonight. It will take at least one more trip back to the Sub for more parts. That leaves you, Rich."

"We're not going to look like much driving around in that thing," Richard pointed to the sad-looking compact ground car sitting in the driveway, his family's other car.

Dayton could relate to Richard's attitude. Tooling around in the Tata with his father was something Dayton never wanted to go through again. Still, if they didn't get out, he thought he'd go crazy.

"I really don't care what these Earthers do," Zara said. "But if I mess with this grav plate for a little more, I swear I'll go insane."

Trenton put the propulsor down. "Let's engage thrusters, then."

Richard looked at each of his friends in turn, then sighed. "Okay."

***

The slow, sluggish Chevy pulled into the Trumball Entertainment Center and found a parking spot way in the back of the lot.

To his left, Dayton could make out a virtual arcade, like the ones on the mining stations, but much, much larger. In front of them, a large collection of exaggerated plasticrete characters like dragons, windmills with oversized blades, and giant apes seemed to taunt players who were putting around a miniature golf course. Finally, to the right, Dayton could see several cages, where men and women were hitting softballs into a 3D construct of a grass-covered field.

Farther in the distance, several imitation rock walls soared above the whole center, with harnessed people climbing up them to reach a hologram of a mountain goat. Once a climber was past a sensor at the top, the goats would cry out.

"Where do we go?" Zara looked around.

"The arcade," Richard said.

Dayton followed Richard in that direction. That arcade was the only thing he recognized readily out of any of this place. Whether it was the training modules aboard *Venture* or the entertainment rings on space stations, he knew virtual games.

Inside, Dayton's senses were nearly overwhelmed by the flashing lights, multi-colored displays, and holographic characters of the games. In one corner, several gamers were dodging blows and feints with holographic boxing opponents. Directly ahead, Dayton saw a 3D street scene where players with plastic weapons exchanged gunfire with holographs of street thugs.

"Grav ball?" Dayton nudged Zara. "Let's see if these Earthers can play ball better than they can throw food."

"I'm in," Trenton smiled.

"Yeah," Zara said. "Even those belters on Meridian Station couldn't score against us, and they practically live in zero-G twenty-four-seven."

"I don't know how to play." Richard looked nervously at the Grav Ball court. "I've never been in zero-G before."

"Don't sweat it," Zara said. "We need someone to play goalie. That position doesn't even go into zero-G so much. All you need to do is block. Stay right in front of the goal. You float up, grab the top. You drift down, grab the bottom, and side to side. You'll get it."

Richard's voice was shaky. "I've never been very good at sports."

"Come on, buddy," Zara said. "Have a little confidence. You can do this."

"He's right." Trenton placed a reassuring hand on Richard's shoulder. "Basically, all you do is block. Just throw your hands up and hit the ball back into the court."

"I've seen those guys on N-ESPN," Richard said. "They do a lot more than that."

"Look," Dayton had been seeing video feeds for months before they arrived. "Stop it with your chest and hands when the grav ball comes at you. That's all there is to it. Everything else is just show."

"Okay," Richard said. "I'll give it a try."

The small prep area just before the court entrance held a number of cubbyholes for shoes and jackets. Several younger kids, perhaps no older than thirteen, were in the process of taking their equipment off. They wore hangdog expressions, and their foreheads beaded with sweat.

"Those guys are the best," one of the kids said to Dayton as he walked in. "They've compacted everyone they've played tonight."

"Let's see how we do against them," Dayton said. The kid, along with his friends, merely shrugged, put their shoes on, and left.

"Hey," Dayton shouted into the court where the unbeatable players were standing. "You guys want to play a round?"

"Sure," the tall one, a blond-haired guy about Dayton's height, said. "We haven't had a good match all night."

The guy came over to Dayton. "Scott." He extended his hand.

"Dayton." Dayton clasped Scott's hand. His grip was firm. A good sign, Dayton thought. He'd seen Scott talking to Allyson in school. Any friend of Allyson's was okay by him.

The rest of the players greeted each other, with Richard giving out weak handshakes and not making much eye contact. It was clear that Richard was nervous around these guys. Anyway, he donned his chest plate padding and placed himself in front of the goal.

All eight players took their starting marks.

Dayton passed his money tube over the activation module, and the grav plates underneath the court came on with a loud clank. Then, the red lights began flashing, and the electronic timer counted down.

Dayton floated free as the gravity disappeared. Motion activators pushed them all in a clockwise direction around the court. Then a *clang* echoed throughout the court as the grav ball shot out of a tube and circled the court counter-clockwise. It was a lot like a ball sent spinning opposite in one of those old roulette games that Dayton saw in an old spy movie. The ball circled around them, just out of reach.

This was the initial challenge, getting the ball, but it was the move that often set the scene for the game. Scott spun in a somersault, and his arm shot out for the ball. It was a practiced maneuver that really impressed Dayton, but still, Scott came up empty-handed.

With a style that belied his bulky, squat form, Trenton positioned his bent legs against the court wall and launched himself in toward the gravity well in the center of the court. His timing proved perfect as he crashed against the far wall, trapping the grav ball in his hands.

Dayton touched the wall to slow his momentum so that he was directly across from the opposing team's goal. Their goalie stood directly in front of the goal on his track that ran in front of the meter-square goal. His helmet was wired to the central computer, and he was ready to pivot left or right by thought alone.

"I'm open," Dayton called out. On cue, Trenton fired the ball over to him.

Dayton caught the ball, but in zero-G, the force of the ball carried Dayton along with it. Dayton's back slammed against the wall.

Scott's friend floated over to Dayton, his hands waving as he tried to distract Dayton from getting a clear shot at the goal. Dayton grunted in frustration, as he had no clear shot now.

Zara launched herself off from the wall and soared underneath Dayton and the defending player. Dayton shot the ball straight down, and Zara caught it before crashing headfirst into the wall.

Her padded helmet must have done the job because Zara executed a perfect flip turn and brought herself even with the goal. Zara threw the ball just to the right of the gravity well, causing it to arc around and slingshot directly at their opponents' goal.

Their goalie, however, proved effective, as he successfully positioned himself in front of the ball and deflected it. The ball careened back toward Dayton, who caught it just as he passed the enemy goal. He fired it at close range, faster than the goalie could react. The ball bounced into the goal and slammed to a stop in the magnetic netting. A loud siren and flashing blue light announced Dayton had scored.

"I set it up," Zara slapped Dayton a high five as she floated past. "You scored it."

The rest of the game was a blur. Dayton had made his mark on the game, but his eyes kept drifting back to the food court, which a player could easily see through the translucent walls. His heart sank when he looked again and saw Allyson and her friends had left. In the end, Dayton's team lost 7–6.

"This is the best game we've had in weeks," Scott said as the players removed their pads and put their shoes back on in the staging area. "You go to CY High, right? You should seriously consider joining the grav team. We lost a ton of good players when last year's senior class graduated. We need some new blood."

"Thanks, maybe I'll look into that."

"Oh great," Zara mumbled as she stood next to Dayton. "Now they're going to use you for your athletics. You know you're being played, right?"

"Don't start," Dayton said. He headed off to retrieve his belongings.

***

The problem with grav ball, Dayton knew, was that you sweated like a warthog after the game. You worked up a sweat, but in zero-G, the beads of sweat either flew off or just stuck to the skin in tiny bubbles. When the game was over and gravity restored all that sweat, it drenched the player like a shower.

Dayton, Zara, Trenton, and Richard sat on the front steps of the entertainment complex, slurping water from bottles. Richard had a large sweat stain running down his chest.

"We almost did it." Zara patted Richard on the shoulder. "For a guy with no experience, you blocked like five shots."

"Yeah." Richard looked at the ground. "But I let seven through."

"Don't be so high-G on yourself, buddy," Trenton said. "You did good. Their goalie let six through. That means he's not much better than you."

"Good point," Dayton said. "He's right. You did that with no experience. You might be a natural."

"I never really tried sports before." Richard perked up. "I did when I was really little, like in little league, but I sucked, so I quit and never went back."

"Things change," Trenton said. "Your coordination probably got a lot better as you got older."

"Oh, come on," Richard said. "Look at me."

"Yeah?" Zara said.

"So?" Trenton shrugged.

"I'm skinny. I had to have vision correction surgery twice," Richard said. "I'm a member of the chess club and get straight As in all my science classes. I'm a geek."

"Not to us," Dayton said. "I think you just proved it to Scott and those guys, too. Didn't you hear what he said after the game?"

"He was talking to you." Richard looked at the ground again.

"He was talking to all of us," Dayton said. "Including you."

A flyer loaded with some guys hovered by the entrance.

From inside the vehicle, several revelers noticed Zara's flight jacket and shouted and hooted at the friends.

"Space geeks."

"Gravity zeros!"

Then they IDed Richard as an Earther. "Look, he's hanging with space losers? Whatsa matter, don't you have any friends?"

Richard turned scarlet.

The driver pointed the front end of the car at a forty-five-degree angle. The grav modules grew bright purple with power, and the vehicle shook violently.

"Five, four, three, two, one—Blastoff!" they all shouted in unison as the vehicle shot up to the sky.

"You see?" Richard looked away in disgust.

Zara waved the whole thing off. "Yes, I do see. And you should see too, Dayton. We'll never fit in with these people. Even if those guys are just a bunch of drunks who need their collective asses kicked."

"Earth people are our people, Zara," Dayton said, with more anger in his voice than he wished was there.

"Not mine," Trenton said.

"What are you talking about? Just because you grew up in heavy gravity, you think you're not human?"

"I look different. I am different," Trenton said stubbornly.

Dayton shook his head. "You guys, we're visiting. We have to get along to get ahead."

"Get ahead where?" Zara spat. "I'm not going anywhere, and neither are you."

Richard put on a brave face, but his eyes looked confused and sad. Dayton realized this wasn't the conversation to be having in front of him.

"Come on, we won tonight," Dayton said, giving Richard a nudge. "Let's take that and go home."

***

It was Saturday morning, and Trenton was over early. He and Dayton had already been working on Old 21 in the garage for a couple of hours, and Margaret had already said his dad would need to give permission for him to keep the flyer at home. That wasn't going to slow down rehabbing it one bit. Dayton hit the remote and opened the gull-wing doors on the surveyor. They climbed in and settled into the familiar positions of driver and systems operator. Dayton called up the flight checklist and read it down, Trenton following line for line.

"Power plant?"

"Check."

"Grav and thruster plates?"

"Check."

"Propulsors?"

"Check."

"Flight computer?"

"Check."

Trenton reached over and handed Dayton a memory module. "Use this. I was able to isolate the frequencies used by traffic cameras and enforcer radar. It'll mask our signature."

"Done deal," Dayton patched the module into the computer. He brought the yoke up, and the surveyor responded. It was maybe half a meter, but the whole vehicle floated steadily in the middle of the garage.

"Now for reverse." Dayton brought the yoke back evenly and touched the retro jets. Old 21 floated gently back out of the garage until he activated the landing gear and set it down on the driveway.

"Not bad," Trenton flipped through his computer console. "All systems seem to be working just fine. Not sure about that rear-right stabilizer. I'll need to keep auto-correcting it, but we should still get altitude."

"In that case," Dayton opened his door. He grabbed up his comm unit and pointed it back toward the garage. Right on cue, the service bot puttered out.

"Give me a hand." He reached down and grabbed the bot's lower handhold. "Bring him inside. He can watch the stabilizer for us."

With practiced precision, the boys fastened the bot into place. Dayton hit a button on the bot's back panel, and it extended its systems connector and plugged into the vehicle. Now, the bot and Old 21 could talk to each other.

"I'm riding up front," Trenton said, grabbing a spare acceleration couch hanging on the garage wall and guiding it onto the fittings in the front passenger side of the vehicle cabin. The seat snapped into place with a loud *click*, and he settled in comfortably. "Now it looks like a regular vehicle. Not that that's a good thing."

The surveyor floated down the street, silent at about half a meter up, while Dayton got a feel for the yoke. It didn't handle as precisely as it used to. There was a certain degree of play in the controls. But it would do.

"We're at the edge of the residential area," Trenton said. "You ready to take the big test?"

"No, but I'll do it anyway." Dayton adjusted the grav plates and pulled back on the yoke. Slowly, the old surveyor's front end lifted until it was at exactly ninety degrees, its front facing the sky. Dayton held his breath as he activated the remaining propulsor units. "What was it they said back at Trumball?"

"Oh yeah," Trenton smiled. "The old-fashioned countdown: five, four, three, two, one, blastoff!"

Dayton punched the propulsors, and they shot into the morning sky. The acceleration pinned them to their seats as the city sprawled beneath them. Suddenly, all was right with the world. Dayton was back in the environment he so loved. It wasn't the same, that was for sure, but it was close enough.

After an hour of pleasure cruising, Dayton dropped Trenton at his home and flew east.

***

It was sheer beauty, seeing the coastline from this altitude. Dayton had seen the vastness of the ocean his first day on earth, but not like this. Now he could enjoy it. Having lived in space where any amount of water was precious, here three-quarters of the planet was covered with the stuff.

The waves, curled and white, crashed against the yellow sands of the beaches, which gave way to the vibrant green of the interior. It was a clash of colors as he piloted Old 21 across an expanse of clouds. Allyson sat beside him in the passenger seat. There was nothing at this altitude but transport planes and shuttles. Allyson seemed nervous at being this high but was getting used to it.

"You've got some seriously weird tunes in here," Allyson said, flipping through the onboard computer's entertainment files. "Look at this. You got something called Latz, Grand Survey, VacuLife, Airlock Kings, Full Bore, The Bulk Heads ..."

"A whole different music scene out there." Dayton kept his eyes on the clouds ahead. His heads-up display, or HUD as it was referred to, told him no other craft was in the immediate area at this altitude. "It's what I know. We picked up some from the colonies and stations we passed, but music is different anywhere you go out there."

"I suppose." Allyson closed the screen on the computer and looked out at the sprawling scenery below.

"Here." Dayton punched up the computer and pivoted the screen toward her. "Log into any music site you want and download some new tunes."

"How did you do this?" Allyson scrolled up and down the screen through the huge number of choices available on Old 21's computer system.

"I'm still in the Agency's network," Dayton said. "From here, I can access anything."

"Now I can get some real music." Allyson logged onto a site and began flipping through the charts. "Wow, this thing is fast. Are you on satellite?"

"It downloads through the link at the Enderi Prime Station." The clouds parted, and Dayton could make out the familiar suburban sprawl below.

Allyson looked up from the screen. "Is that home?"

"Yep."

"Are we at the end of the ride?"

"Not until you tell me if you'd go to the dance with me."

"If I say yes, can we keep flying?"

"Yes."

"Okay, yes."

He didn't dare ask her a second time. He just grinned and waggled the wings so he and Allyson shook gently in their seats as Allyson threw her head back and laughed.

EIGHTEEN

"Dayton?"

Was that what he heard? Dayton stirred in his sheets.

"Wake up."

Slowly, he opened his eyes and peeked at the comm unit on his nightstand. It read 6 a.m., thirty minutes before the thing was set to go off. Yep, he was being denied sleep, no doubt a grand follow-up to Margaret's early morning call to his father.

Her voice persisted. "Dayton, wake up."

He had always been bothered by the harsh way these comm unit alarms blasted him awake in the morning. Usually, that happened in the field. The biometers aboard *Venture* would gently stimulate your senses until you were up. Even so, Margaret's voice was a hundred times worse than the alarm.

"Yes?" he said, his head lifting mere centimeters from his pillow. His eyes could see only a blur around him.

"Are you awake?"

"I just said 'yes.'"

"You need to get the trash out," Margaret's image came into focus. She was standing in the doorway.

"Yeah, fine. Give me a second," Dayton said as he sat up in bed. "I'll take care of it."

"Hurry," Margaret said. "You need to get that trash out. I can hear the garbage man coming."

Margaret had exceptional hearing, Dayton thought. The last time she "heard" the garbage man it was 5:30 a.m., yet the man didn't arrive until sometime late that afternoon. Now it was 6 a.m., and likely, the garbage collector wouldn't actually show up for hours.

Dayton reached over and grabbed his hand held. He flipped the menu till he got to the proximity scanner. Just as he thought, there were no large vehicles within a three-kilometer radius of the house.

He held up the small computer. "No one is coming," he said.

"No," Margaret insisted. "Your gadget is wrong. I hear him. Take the trash out."

Yeah, sure, the hand scanner could detect micro fissures in a toxic atmosphere at high pressure, but it couldn't pick up something the size of a garbage truck coming down a city street. "I'll take care of it," he said. With that, he threw his comforter over his head, indicating this conversation was over.

Dayton heard Margaret head down the hall, and with that, he rolled over and picked up a controller unit from his drawer. He pressed a series of buttons on the touchscreen and pressed enter. He heard an electronic whirring and a series of clanks in response.

The nagging voice of Margaret came from his doorway. It was now 6:20 a.m. "Get up." Margaret was starting to sound like one of those warning announcements on the ship. Those were at least followed by a klaxon wailing in your ear. Right now, he really missed those klaxons. "You need to get the garbage out. You said you'd take it out."

"No." Dayton propped himself up. "I said I'd take care of it, and I did."

"You used those robot things, didn't you?" Margaret stood there, hands on her hips again. "You know how I feel about that."

"Yes, I know how you feel about that." Dayton flung the sheets off his body and sprung to the sitting position. "It would be impossible for me to *not* know, seeing as you never stop about it. But guess what? I believe in robots. In fact, I believe they can take the trash out every morning because that's what I programmed them to do. I also believe they can do the dishes, the windows, the carpet, clean the bathroom, dust, and just about anything else that needs doing around here that you seem to think is so important."

"It makes people lazy," Margaret said, and not for the first time. "That is what you're becoming. Look at you. Sitting there in bed. I doubt your father would approve."

"I'm sitting in bed because it's not even 6:30 a.m. in the morning, and you know what my father would say?" Dayton asked. He shot up and made his way to the door. He stormed out in such a way that Margaret yielded as he came through the door. Dayton stopped and faced her in the hall. "My father would be glad the robots helped him on *Venture*. He knows which things that are important. Taking out trash isn't it."

"Listen here." Margaret put her hands on her hips. "Your father put me in charge. Now, we will run things by the rules I set. Do you understand me, Dennis?"

Dennis?

"Who's Dennis?" Dayton asked.

But Margaret's face had gone blank.

"Oh, no," Margaret said as she struggled with this development. "No, you're not Dennis. No, of course not. I'm sorry. Just, can you meet me halfway on this?"

"All right," Dayton said. "I'll come up with a compromise."

Margaret attempted a smile and walked back down the hall. This left Dayton with two questions. How does one compromise on robots taking the trash out?

And who was Dennis?

***

"Hey!" Bradford's voice echoed in the crowded high school hall behind Dayton.

Great, Dayton thought, *this guy again.*

"What?" He turned to face him.

"Allyson's not going to the dance with you." As Bradford said it, Dayton noticed he had three of his followers in line behind him.

"Actually, yeah, she is," Dayton shot back. He held up his eduTablet, which had two access codes for the dance, just purchased.

"Oh. Look. He bought tickets," Bradford whined. "Well, you wasted your money. You can take that freak with the multi-colored hair instead."

Dayton looked at all four of them, sizing things up.

"What's the matter? Did I insult your real girlfriend? Gonna kick my ass?"

Dayton cracked a smile. "I'll let Zara kick your butt. She'd have no trouble with you."

"Allyson and I aren't broken up."

"She seems to think you are."

"You calling me a liar?"

"Yes."

Without another word, Bradford lunged. Dayton threw up his arms only to find Bradford's target was his eduTablet. He pulled his hands away, but it was too late. Bradford's fists grabbed the tablet and yanked it away.

"You aren't going without this," Bradford yelled as he slammed the eduTablet down on the duracrete floor. The tablet shattered on impact, sending fragments of circuit board, fiber optic cable, and data crystals flying in all directions.

The crowd in the hall went silent.

And Dayton had had enough.

He flew across the distance before Bradford even knew what hit him. WHAM! In the blink of an eye, Dayton was on top of him, pinning him to the ground.

"You're paying for that." Dayton planted his knees on either side of Bradford's chest, immobilizing him. "You try to interfere with Allyson and me again, and I'm going to take you out and beat you so fast it'll make your gyros stop. If you call Zara a freak again, I'll break both your arms off and throw them into the reclamation unit."

The three followers just stood there, like the rest of the

hall. *Just like dealing with thugs on mining colonies*, Dayton thought. *Take out the leader, and the rest will fold.*

"Well?" Dayton said to them. "Anyone else want to smash my stuff?"

Someone blew a whistle from behind. Turning, he saw Coach Flagel and a pair of duty bots patrolling the halls.

"All of you," the coach shouted. "Get to the principal's office right now. Move!"

***

Dayton glanced around Principal Ramirez's office. It wasn't quite as welcoming as it had been the first time he had been there. Back then, the man talked a lot. Now, Principal Ramirez just sat behind his desk, fingers steepled, staring daggers into them both. The fragments that were once Dayton's eduTablet lay on the desk in front of him. This was a new one. Being hauled before Milly, the old guy would never stop yammering. It was rough, but at least you knew where you stood. Here, it was the silent treatment. And that ground on Dayton.

"So, Bradford, you smashed Dayton's gear to the ground," Principal Ramirez said at last. "You destroyed private property. And I understand this was about a girl?"

"Yeah, well ..." Bradford showed a lack of command of the English language as he brushed off the charges.

"He just grabbed it out of my hand," Dayton said.

"Quiet, Mister Murdoch." Principal Ramirez held up a hand. "Bradford's vandalism doesn't give you the right to assault him. As far as I'm concerned, you're both at fault for this."

Dayton knew when to back off. He was mad. Very angry. He wanted to smash something of Bradford's to get even. But he knew this was the last instinct to follow right now.

"As of now," Principal Ramirez said, taking a firm, though notably lighter tone, "You are both suspended from the dance.

I feel that's only fitting since witnesses tell me that's what this came down to—taking Allyson Curtis to the dance?"

"She was going with me," Bradford said.

"No, she wasn't." Dayton shot back.

"Stop it," the principal raised his voice just enough to show he was in charge. Like there was any doubt of that.

"Fine," Bradford said. "Am I dismissed?"

"Your parents have already been sent the charges for Mister Murdoch's gear. I'm sure they'll have plenty to say to you when you get home." He pivoted to face Dayton. "A file on this incident will be sent to your caretaker."

"Yeah." He didn't dare say more.

"Well, that's it then. No dance for either of you. Dismissed."

Dayton felt all the blood rush out of his face. This couldn't be happening. "Wait."

Ramirez raised an eyebrow.

"Isn't there ... couldn't there be ..."

"What are you getting at, young man?"

"What I mean is, there's gotta be something we can do. Something to maybe make it right—"

"You mean earn your way back? Hmmm ..." Ramirez crinkled his eyebrows in thought. "If you two are interested in making this up, perhaps there's a way ..."

Dayton felt a ray of hope. There had to be a way out of this.

"You could possibly do some environmental work at the beach."

"No," Bradford said. "I think this whole thing is bull—uh, not good."

"Well, if that's the way you feel," Principal Ramirez said. "But if you still want to go to the dance ... you both could help out The Bay Project with cleaning up the mounds of dead fish washing up on the beach." He printed out a pair of disciplinary contracts, one in each of their names. They stated that they were to make themselves useful to the local environmental agency. The contracts were on ClearScan plastic, with a sensor square at either end of the bottom of the sheet. The lower left-hand corner was for acceptance. The lower right for refusal.

Dayton scanned the contract that went on and on about the removal of waste from the beach area and the possibility of aiding in any other conservation efforts "deemed essential" to the waterfront, whatever that meant. Dayton thought it might be left vague on purpose.

"A copy of this offer has been sent to your respective parents or guardians," Principal Ramirez said. "Just in case you have a change of heart in the matter."

"Ewwww," Bradford scrunched up his face as he read the contract. "I'm not going to deal with piles of slimy dead fish. It stinks." He pressed his right thumb on the lower right-hand square with a firmness that left no doubt about how he felt.

"I'll do it," Dayton said, almost before he realized he'd said it. Then he pressed his thumb to the left-bottom of his contract. It beeped in recognition.

"Oh, good luck," Bradford smirked. "You spend five milliseconds around those dead fish, you're gonna stink so bad they won't even LET you into the dance. You're gonna get all slimy and sick. That goo leaks into your skin and makes you all sick and zombie-like. You're gonna look and smell like a zombie."

"Thanks for your concern," Dayton retorted with sarcasm. "I'll wear protective gear."

"Not gonna help," Bradford said. "Even that space gear you live in won't do you any good. You're doomed."

"That will be enough of that," the principal said. "If you don't want to go—"

"I don't."

"If. You. Don't. Want. To. Go … That is your decision. Allow Mister Murdoch to make his decision in peace. No one is going to put anyone at risk for anything."

Bradford tossed the contract onto the principal's desk and

turned his back. Without another word, he walked out.

"You are dismissed," Principal Ramirez said as an after-thought. He took the contract and inserted it into his auto-filer, where it would be added to Bradford's permanent record.

"You accepted," Principal Ramirez said, sounding both delighted and surprised.

"You mean do I care if I get dirty and smelly?" Dayton asked. "No. I knew when I leaped on Bradford, there might be a chewing out. Which this kind of is."

"And the punishment?"

"Well, I'm disappointed," Dayton said. "But then again, it's a punishment. I'm not supposed to like it."

"Are you aware of the catastrophe that hit our beaches?"

"A catastrophe?"

"Yes," Principal Ramirez said. "The bay has been hit very hard by that new bio-engineered Ecto-Coli bacterium. Some company spilled a batch during a mishap, and now it's ruined most of the water near the shore. There are dead fish choking the beaches. No one can swim in there without getting sick. I'm not going to lie to you; it does smell. But if you can find a way to help out and do a good job, I'll let you go to the dance."

"Help out?" Dayton mulled the thought over. "Yeah, I think I can do something. Can I organize a cleanup? You know, get more hands involved?"

"Absolutely," Principal Ramirez stood up.

***

Dayton was out and down the hall, and already his mind was on damage control. First, he had to talk to Allyson. Tell her the dance was still on with them no matter what she might hear.

Margaret would be ready with a full blast once she got word of the fight. He needed to talk her down. And Dad. Oh boy, he had promised no more fighting.

He needed to talk this out with someone. Zara would likely go negative, and Trenton was too busy at the moment. But there was Richard. The guy was on a schedule. He'd be in the main library right about now. And probably in the same study cube he always took.

Dayton shot in, past the library bot. It hummed to action and spun its cylindrical head to face him. But Dayton continued on, and the bot settled back into its station at the information counter.

"Richard," Dayton called when he saw his friend in his usual spot at the usual time.

Sssshhhhhh. An electronic voice emanated from the library bot. Those things were worse than Yard Duty bots when it came to enforcing the rules.

"Richard," Dayton said in a low tone.

Richard pulled his VR headset off and blinked at Dayton, his eyes refocusing.

"Yeah," he said. "What's up?"

"Ramirez suspended me from the dance for fighting Bradford."

"What?" Richard's thin face fell.

"But I think I have a way to go to the dance," Dayton said, casting a side glance at the librarian bot. It looked in his direction as if expecting trouble.

"If Ramirez says no? No way."

"Well, yes," Dayton said. "If I help out with the clean up on The Bay Project or something. You know the biohazard down there?"

"Everyone does," Richard said. "You going to pick up some dead fish??"

"I was shooting for something a little bigger ..."

"Go on."

"Help out the bay," Dayton reflected. "Lots of dead biologicals."

"You mean dead fish?"

"Exactly," Dayton said. "We encountered something like that on Malpar Four."

"They had dead fish on Malpar Four?"

"No, not dead fish. The colony was never what you'd call 'green' or clean. They fumigated one time, and next thing they knew, they were hip-deep in dead rats."

Ssshhhhh. The electronic voice shushed them again from behind the information counter. Dayton lowered his voice to a whisper, and Richard scooted closer. "We hooked up scoops to the underside of some grav platforms," Dayton said more softly, though his enthusiasm was hard to hold back. "Then we just sucked all the dead rats up. Problem is I'm going to need help to set this up for the fish."

"Help? You mean me?"

"Your help and more. But what can I offer the other kids to recruit them?"

"You could make it part of the volunteer requirement," Richard said after a minor pause. "You know, everyone has to have credits for doing volunteer work."

"The principal didn't say anything to me about it," Dayton said.

"That's because everybody just knows." Richard set his VR goggles down. "Just say it's a great project and have everyone sign up at the beach monitor station."

"Picking up smelly fish is a great project?"

Richard shrugged. "You might have to spin it a little."

"That'll work," Dayton said. "Meet me at my locker at the next class change; we need to do some enlisting." He hurried out of the library before the robot could shush him again. His comm unit, immune to the school's communications dampening field, beeped. He checked the ID. It was Dad. The dampening field, set up to keep the students off their comm devices and social networks, would have saved him this time. But no, *Venture* equipment, created to break through all manner of electromagnetic storms and other interference, worked fine. Oh, the irony.

Dayton bolted into the library entrance hall. At the end nearest to the entrance were holo-imaging chambers. Dayton entered the first open one, and the door swished shut. He placed his comm unit into the touchscreen console, and a life-size image of his dad sprung up on the disc in front of him.

The image was clear, as was the disapproving look on Dad's face. The background, what little Dayton could see of it, looked like the metallic bulkheads of a space habitat.

"I know," Dayton cut to the point. "I promised no more fighting."

"You did," Dad said. "And what did you do?"

"Fought."

"This was over a girl?" Dad asked, reading a hard copy printout of the incident, still in his hands.

"It started that way," Dayton said. "Look, the guy smashed my tablet. I got mad."

"This is not some frontier mining settlement where you can punch someone out for looking at you wrong. They have laws."

"I already got a dose of their laws, as if I needed more. I can't go to the dance now. Until I do some cleanup at the beach."

"All right," Dad said. "Picking up trash for a day isn't going to hurt."

"Well, it's dead biologicals, actually," Dayton said. "I was thinking maybe try a pick-up job like the *Venture* did at Malpar Four. Only I know you were the one that put it together."

Dad's eyes went wide. "Okay," he said. "Do you want to know the mechanics?"

"Yeah," Dayton said. "How did you make it happen?"

Dad thought for a moment. "Take vacuum-sealed lines, fuel hoses should do, and connect them to the intake manifold of the grav engine."

"How?" Dayton asked. "The hoses won't connect to a manifold. It's a totally different fitting."

"Use a type-A universal fitting," Dad said. "A two-way clamp. Then lock it up tight with some auto-foam."

"Isn't the intake of all that dead material going to lessen the power to the grav motors?"

"We thought so, too," Dad said. "And it will. So, when you come in over the dead fish, gun the engines. Do it fast and watch the throttle."

"I knew there had to be a trick to it," Dayton said. Mentally, he was imagining this.

"I retrofitted the scoops?" Dad looked off-holocam. "But our great friend here was the one who actually did the flying."

His dad scooted off-holoscreen. Turco took his place. He flashed a friendly grin.

"You been listening?" Dayton asked, knowing the answer already.

"Of course," Turco said. "You guys are talking about my famous rat-carcass pickup sortie. My ears naturally drifted over when that happened."

"Dad said I need to gun the engines at the point where the stuff is sucked into the scoops?"

"I'm not going to lie to you, kid," Turco looked off holo-cam, as if checking to see if Dad was still nearby. "I almost crashed. It was one of those split-millisecond moves that no one but the pilot notices. What kind of grav are you going to use?"

"I don't know," Dayton said. "Probably an old carrier. I can usually check one of those out."

"Not a precision vehicle," Turco said. "But it should do the job. I had a load lifter for my run. How much are they making you vacuum up?"

"They didn't give me a number," Dayton said. "I figured enough to fill the grav bus' cargo compartment."

"Good, we can shoot for that," Turco said. "Now, where are you headed after the pickup?"

"After?"

"You do plan on dumping the fish off somewhere, don't you? You don't want to take it home with you."

"Oh yeah, that ..." Dayton hadn't thought this through. "I could take it to a city recyclomat, I suppose."

"Good," Turco said. "Nice to see the Earth sun hasn't melted your brain, at least yet. Okay, take it there. Recyclomats have doors at the top, so disposal shouldn't be a problem. Just hover over the mouth and dump it all."

"But back to the actual piloting," Dayton said.

"Sure. When you come in, come in low, maybe half a meter off the ground. The split second you hear and feel the fish being sucked up, gun the motors, then ease off at least forty percent when the last of the stuff shoots through into the cargo hold. Otherwise, you'll overshoot."

Turco's holo-image winked out, leaving Dayton in the darkness of the holo chamber.

But he didn't feel alone.

NINETEEN

He sent out a group comm for everyone to meet him at the lockers during their ten-minute hydration break that was coming up.

Allyson and her friend Karen arrived first. Karen was kind of good-looking, although Dayton didn't think she was as outstanding as Allyson. She had long, straight hair, dark eyes, and very white skin. Then came Scott, Zara, Trenton, and several members of the grav ball team. Their expressions were concerned, worried, and unsure. Richard was last, looking a little timid.

"I heard," Allyson said as Dayton got closer. "You fought Bradford, and now you can't go to the dance?"

"Oh no," Dayton said. "I am going to that dance. WE are going. To that dance. I'm just gonna be a little busy for the next couple of days. I have a plan."

"Oh boy," Zara rolled her eyes. "I know what that means ..."

"A plan?" Allyson laughed. "With you, that could be anything."

"Do you want some extra credit?" Dayton asked the group.

They glanced at one another, searching for some thought to bring to the forefront. Dayton was into uncharted and rather unpopular waters right now. Clearly, more guidance was needed.

"It's a beach cleanup project," Dayton said. "Anyone who volunteers gets credit toward their volunteer requirements, isn't that right, Richard?"

"I'll do it," Richard said, if somewhat sheepishly. "Anything's better than admin work at the Bureau of Statistics downtown."

"Oh, that's right, we gotta do that volunteer thing," Zara

said, practically spitting the last two words out. "But I'm wearing my rescue suit. I've been in that drink once, and I know how it smells."

"You won't need to go in the water," Dayton said. "Just work on the shore. That's it; just collect all the dead fish in a big row about two meters wide."

"And get full credit?" Scott asked. "Just for moving deceased aquatic life around?"

Good. Dayton was getting some takers. "Just bring some tools."

"We don't even have to, like, dump it anywhere? We're in." His fellow grav ball players nodded in agreement.

"Wait a millisecond," Zara said. "A row? Are you planning on pulling a Malpar Four?"

"Oh, I heard about that," Trenton said. "This might actually be fun. Do I get any extra credit for helping you with the reclamation scoops? Or maybe FINDING reclamation scoops?"

"Sure, at least with me," Dayton said. "Then Saturday, 9 a.m. at Avenue I at Monitor Station One-One-Five-Three. Zara, you know what this is all about, so I need you to mark off the rows in the sand and check their height. You also know what clogs up fuel scoops, so keep an eye out for that."

"Does that mean I get to direct everyone around?" Zara's eyes lit up, a rare occurrence. "Like maybe using a holographic pointer?"

"Do whatever it takes," Dayton said. "Just make sure it meets the measurements. Scott, you and the guys just start moving dead bio—I mean the dead fish, I don't care how. Push it. Pull it. Drag it. Whatever. Just put it where Zara marks it off."

"What's my part?" Richard said.

"You wanted to be part of a *Venture* crew, right?" Dayton said. "This'll be close. You and me together on the grav carrier."

"We need to make a trip to the Sub again," Trenton said. "Start crawling through the piles of spares to make the vacuum."

"Hey, I love digging through spare parts," Zara said.

The chime sounded, signaling class was about to begin.

"And us?" Allyson said as the others walked away. Karen stood by her side.

"Would you mind helping out Scott?" Dayton answered with a question.

"Okay," Allyson and Karen said in unison.

That was easy.

"But," Allyson said, "and this is a big 'but.' We each want a set of those shipboard envirosuits."

"Sure," Dayton said.

"And we want to keep them," Karen added. Allyson nodded in agreement.

"Deal," Dayton said. "After you're done there, you may not WANT to keep them, but sure, keep 'em."

"Pleasure doing business with you, fly boy." Allyson landed a peck on Dayton's cheek. Dayton watched her leave. There she was, the whole reason he was doing this. And yet, she was all ready to help out. Would she have ever done that for Bradford? He smiled.

No. She wouldn't have.

***

The gigantic grav carrier was angled in the driveway at Dayton's house, so it mostly stayed out of the street. Luckily, it was morning on a Saturday, and no one seemed to mind. Dayton had found a slightly ragged Bay Project banner in the dumpster behind the school, and he hung it across the carrier so it gave the idea it was there for a community project. It would cut down on complaints, he thought.

"You know," Trenton said, his welding torch gleaming as he soldered the right fuel hose to the ram scoop under the grav bus. "If the guys at the Sub knew what we were doing to their vehicle, they would kill us."

"I told them I had a socially-conscious purpose for this thing," Dayton said. "We're covered."

"Socially conscious." Trenton blew a raspberry through his lips. "What did you say?"

"I left it vague."

"You're a real master diplomat," Trenton said. "We're home-free."

"Pressure is holding, on the left one anyway," Richard said from his seat near the back of the cockpit. "Haven't fired up the right one yet."

A final grunt from Trenton told Dayton they were done. "Try it now," Trenton's muffled voice came from under the bus.

Richard set the series of buttons on the touchscreen control panel in motion. The digital readouts shot into the triple digits and then stabilized. "I think we're good," he said.

The hoses and scoops were ready. Dayton glanced at his chronometer. It was just about time to get going. He'd been able to retrieve the old grav carrier from the Sub again; it was a floater that had no permanent home or repair bay. The guys at the Sub didn't care what happened to it. It probably depreciated off the books a long time ago.

"Get on board," Dayton called to Trenton. "You'll get to see Zara directing Earthers around. You'll probably never see her happier."

Trenton jumped in and buckled up. Dayton took the old carrier up in the air. It was slow and clumsy to handle, but it obeyed his steering. He brought it level. Off in the distance, he could see the blue, flat-topped steel pyramid of the city's local recyclomat. That technical wonder would be his drop-off point once he collected the fish. Grav waste carriers dumped their garbage into the top maw, where a series of chemical and mechanical processes turned scrap and junk into an eco-friendly paste suitable for everything from weatherproofing to construction blocks to ordinary plasticware. He considered it a "Margaret" kind of thing but useful.

The coordinates led them to Avenue I, Monitor Station 1153. His volunteers were all down there, gathered and waiting for him—Zara, Allyson, Scott, Karen, Richard and Trenton. They had managed a row of rotting fish several meters long and then about a meter wide. Allyson was waving up at him happily, and the others followed her lead.

Perfect.

The shoreline shot by about a dozen meters below. Lifeless fish floated on sickly yellow foam on top of the water, lapping at the shore. Dayton kept the bulky grav carrier on target.

"One thing about you," Allyson's voice came over his headset. "Never a dull date."

"How's the environsuit?" Dayton laughed.

"It's kinda nice," Allyson's voice said. "I still think your jacket is better, though."

"I don't like the sound of that," Dayton said. "But anyway, you guys need to back off a few meters. I'm going to kick up a ton of that sand."

"That's what I've been saying all along," Zara said. "But do they listen? No. Not even your 'girlfriend' believed me when I told them about sandstorms on Aytle Three, but they're about to live out one of those when you hit the beach ..."

"Okay, okay," Dayton said. "You were right. They were wrong. He knew from years of mission teams with Zara that she had to be recognized as right. Otherwise, she'd never let up.

***

They worked on the beach for hours. Zara seemed rather bossy, and then, as Dayton was collecting rotting fish carcasses, he heard Zara and Scott arguing.

"Why do you say that?" Zara's voice echoed.

"I was just asking," Scott replied in a bit of a defensive tone.

"What is going on?" Dayton marched over to the two.

"He said I have ugly hands," Zara yelled as much as spoke. "When I was putting on my bio-hazard gloves, he assumed I had an animal that mauled me."

"I didn't say that," Scott said. "I just saw that she had some scratches on her hands and asked if she played with her cat at all."

"You Earthers and your comfy lives have no idea what we've been through," Zara said. She pulled off her bio glove and showed off her scared hand. "This! This is the result of work. You have no idea!"

"Okay, I'm sorry," Scott said, throwing up his hands. "God, you're a little defensive."

"Oh, you want defensive?" Zara shouted.

"Enough," Dayton said. "Zara, drop it. He apologized."

"Oh, fine," she said. "Take his side."

"I'm not taking anyone's side."

"Yes, you are," Zara said and marched off.

"Seriously," Allyson came up beside Dayton. "She is getting more and more hostile. Someone needs to have a talk with her about life."

"She'll be fine," Dayton said. "It just takes her longer to acclimate around here than others. You'll see."

"I hope so," Allyson said, without any real conviction. She looked at the gathered trash and dead fish. "I think we're about ready."

***

The grav carrier held its own, creak by creak, groan by groan. He felt the old metal under his boots vibrate, shaking due to misaligned maneuver jets. Nothing he could do about that now. Just realigning the ones on Old 21 took two nights, and Old 21 was a LOT smaller.

There was some give to the stick, and for a brief second, Dayton thought he would crash. He was used to the precise response of Old 21. This old bus was neglected, poorly maintained. What was the saying he heard from the Earth pilots at the Sub? Oh yeah, it maneuvered like a bathtub.

He flipped on the giant vacuum and pulled even with the beach, kicking up sand just like he knew he would. The line of junk got closer until, finally, he flew directly over it. He slowed, lowering the carrier until the scoops were at sand level.

A cacophony of clatters, bangs, pops, grinds, and grating filled his ears, even through the headset. The sound was all around him, enveloped by the sand, shot through fuel hoses, slamming into the metal hold. But it was music to Dayton's ears. His new ticket to the dance.

"Pressure's holding," Richard shouted from behind him. "Vacuum is strong at Three-Fifty-three. We're at eighty-three percent capacity."

"Almost there," Dayton said, as much to himself as Richard.

"We're shaking," Richard shouted.

Dayton even heard the groan of metal flexing below his boots. Maybe he should have studied the schematics of the grav carrier first. Just to see if it could handle this kind of work. Good idea, just a little late.

"We're fine," Dayton said, though he noticed the stick was twitching, and he used both hands to hold it steady.

Suddenly, they were at the end of the whole morbid line. The shaking stopped. The all-enveloping noise stopped. Only the straining sound of the engine was left to assault their ears. Seconds later, he heard cheers erupt over his headset. He pulled the carrier up, only to hear Allyson cry, "You did it."

Bringing the carrier out over the yellowish water, he leaned in for a wide turn, possibly the best the old bus could do. He shot back over the monitor station. Below was a clean trench where the line of dead fish used to be. The sand looked clean and pressed.

Dayton brought the carrier down on the sand. Everyone came around, high-fiving him, except for Allyson. He got a hug from her. A crowd of onlookers, busy on the pedestrian path, were stopped in their tracks, mouths open.

He pulled the access seal to the carrier's hold. It was stuffed with all manner of deceased aquatic biologicals. The stink was awful.

"Looks good." Allyson stood beside him, peering into the dark hold. She pulled off her headgear, and even with her face exhausted, her cheeks ruddier, and her hair tied up in a bun, Dayton found her beautiful. She sure had a nice figure for a girl wearing an environsuit.

"Next stop the recyclomat," Dayton said. "Then I guess we're done here."

"Can I come aboard, Captain?" Allyson asked.

"Of course," Dayton replied, bowing and sweeping his arm dramatically.

"Can we all go over?" Scott asked. "I've never seen the recyclomat working up close."

"Well, yeah, sure," Dayton said.

Allyson climbed in through the open door with the clear intent of taking the co-pilot's station. That was until Zara pushed her way past.

"Shotgun," Zara said, not even looking at Allyson but making sure she could hear.

Dayton glared at Zara.

"What?" Zara said, shrugging. "You need a co-pilot if something goes wrong over there."

"You weren't too eager to be a co-pilot before this," he said, giving her a warning look.

"And now I am," Zara said flatly. "You need me."

"It's okay, Dayton," Allyson took a seat next to Karen. She didn't look annoyed, either. Another reason to love her.

A little more clanking and grinding and Dayton brought the old bus into the air. The trip to the recyclomat was tense, and no one said much. That made the five-minute trip seem more like five hours. The recyclomat was easy to spot, a large blue-and-white pyramid twenty stories high and about half that wide at the base. Modern technology in all its glory, the recyclomat and others like it had a large maw at its flat peak. The automated perimeter scanner identified their cargo, and the roof-mounted clamshell doors at the top of the metal pyramid opened. Dayton brought the grav carrier directly over the waiting jaws and released its bay doors.

The collected fish fell into the recyclomat, sending up a wave of heat. Dayton rushed to compensate for the eruption of hot air, but no one seemed alarmed by it. As a pilot, Dayton could feel every slight error, and with an audience aboard, it made him a little sensitive.

The doors to the recyclomat sealed once again. That meant it had worked. Cheers broke out behind him. Dayton pulled away, taking in the rush of a decided victory. It had taken all morning and a good part of last night, but he'd done it. He couldn't wait to see Principal Ramirez.

"Let's go," Allyson called from the back. "Can you drop us off at the Monitoring Station? We need to get our vehicles."

"No problem."

Back to the beach. No sooner had they arrived than Dayton saw a terrible problem. The others saw it, too, and they let out gasps.

The putrid fish was all back, or at least more of the same. The yellowish waves, deadly in their bacterial infestation, had deposited even more of them onto the beach. They'd been gone less than fifteen minutes, and it was as if they'd never done anything to begin with.

"What the —" Scott said from behind Dayton. "The fish. They're all back."

"This was a fine way to waste time," Zara said. "Looks like we REALLY made a difference, didn't we?"

"Shut up, Zara," Dayton snapped.

He brought the grav carrier down, and everyone scrambled off. Everyone but Richard, Allyson, and Zara.

"What are you going to do?" Allyson asked.

"It's not a complete loss," Dayton said. "You guys checked in with the rescue teams at the monitor station. You'll get credit for all the work you did."

"But what about you guys?" Allyson moved slightly closer. "You have no proof now you did anything."

"I know." Dayton looked at the concern on Richard's face. Trenton didn't look too thrilled, either. "Can you show this work log to the rescue guys? It has Richard's and Trenton's information on it. Zara's there, too."

"Sure." Allyson took the log pad. "That'll take care of them. But what about you?"

"I'm going to have to work that one out," Dayton said.

Pulling up from the beach, he leveled the grav bus and headed back to the Sub.

He really didn't know what he was going to do.

***

"So, what do we learn from Nietzsche?" Mister Segramson asked as a hologram of Friedrich Wilhelm Nietzsche spun in the center of the class. It was a grainy image of a man with plumed hair and a bushy handlebar mustache. It was in black and white, meaning the man lived long ago, most likely.

"He invented Nihilism," one guy at the back of the class-room said.

"He is closely associated with it, yes. Who can tell us more about the history of Nihilism, the concept that values do not exist but are falsely invented," Segramson asked, "that life is without meaning, purpose, or intrinsic value?"

"He had a lot of time on his hands," Dayton mumbled, but the teacher heard him anyway.

"Dayton?" Segramson said, his eyes wide with surprise. "You have a comment?"

"I was just thinking this Nietzsche guy must've had a lot

197

of time on his hands. It seems like all he did was worry about small stuff."

The class laughed, but the teacher was quick to silence it. "That's very interesting," he said. "Why do you say that?"

"I mean, when you're working, you don't have time to overthink stuff like that. I don't think he contributed a lot to society."

"Maybe, but maybe not." Segramson smiled. "Nietzsche's philosophical outlook has inspired generations of authors and philosophers. To him, life was to ponder. He asked the questions we all ask ourselves at one time or another."

"He did?" Dayton asked. *For people on Earth, maybe*, he thought.

"I can see I've given you a great deal to think about." Mister Segramson flipped the hologram off. "Meanwhile, Mister Murdoch, I have a message here that Principal Ramirez would like to see you."

***

"Frankly, I'm disappointed," Principal Ramirez said, frowning over his glasses. "I have the receipt from the recyclomat, and the grav carrier did drop off a load, but there's no evidence at all that it made a dent on the beach. Did you happen to get a holophoto of the clean beach before the next wave of fish flooded in?"

Dayton hung his head. "We … I … didn't think to take one. It all happened so fast."

Ramirez shook his head.

"What does this mean for me going to the dance?" Dayton asked.

Ramirez grunted a bit and took off his glasses to clean them. "I know Bradford's parents pretty well. They will claim you didn't do anything, doctored up any evidence, and press their attack. I need irrefutable evidence."

"In other words, you know these people, and they'll make

trouble?" What Dayton didn't say was, *And I'm just one of those unimportant space kids, and you won't stand up for me.* Instead, he jumped in. "Look, I don't like unfinished business any more than you. Please, Principal Ramirez, let me take another crack at this. There's still time to earn my way back in, isn't there?

A long sigh came out of the principal. "Sure, go ahead and try it." He sounded about as hopeful as a parachutist with a broken rip cord.

TWENTY

"Now that I see it in the light ..." Brock said from his hospital bed. The gauze pack had come off some days ago, revealing a new arm where the old one was burnt and boiled. "I still say it's darker than the original." The boy couldn't help but stare at his new limb, turning it over the way an art critic would rotate a fine holo sculpture.

"Okay," Dayton said. "So, you get to suntan the other arm till it matches. Be glad you HAVE an arm."

"Hey, I got nothing to do till they let me out," Brock said. "Unless you have something for me? A holo game, perhaps?"

"No." Dayton reached around to the small of his back. "If the crew saw one in there, they'd all want one. So, they didn't see it."

Dayton came around his mid-section with a new Ersatz holotab. Brock's face lit up.

"After surviving a plasma burning like you did, how could I say no?" Dayton said. "Just do me a favor? Don't rub it in anyone's face."

"Naw," Brock flipped through the touchscreen. The Ersatz logo lit up, spinning above the tablet. "I'm in this room by myself all the time anyway."

Outside the room, the *Venture* children played with their new devices and ate candy that Dayton had just distributed.

Brock looked up from the tablet, no small feat considering his enthusiasm for the thing. "Looking forward to the dance? With that Allyson girl?"

"How do you know about that ...and Allyson?"

"How do you think?" Brock shrugged. "Turco and I talk a lot, you know."

Dayton sighed and sat down at the edge of Brock's bed. "I

took another grav truck out and converted the fuel scoops to suck up dead fish at the beach."

"Yeah," Brock said. "Like we did on our deployment to Braundel Seven that time?"

"It was Malpar Four, actually. We've been to so many different planets I can't keep 'em all straight either."

"Doesn't matter. Back to that grav truck you were talking about. Was it kind of like a big vacubot? Did it work?"

"Well, yes," Dayton said. "Sort of. I got all the fish for like a dozen meters or so of the beach. So, I took the full load of that junk to the recyclomat. Then I flew back. But by then, that bio-hazard tide had just washed up more dead fish. It erased any proof I did that. Then I had to get the grav carrier back."

"Oh," Brock said.

"Uh huh," Dayton said, dejected. "I spend hours rigging up those hoses. And for what? For the ocean to spill more dead fish on the beach and ruin everything all over? How can I prove I did my job to Principal Ramirez?"

"You could do it again," Brock said. "Video record it this time. Just rig up a nav beacon. That should do it."

"I thought of that, but no." Dayton shook his head. "When I returned the carrier to the depot, it stank so bad the foreman said he'd never let me have another one."

"Oooh," Brock said. "Tough break."

The two sat for a few moments, with only the animated sounds of the *Venture* children playing outside in the halls to break up the silence.

"I need help, Brock. I need to prove that I helped the Bay so I can take Allyson to the dance."

"Okay," Brock said as he patted the bed with his new arm. "You did me a favor with this game tablet, so I'm gonna help YOU out."

"Oh really?" Dayton said with wide eyes. Logic and necessity cut short any smart remarks. Bottom line was he needed help from someone, anyone.

"While you were out conquering the stars, do you remember that problem we had with the water tanks on *Venture*?"

Dayton did remember. And yes, Brock had been one of the maintenance techs assigned to solve that problem. "The problem we had with that bacterium that kind of grew out of nowhere."

"Yeah," Brock said. "The envirotechs made that enzyme stuff that ate it away. So, if the enzymes could eat up *that* bacteria, are the bacteria that makes the water yellow at the beach any different?"

"Probably not. But I have no idea how to solve the problem. "

Brock smiled. "I think I can help you out. Give me a day or two."

***

The Skye Cafe was busy and clattering as Dayton and Allyson enjoyed steaming platters of burgers and fries. The place was located midway between Los Angeles and San Diego, overlooking San Juan Capistrano with its sparkling beaches and brilliant cliffs. They had parked Old 21 right outside the cafe on the landing pad. Dayton was nervous about his meeting with the principal but kept quiet about it until he had a plan in place.

Allyson looked at their plates. "Enjoyed it?" She cleaned her fork with a napkin, an odd habit he found endearing, even though it didn't make much sense. Allyson played with her straw. "Karen will want to know all about this latest adventure."

"I'm sure you're going to give her a real extensive debriefing."

"She's tried to link in with me and message me like a hundred times," Allyson laughed.

"Well, we don't want to keep her waiting," Dayton said.

Allyson dropped the straw and grabbed his hand. "There's a group of older guys coming over here."

He looked quickly to see five men in jackets with car club patches walking over. He'd seen them eyeing Old 21 in the parking lot when they pulled in. "That's okay," Dayton smiled. Car club guys would appreciate an old flyer.

"Hey," one of the club members stood over the table. He was tall, with a dark complexion and angular features. His dark hair, medium length about his shoulders, barely covered the tattoos around his neck. His eyes were large and brown and seemed more at home on a curious child than a man in his twenties. He looked directly at Dayton. "That's a nice flyer you got out there. What make is that?"

"It's an old surveyor."

"I like that; it has sand-blasted paint scars. Looks good that way," the man said. He rolled up his sleeve, revealing a tattoo on his bicep that read "AirFlow Xtreme," with a cartoon image of a buffed-out flyer. "Name is Vance. We all belong to AirFlow Extreme."

"Nice tat." Dayton rolled up his sleeve to reveal that his own bicep had a tattoo as well. Dayton's was a starburst, with the words *354th Survey Squadron* circling the burst's outer halo. "This is the crew I belonged to."

"I didn't know you had a tat." Allyson's mouth fell open.

"Got this when I made pilot." Dayton showed the design off.

"Look at the detail on that thing." Vance bent over to get a closer look. "What graphitat did that kind of work?"

"Graphitat?" Dayton unrolled his sleeve. "No room for tattoo machines out there. This was done by a flight engineer. He was a big-time tattoo artist before he came out to space."

"The man is talented." Vance looked back at Dayton. "So, you must be pretty good at the controls. You ever do any racing?"

"Not much." Dayton liked to race, but now was not the

time to talk racing with Allyson present.

"Well, you want to give it a try?" Vance looked to his friends, who were smiling and nodding.

"I don't think so. I have company."

"I got ya," Vance said, nodding with a smile to Allyson.

He pressed a comm pad on his wrist, and Dayton's pad beeped in recognition. "Just to let you know where we hang out. You know, if you want to see what we're all about."

"Sounds good," Dayton said.

"You know you could race him," Allyson said after Vance was some distance away.

"No," Dayton said. "Today is all about us."

"I'm impressed," Allyson said. "A lot of guys would get all machismo on me and take off racing."

"I'm not a lot of guys."

"No," Allyson said. "You're not."

***

"Well, this was an insanely different date for me," Allyson laughed. After leaving the cafe, they had gone flying to see the old Spanish mission, a religious center founded in 1776. Now, they pulled up on the dark street in front of her house. Dayton settled Old 21 down next to the curb and said, "Of course it was different. That was my plan."

Allyson's eyes sparkled, even in the near darkness that enveloped them. "What are we?"

"Huh?" Dayton cocked his head. He didn't know where that question came from and sure as hell didn't know how to answer it.

"I mean, what is this?" She motioned between the two of them. "What are we?"

"I don't know," Dayton said. "What do you want us to be?"

"Well." Allyson smiled as she looked up at the roof of the surveyor. "I don't know. I thought a commitment might be a thought."

"A thought?" Dayton saw where she was going with this, but he drew a blank.

She grabbed his hand lightly. "There must have been girls on *Venture*. What did you do?"

Dayton squeezed her hand, and their fingers interlaced. "Up until now, I haven't really had one, a girlfriend."

"You're kidding." Allyson smiled. "So, you don't know what to do?"

"Not really, no," Dayton said.

"Cool," Allyson said as she leaned over and kissed him.

Her lips felt so different from any girl he'd ever kissed. He didn't know if it was the fact that she'd grown up on Earth, had never been in a pressurization chamber, or what, but he liked it. Dayton had always had little trouble meeting girls. He showed up as a crew member on *Venture* and was the center of attention. But, in the end, all these hook-ups ended after only a few weeks, sometimes days. As such, a permanent relationship was something he had never experienced. He knew the meeting part. He knew the getting-to-know-you part, but not the maintenance or sustaining part. And that made him feel under-equipped right now.

Dayton's comm vibrated. He was so into Allyson that, at first, he didn't even notice it. But on the third buzz, he grabbed it and took a peek. It was a message from Brock:

Hey, Venture buddy:

I talked to the techs. They can meet you tomorrow 8 a.m. at the Monitor Station.

See ya.

"What's that?" Allyson asked, pointing to his comm unit.

"The answer I was waiting for," Dayton said. "My new ticket to the dance."

The comforting darkness of the surveyor suddenly filled with light. Dayton saw the porch light turrets from Allyson's house were on and were rotating their way. A dark figure marched off the porch and down to the end of the driveway.

"Allyson." The figure's voice was deep. "You're late."

"I know, Dad," Allyson said. She turned back to Dayton. "I better go."

"No problem," Dayton said.

Allyson opened the gull-wing door and stepped out, but by that time, the figure of William was standing right next to Dayton's side of Old 21. He leaned over into the cockpit.

"Hi," he extended his hand. "Good to see you again. Did you two have fun?"

"Yes, Allyson is showing me so much around here." He shook the man's hand, finding it to be firm but not challenging.

"Hi, Dad," Allyson said with hesitation and embarrassment. "We've been seeing the sights."

"Impressive," Allyson's father said as he stepped back and looked Old 21 up and down. "This is one of those early PSVs, a type R if I'm not mistaken."

"Type RE, to be exact," Dayton popped the gull-wing on his side and stepped out. "I modified her to be driven like a regular civilian flyer."

"Allyson said you were working on something big in your garage." William bent over to look at the grav modules. "You know, we used to work on these down at GravaMetrics. We always had a problem with the counterpoints."

Dayton popped the rear access panel near the passenger's side grav module. "We had trouble with those for years. Our machine shop finally discovered if you reverse the counterpoints, the whole module stabilizes without the need to manually readjust."

"That's them." William's eyes went wide when he saw the inner workings of the module. "I remember those now. Wow. What an easy solution you came up with."

"Before we reversed them, we had to realign for every mission." Dayton smiled at Allyson, who returned the smile but rolled her eyes. "We manufactured a small cross-point harmonizer to bridge the gap. It made all the difference."

"You actually had to build another part entirely?" William looked embarrassed. "I guess GravaMetrics really dropped the ball on this one."

"It wasn't so bad, really," Dayton said.

"You must tell me about that, but first, let me take care of something." William pulled a remote out of his pocket. Within seconds, the ButlerBot appeared.

"Do you like mango smoothies?" William looked at Dayton, who shrugged.

"Never had one before."

"Perfect. You're going to love them. Now, please, tell me all about how you tripled the range on this thing."

Dayton realized that while the date was over, the night certainly wasn't.

***

"Where are they?" Richard said, his hair blowing in the offshore breeze. It was the next morning, bright and windy, as a few seagulls scrounged beach trash. "They said eight, right?" He pinched his nose at the smell coming from the beach. The sickly-looking water was jammed with rotting fish. Yet again.

"They'll be here," Dayton said. "Brock has never missed a shift."

The whining, whirring sounds of heavy grav motors announced the arrival of an Agency loader. It was painted a long time ago in a construction-yellow color with dayglow-orange stripes. It kicked up extraordinarily little sand as it touched down.

Once settled, the heavy cargo door at the back popped open. Brock, looking as strong as Dayton had seen him since they got to Earth, led three techs down the aft ramp. Dressed in white lab coats, the techs trudged across the sand. Already, they had surveyed the bay and were carrying beakers, chemistry kits, and portable scanners.

"This is Tojun." Brock motioned to a small-framed Asian man. Dayton didn't think he'd met the man before. It was doubtful their paths crossed much back on *Venture*.

"Hey, Tojun." Dayton extended his hand.

Tojun glanced at Dayton, then turned back to his equipment.

"You wanted that bio-pollutant removed?" Tojun said simply, not looking at Dayton.

"Yes," Dayton said. "It's been a bio-hazard here for a long time. I was hoping the enzymes we used in the water tanks back on *Venture* could help."

"Probably," Tojun said after some silence.

Hours ticked by. The techs didn't say much, even to each other, but they worked feverishly.

Every now and then, they would ask for samples of ocean water or some of that sickly yellow foam, and he and Richard scrambled to collect them.

Brock and Richard seemed to get along right off. Which figured; they both loved science. Dayton also knew Brock was just waiting to get to know someone outside of the hospital ward. Richard, for his part, wanted to meet all of *Venture*'s crew.

"You really think your scientist guys can defeat that stuff?" Richard asked, casting a wary eye at the yellowish water foaming up on the sand a meter away from them. "Water and Power has been trying to get that stuff for years. All they can do is dump chloro-emulsifiers to make sure it stays out of the drinking water at the desalination plants."

"These guys will get it," Brock said. "They're the best."

"Flight Commander Murdoch," Tojun said, raising a beaker of polluted, contaminated water for Dayton to see. "We're ready to try."

Richard looked in surprise at the use of Dayton's *Venture*

job title. On Earth, it usually belonged to a much older person.

Tojun reached out and handed Dayton a dropper. It was clear he wanted Dayton to do the honors.

Dayton added a dropper of frothing enzymes to the beaker filled with sea water. The foaming started with the drop and then grew outward.

"Looks like you have something there," Richard said.

"We do." Tojun looked at the beaker through a magnification loop. "I think it worked. Here, Flight Officer Murdoch. See for yourself."

Dayton pulled the electron eyepiece and focused on the beaker once again, though this time in the field. The Ecto-Coli bacteria was there, long rods of it bunched together at the micrometer level. Then he saw it: the enzymes feasting on the Ecto-Coli. They looked like globules of pure water, expanding over the rods of bacteria and enveloping them. The enzymes multiplied, thousands of them expanding by the millisecond. Dayton's whole myopic view filled with the enzymes, fat and sated.

"The water's clear," Richard said from behind him.

"Not just yet," Brock said. The enzymes, now full of their meals, dissipated. They disintegrated into pure water droplets, their function in life complete.

"Okay," Tojun said. "Now we've done it."

"We still need to submit this to the City Board, right?" Richard asked as the techs walked away with their equipment, back to their flight vehicle. They didn't hear the question.

"True," Brock said. "But first, we have to log it. Once we get that done, we can submit it to the local government. Just like we did on Malpar Four."

"No," Dayton said. He grabbed the foaming container filled with billions of the enzymes. "That would take too long. I need to be at the dance."

"What are you—" Brock stopped talking as Dayton emptied the container into a crashing wave.

Richard's eyes bulged out. "You can't just throw that stuff in the water."

"I just did," Dayton said. "It'll be fine. The techs said so. I've seen this stuff work on the ship. It eats the bacteria, which causes a chemical reaction that turns them into plain water afterward. I mean, the ocean will lose some salinity, but that will equalize."

"But you ..." Richard looked at the water. A circle of clear water formed where Dayton emptied the container. The edges were foaming, expanding.

"Gotta go," Brock said. "I need a lift back to the hospital." He pointed to where the techs were waving him back and shivered a bit. "I've probably been out long enough."

"What? Now we're just leaving?" Richard protested.

"Oh, right," Dayton snapped his fingers in realization. "We need to call the Sanitation Department to pick up the last of these fish. They won't be a problem going forward."

"And then?" Richard said, looking out at the changing water.

"We're done here," Dayton said. "Principal Ramirez said to help the bay."

"We didn't just help it," Richard said, eyes widening as the water brightened and cleared. "We cured it."

"Look, I told you," Dayton said. "I'm going to that dance. Do you know how to call the Sanitation Department for service?"

"Can do," Richard answered, pulling out his comm.

"Let's wait for the sanitation guys so we can holo-image scan the beach when it's clean. Then we can get it to Principal Ramirez."

TWENTY-ONE

"Preliminary testing by DWP shows the Ecto-Coli is completely removed from bay waters," Principal Ramirez said, looking over his glasses. "It's now being reported as clear as far north as Malibu. They say the salt content of the water is down slightly."

Dayton's face fell a bit. "Sorry about that. The techs couldn't compensate for those factors. Analysis showed it was within the margin of error."

"Do you realize what you did?" Principal Ramirez said flatly.

"You said if I helped the bay, I could go to the dance," Dayton said. "So I helped the bay. Can I go to the dance?"

"I am impressed, if a little scared," Principal Ramirez said. "And the Environmental Agency is all over this now. They will be testing, retesting, and probably detaining you for questioning to see if any permanent harm was done to the Bay. This isn't over for you yet. You realize that, right? You could be facing some severe charges."

"Yeah," Dayton said. "But they won't find anything. I mean, the process is safe. We have been using it on *Venture* for years and years. I can still go to the dance, right?"

"For that, yes. I can do that." Principal Ramirez tapped the touchscreen on his computer. "Done. You are all clear."

"Awesome," Dayton said. His heart rose with the tap on that screen. "That means I have to get my vehicle ready."

Principal Ramirez's face folded into a worried look. "Vehicle? You mean that old, ahem, that flyer?"

"Yes, Old Twenty-One. That's mine."

"About that," the principal said. "With everything else that's been going around, I haven't had time to talk to you about this. I'm afraid your flyer isn't classified as a Class-C vehicle. That means it can't come onto school property."

"What?" Dayton's heart plopped back down into the pit of his stomach. "You're joking. There's nothing wrong with it."

"I'm sorry," Principal Ramirez said. "If it were up to me, I'd let it go, but it's the law."

"But I have an operator's license." Dayton felt the blood drain from his cheeks. "I know it's not a driver's license, but the police said it was okay."

"Yes," Principal Ramirez nodded slowly. "I have no doubt you're as skilled a driver as most adults. But it's not about that. It's about the equipment. Your flyer just isn't a car."

Dayton made a choking noise. He was about to pound his fist on the table when he remembered where he was. Principal Ramirez wasn't the message, only the messenger.

He took a deep breath and presented himself. "Thank you for telling me," he said flatly.

"I know," Principal Ramirez said, and with the tone Dayton had become fond of. "Look, you can still go to the dance. Just take another car. I'm sure your family has another one you can use."

The whole trip home, Dayton knew there was but ONE other choice.

The Tata.

***

Dayton stared out the front window of his house, the one that looked out over the driveway. Sitting just off to the side was the Tata, a vehicle so cheaply made it looked as if the next gust of wind could blow it apart.

How could he take Allyson to the dance in that? He imagined the looks they'd get pulling up to the dance in that—that thing.

"Dinner's ready," Margaret called from the dining room.

"Did you want some extra vegegravy?"

"Oh, wonderful," Dayton said under his breath as he pulled away from the window. Now, he had another one of Margaret's concoctions to keep down. This day just kept getting better. Ever since the woman found out he had cleaned up the bay, she looked at him differently—with a smile he found unsettling and weird.

"You've been staring out that window all afternoon," Margaret said as he sat down. "Is there something you want to talk about?"

"No," Dayton said reflexively. "It's just all these rules. Principal Ramirez says I can't take Old Twenty-One to the dance because it's not a registered Class C or something."

"Oh," Margaret said. Her face frowned. "That isn't right. You're an eco-warrior now. You don't need to be treated like this."

"Yeah, I don't know about the whole eco-warrior thing. I just want to take my flyer to the dance. The only option is that Tata. That thing is an embarrassment."

"Our cause won't stand for this." Margaret threw down her fork. "C'mon, we're going to talk to your principal. Right now."

"But it's dinner. He won't be at his office this late."

"I know." Margaret picked up her keys. "We're going to his house."

"You know where he lives?" Dayton stood up.

"I certainly do." She motioned Dayton out the front door and into the driveway.

"Isn't he going to be mad we bugged him at home?" Dayton said as he shut the rickety door on the Tata.

"Not as mad as I am right now." Margaret cranked up the starter, and its feeble engine sprang to life, squeaking and groaning. "You let me worry about him."

"But I don't think it's his fault."

"He's the principal," Margaret yelled as much as stated.

"He can't just throw something like that out there and then leave you to the wolves."

"I don't think he has any pets," Dayton said. "You have to get a permit to have a wolf, right?"

Margaret sighed. "Just let me straighten this out."

The principal's house was a townhome with shiny black glass and yellow stucco in a housing tract not far from the mall. Dayton noticed how clean everything was as they walked onto the porch. That figured.

The visitor sensor was triggered, and a chime went off within the house. In seconds, the door slid open, revealing Principal Ramirez in sweats. "Margaret?" he sounded and looked surprised.

"Hello, Ruben," Margaret said. "We need to talk."

Principal Ramirez moved aside and motioned them in. Like the porch, the place was clean inside, almost sterile, with off-white endurofiber carpeting and streamlined black furniture with white piping.

They sat down on an overstuffed couch.

"Dayton tells me you won't allow him to bring his flyer on campus," Margaret said.

"That's correct. It's the law. I can't do anything about that. I am sorry to have to bear this news, but I can't do anything about it."

Margaret's lips pursed. "When you signed off on the *Venture* kids attending your school, you agreed to look after their emotional and physical well-being. Even going beyond the normal job to do so. That includes being an advisor. By your own admission, these kids have enough to worry about without all their aspirations dashed to bits."

"I do take an active interest in my students," Principal Ramirez said. "But I don't see what I can do in this case."

"Counsel him," Margaret said without missing a beat. "Advise him. Tell him how to make his flyer acceptable by school standards."

"Honestly, Margaret," Principal Ramirez said, "I'm an educator, not a vehicle tech. If I were, I would help him out."

"Ruben ..." Margaret cocked her head to the side as she spoke. "My nephew is the tech. All you need to do is find out what he needs to do. And Dayton will do it. You have no idea about this kid's technical skills."

"After that incident with the bay, I'm beginning to find out." The principal grabbed an electronic tablet beside him on the seat. "I suppose we can see what needs to be done to make it street-legal. Do you have the specs on the vehicle as it stands now?"

"Yeah," Dayton pressed the touch screen on his comm units and beamed the specs to the tablet. "That's everything I've done to it."

The man swiped around on his touchpad. "Okay," he said at last. He beamed back some data to Dayton. "I ran a check with the Department of Vehicle Services. You'll need to make the modifications listed there. Once you do, have Margaret take the flyer in for an inspection on-site. Once it passes that, you're legal."

Dayton dove into the new data that listed back-up lights, proof of zero emissions, turn signals, and a few other things.

He could do this.

What was better was that he could do it all by the dance.

And weirdest of all, he had Margaret to thank for it.

Margaret.

***

Dayton dropped Old 21 even with the curb outside Allyson's house. He checked his reflection in the portable holo mirror. He swiped front, left, right, and behind his small holographic self. He hoped he looked good from all angles. He'd spent time playing with his hair, getting it just the way Allyson liked it. Clothing, while still a struggle, was less intense. He decided to mix it up, going with the metallic-blue dress shirt with a circuit board pattern, along with black jeans and a pair of onyx shoes that kind of looked like his own shipboard boots.

The hologram popped off.

There was a ticking sound against the window. Allyson's dog was scratching at the glass, propped up on his front paws. His big, dark eyes stared from the other side of the glass.

"Hey, buddy." Dayton opened the gull-wing door. Lysander hopped into the front passenger seat, pivoted to a seating position, and swiped his tongue across Dayton's left cheek.

"Lysander!" Allyson appeared at the raised door. She was all smiles. "He really likes you."

"That's fine; I like him too."

"No, you don't understand," Allyson said as Dayton fought off another round of licking. "He doesn't like just everybody." She grabbed Lysander's collar. "C'mon, we don't need your hair all over us tonight." She piled into the passenger seat and brought the gull-wing door down. "Let's go."

"Don't you think I should say 'hi' to your father?" Dayton asked.

"No," Allyson said flatly. "You and my dad would start talking cars, and we'd be stuck here all night. Just go."

Dayton brought Old 21 over the treetops and into the sky. Next stop, Scott's house.

"You got dog slobber on your left cheek." She reached out her finger and flicked it off.

Just weeks ago, his voice had failed him just thinking about talking to her. Now, it was as easy as a pre-flight auto sequence. That was progress.

The avionic alarm whined. "We're here at Scott's house," he said

The place was buzzing with activity. Everyone was gathered on the front lawn in groups. Scott was standing next to Karen, and everyone waved at their approach. Once the hugs and handshakes died down, Scott motioned Dayton to follow him to the front porch, away from everyone.

"This could be it for you, my friend," Scott said as he and Dayton sat on the back porch in a pair of identically matched, all-weather servo grav chairs.

"What do you mean?" Dayton noticed the grav chair was a little unstable, but this really caught his attention.

"Allyson likes you," Scott said. "I never saw her like this when she was with Bradford. She'll probably want to commit tonight."

"Uh, commit?" Dayton knew he sounded like an ignorant fool, but at this point, he didn't care. Input was needed.

"You know, commitment," Scott said. "The old B-friend, G-friend thing?"

"Oh, commitment like that," Dayton said. "Hmmm, so that's what she was talking about."

"What do you mean?" Scott asked.

"Never mind," Dayton said. "So, does the girl bring it up first? How exactly does that work here?"

"Traditionally, the guy brings it up," Scott said. "But the girl can bring it up, too."

"Is there anything I need to do?"

"No, just roll with it. Should be good."

Dayton's head felt light, and his airways constricted. He forced himself to gulp air when he realized he'd stopped breathing. Suddenly, there was a lot more on the launch pad than just going to a dance together.

"You okay, bud?" Scott asked. "Your face just went totally white."

"Yeah, yeah," Dayton said. "I'm fine. Just a lot to take in, you know?"

"Relax." Scott patted him on the shoulder. "You got this. C'mon bud. You fell from orbit, for crying out loud. You can handle a little social sitch."

Dayton caught sight of Allyson across the yard. At this distance, he took full view of her. She wore a blue emo-fiber dress that hugged her body and periodically changed to red. Her legs—Dayton had never seen them before—looked great, dark and shapely, as she stood there in black stilettos.

"Let's get this party started," Scott said, motioning Dayton to follow him back to the crowd.

They walked toward her, and Dayton's heart raced when he connected eyes with her. She had a hopeful look on her face, like she cared that he liked what he was seeing. "You look more than awesome," he said.

"You noticed," Allyson said. She turned a little pink in the face. "Why are you looking at me like that?"

"No reason." Dayton felt the blood leave his face, and his head got light.

"What did Scott tell you?" Allyson's face lit up like she was putting two and two together.

"He said it was time to go," Dayton said. And with that, he motioned Allyson back down the walk.

The next thing he knew, Scott was walking next to him. "Karen and I will take my Dad's Beemer," he said. "You and Allyson be okay taking your spaceship?"

"Sure." He turned to Scott just as he felt Allyson squeeze his hand. "See you there."

Old 21 lifted off as the other vehicles either sped down the street or launched in their own direction. Once he had Old 21 stable and moving, he grasped Allyson's hand again. It sent a warm feeling to his core.

"Nervous?"

"Nah."

"Liar."

"Yeah."

"Don't traum it," Allyson said, patting his hand. "You don't even have to dance. A lot of people just like the sosh part of it all. You know, hang out with friends?"

"I want to dance," Dayton said. "I watched holovideos on dance techniques. I even used that one where you stand in the holo-dancer and imitate his moves."

"You've been taking this serious, haven't you?"

"I don't want to embarrass myself."

"Or me."

"Well, yeah, you too."

Dayton followed the road, keeping pace with everyone on the ground. He didn't want to arrive first. *No,* he thought, it was best if he came in with everyone else. That left less to worry about. If he came in on time, not before, he could just follow the crowd. Tonight, he was doing what they did.

After congregating in the parking lot, the crowd moved into the gym. The place didn't look at all like it had in gym class. It was dark, with streams of lights shooting against the walls. Streamers cascaded from the ceiling. The holo-emitters, a commercial rental kind, created a conceptual Garden of Eden with palms, rose bushes, and tree-lined bubbling brooks. Someone had strung up one of those glitter balls in the center of the ceiling and directed light beams on it. The effect was like an old 1970s non-holographic video he saw years ago. It looked cheesy then, and it looked cheesy now, but he didn't care.

For the first time since he arrived, Dayton thought the music was too loud. It thumped and bumped with a beat that was not quite as wild as he was used to in colony dome concerts, but the audio was there, and it was powerful. Along with that, the constant thrum of voices filled his ears.

A stage was set up on one side of the gym. Six speakers, each at least a meter square but only millimeters thick, pulsed to the beat. The speakers must've had holo-emitters on them because they displayed green, blue, and yellow holograms of dancing human figures. And behind the board, working the holo controls, stood Trenton.

There was no mistaking the heavy worlder, though he looked the part of a party DJ with his black-and-white tuxedo shirt, somehow sized to fit him perfectly. On his head were wire-thin headphones, and he looked through a holographic vizor that covered his right eye with a square of green glass.

"You?" Dayton shook hands with his heavy friend.

"Me," Trenton said. "I used to do these things all the time back home. But here, I can pick up a few creds for my work."

"This place just got cool," Dayton said.

"Oh, I'll show 'em how it's done," Trenton said, his head nodding with the tempo. "You watch this. They are about to get schooled."

Dayton whirled around to find Allyson had wandered off to talk to Karen. Her face lit up when he approached.

"This thing needs to get going." Allyson swept the floor with a wave of her delicate hand.

She was right about that. Only a portion of the students were on the dance floor. The rest were in a ring around the periphery of the gym or stood outside talking.

"So, what do we do?" He had to yell at her over the music.

"What do you want to do?" Allyson had that little smile on her face. Clearly, she enjoyed it whenever Dayton was exposed to something new.

"I can tell you what we're going to do." Karen grabbed Scott by the shirt and Dayton by the shoulder. "Dance."

Allyson followed as they made their way onto the floor. Dayton's breath steadied, and his heart slowed. He felt relief. He'd been paranoid to imagine his first time dancing would be alone, in full view of everyone. Instead, he was comforted by the masses of dancers. Karen stopped their little group on the edges of the dance floor, but Dayton playfully pushed Karen a little further in until they were surrounded.

It was as if some pin had been released.

He started to move like the dancer in the holovids but soon realized everyone was just doing their own thing. He let loose and moved with the music, up and down, side to side. One song, then another, then another after that. Dayton lost count.

No longer was he a chip in a machine. He was just here to have fun. Now, he pulsed and gyrated in a crowd that was doing the same thing. Trenton must've put the magic on because, within a few minutes, they were surrounded by dancers. The music morphed in and out of songs with matching beats, and Dayton recognized some of the outworlder bands that Trenton was slipping into the mix.

"C'mon," Allyson shouted. "We need to get some air." She led him by the hand to the outside courtyard. Other students were there; a couple high-fived Dayton. It felt great. He wasn't being looked down on. It was the opposite of that.

"We didn't have to stop," Dayton said.

"Uh, yeah, we did," Allyson said as she reached over to a table and picked up a sponge towel. She handed it to him. "You are going to sweat out all your fluids."

As if on cue, sweat poured down his face. His sleeves were wet and clung to his arms. He noticed how cool the air was and how slick he felt. "I haven't worked out like that in a long time."

"You were really going at it," Allyson said. "When you try something new, you really dive into it."

He rubbed his sweaty temples. His hair was matted. All that styling had gone to waste, but he didn't care. Taking Allyson's hand again, he led her to a stone bench.

Her hand reached up and caressed his cheek. "How do you feel?"

"Good," Dayton said. "You, my clothes, my hair, and this dance. This is all coming together."

"I've earned a place in your goals?"

"Allyson," he said, taking both her hands in his. "You are the goal. All this other stuff? Doesn't matter. I think I liked you from the first time I saw you."

"Oh really?" Allyson said with a gasp. "When you were all dangling up there from parachute cords? I was the one you were thinking of?" She let out a laugh.

"Yeah, I noticed you. Even though I was hanging."

"I want you to know something," Allyson said. "I've been thinking ... do you want to—"

"Oh no ..." Dayton spotted familiar shipboard clothing, several sets of it, walking out of the dance.

"What?" Allyson said. She turned around.

Zara was there. She'd brought several others with her, all *Venture* children. Their heavy-duty cargo pants and pressure jackets made them stand out like nav beacons in an asteroid field. He recognized the others, a few personnel from maintenance. He hadn't seen them in months, but they looked guarded and angry.

"Are they here to make trouble?"

"I doubt it," Dayton said, although he sounded unsure.

"I thought they hated us," Allyson said. "Why are they here?"

It was a good question. One Dayton needed an answer to.

"Don't." Allyson grabbed his arm as he rose. She knew what he was thinking.

"But maybe I can talk to them," he said.

"Just let it happen." Allyson pulled him back down. "You aren't responsible for their actions. Don't be a cop."

Dayton sat. Allyson pulled him tight, resting her head on his shoulder. Her long, flowing hair offered up the scent of wildflowers. His right hand found hers, and he held onto it tightly.

"You didn't put an energy pistol to their heads and make them come," she said softly. "They don't like us, and yet they show up here anyway. You know they're looking for trouble."

Allyson was right. He couldn't control Zara or anyone else. He closed his eyes, willing the whole scene to go away. The tromping of deck boots was getting closer, his heartbeat faster with every footfall.

"So here you are," Zara's voice boomed at him. "Playing Earther type again? I almost didn't recognize you among these monotons. You look just like them."

"Hi, Zara," Allyson said.

"Hi, Zara," Zara mimicked with her best combination of sarcasm and disdain.

"What are you doing here?" Dayton asked. "I didn't think this was your kind of venue."

"I can go where I want, right?" She forced a laugh. "I mean, we're free here, right? So why not?"

"I think 'Why?' is a better question," Dayton said.

"Whatever," Zara waved the comment off. "Just stay here and be a good little trog. Someone has to show these Earth huggers how to have a good time." She stormed off, back to the band of *Venture* kids.

"I got a bad feeling about this," Dayton said.

"I know; me too," Allyson said. "Why can't they just go someplace else?"

The voices got louder, followed by shoving. Dayton recognized the hair and the sneering voice.

"Bradford!" Allyson cried. "He's not supposed to be here."

The crowd surrounded Bradford and Zara.

"So, step out," Bradford called, shoving her. Zara was forced back two steps, but being used to heavier gravity had its benefits. She shoved Bradford, who fell into his friends as they all tumbled backward to the ground.

Some other students rushed Zara, taking up for Bradford, but by then, Zara's four friends had moved to intercept them. Arms and legs flew as they pushed and pulled and slapped.

"I got to put an end to this," Dayton said to Allyson as he moved into the fight.

Allyson said something, but he didn't hear what it was. Pushing his way into the crowd, he waded into the center, dodging elbows and flying feet. At the center, he found Zara on top of Bradford. He reached down and pulled Zara off with such force that both he and Zara landed on their backs. Both of them scrambled to their feet, and the next thing, Zara was staring him in the eye.

"Enough!" Dayton said so loudly that it stopped the melee.

"I knew it," Zara yelled back. "You're protecting them. You are a sell-out, Murdoch."

"Attention. Attention." Trenton's amplified voice boomed over the speakers. The music shut down, and the general alarm sounded its "*beep-beep-beep*" in the distance.

"Attention. Attention," Trenton repeated. "This is a Code Niner. Now, everyone, let's get back on the dance floor."

Trenton was disguising it, but he just gave a warning. A Code Niner aboard *Venture* meant the enforcers were on their way. The message was clear: break it up now, or they'd be in trouble.

"You hear that?" Dayton shouted. "Get out of here before you get us all in trouble."

"Let's go," Zara said to the crewmate beside her. Both kids stared Dayton down like mad dogs. "I think we know who our friends are."

"I didn't need your help, space case," said a voice. Bradford stomped up to them.

Zara raised her fists, so Dayton stepped in front of her, blocking her with his back.

"Oh, yes, you needed my help," Dayton said. "Whether you believe it or not, I just kept you from getting your butt kicked."

"I can handle her. Get out of the way," Bradford said.

"Oh yeah," Dayton laughed. "You were doing a great job on your back. She was pinning you."

"Shut up, space case," Bradford yelled.

"Wʜᴀᴛ's ɢᴏɪɴɢ ᴏɴ ᴏᴜᴛ ʜᴇʀᴇ?" Principal Ramirez's voice came loud and clear as he pushed through the crowd. "Bʀᴀᴅꜰᴏʀᴅ Fʟᴏʀᴅᴇʟɪs. You're not supposed to be here."

Everyone turned to see Principal Ramirez striding up.

"Every one of you get back inside," the principal commanded. "Bradford, you must leave."

"We weren't fighting," Dayton threw up his arms like a surrendering soldier, "I broke up a fight."

"It's true," Allyson said, coming to his side.

Several kids nodded in agreement.

"Everyone. Back in the gym," Principal Ramirez said.

Dayton gathered Allyson and headed inside.

When he looked back, Zara was gone. Turning around, he spotted Bradford walking out. Bradford looked back for just a split second, bitter and angry. And it was all focused on Dayton.

TWENTY-TWO

The next morning, Dayton woke early and went out to the garage. He could think things through better when his hands were busy. Picking up a wrench, he wrestled with the bolts that held the driver's side brake lights on Old 21. He activated one of the robots to repeatedly press the brake actuator to make sure he was getting a connection. For some reason, one of the brake lights activated fine when the pedal was pushed; however, the other did not.

But his mind wasn't really on the task. Instead, he was worried about Zara. He heard a sound from behind, and like magic, she was there.

"You sided against me." Zara's face was red, and her eyes were on fire.

"I did not. You showed up to make trouble." Dayton threw the power wrench down. "We're stuck here for the time being. It might do you some good to try and make friends, too, you know."

"With the Earthers?" Zara's eyes grew wide. Dayton could see the bitterness and anger in those two brown orbs. "They hate us. They think they're better than us."

"Some do, yes. They're not all bad. Look at Richard, for example."

"The only reason Richard hangs out with us is because they don't accept him, either." She stormed back and forth in the small area between the surveyor and the second work-bench. "It's that queen bee girl, isn't it? She's changed you, turned you against us."

"Don't call Allyson a queen bee." Dayton stood up.

"Aha!" Zara sounded like a prosecuting attorney. "So that's it. It's her, isn't it? You're just trying to impress her, I bet."

"You know what?" He waved his hands. "That's enough. Just because I'm trying to make new friends doesn't automatically mean I am against my old friends. I'm sorry you can't see that."

"End game." Zara turned around and walked back to her grav bike. "She's never going to understand you, you know. No way an Earther gets you, but you'll find out about that in another rotation or so of this planet."

Without another word, she hit the ignition button and rose up. When she reached treetop level, she threw the grav cycle's propulsor on and headed off into the sky.

Dayton turned to the videophone mounted on the second bench. "Call Richard. Home." The videophone flashed on, showing the screen saver image of him and Allyson at the mall together. A small red panel light and intermittent beeping showed that the call was being placed.

Richard's face flashed on the screen. He had just climbed out of the shower. The room behind had steam clouds rising to the ceiling. Richard wore only a towel tied to his midsection.

"What's up?" he said, looking a bit surprised.

Dayton didn't bother with small talk. "Do you think I've sold out?"

"Huh? What do you mean?"

"I mean my hair and clothes." Dayton pressed his left hand against his chest. He was wearing a technician's jump suit but tried to illustrate the point. "Zara thinks I've turned on her."

Richard looked sympathetic. "Look, I don't understand how girls think. I'm a geek. I hang out with other geeks. I'm a chess club member, a computer club member. I'm a future engineer."

Dayton, like every other member of the *Venture* crew, held a great deal of respect for engineers. It was the engineers who helped save the ship, designed the automated systems, the surveyors, and practically everything they used or depended upon for their survival. Every mission's success depended on engineers. But Richard couldn't help him with this. Perhaps his father could explain all this. "I'm going to comm my dad. I'll catch up with you later." Richard disappeared from the screen, and the comm company's logo spun digitally in front of him. Then it winked out, replaced by Turco. The man's eyes went wide when he recognized him. "Hey, buddy. How're you doing?"

"Pretty good. Just wanted to know if my father was around."

Turco's head darted off-camera. "Hey, Professor Murdoch. I got your offspring on the comm." He exited right off-screen. What Dayton saw was a white paneled wall with black piping, where digital instrument panels blinked on and off in many colors, showing bar graphs, spectral analysis, and other read-outs. It was clear from Turco's hair sticking out in places that they were in a null-gravity environment. Obviously, they were training for something in space.

"Hey." Dad's face brightened when he saw Dayton.

"I have a few questions."

"About ..." Dad let on slowly. They both knew the comm was being monitored. Asking questions was a great way to get cut off. And in more trouble.

"No," Dayton said. "Not about that. About, you know, school and stuff."

"Okay, then. Ask away."

"Zara thinks I'm a sellout. She says I spend too much time with my new friends and forget about her. I have tried to get her to hang out with us, but she won't."

"I was afraid this might happen." Dad stopped, set down his stylus, and turned his full attention to Dayton. "You two were good friends aboard the ship, but you're really very different people when it comes down to it."

"Do you think she's right?"

"From her standpoint, she is; from your standpoint, no."

"Okay," Dayton hesitated. "Now, I'm completely confused."

Father laughed. "It's a confusing thing. You see, everyone in school falls into one group or another, depending on who they are."

"That means Zara and I are in different groups?"

"Exactly. You're doing what comes naturally."

"So, this is like that natural selection we learned about?"

"Kind of. In school, people with different personalities tend to group with different groups. It happens all through life, but nowhere like high school."

"So, Zara's angry about this?"

"She sees her world coming unglued. She doesn't like change. You seem to be coping with that change better than she is. You are making friends, pursuing interests, while she seems stuck on the way things used to be."

"We always got along fine aboard *Venture*."

"Sure," Dad laughed again, obviously amused by the topic. "But not now. Now, it's a completely different social landscape. Son, it's a whole new world, in more than one way."

"Zara's a good person, though."

"It's not who's good and bad," Dad said. "We should wind up about now. The time ..."

The screen blinked out, leaving Dayton feeling isolated. How was he going to solve this? He reached over and picked up the laser measuring device. He had a lot of thinking to work out.

***

The next day, as the cafeteria food dispenser served his morning coffee and fruit bar, he still felt uncomfortable about Zara calling Allyson a queen bee and accusing him of taking sides.

"Hey you," Allyson came up to his side. She looked good in her faded stone-washed jeans, black tank top, and sandals. Of course, the black top was poking out from under Dayton's flight jacket.

Dayton smiled at her and took a tentative sip of his coffee. They were using that Brazilian nut blend again, and it was screeching hot. Allyson tugged. He looked in that direction. Bradford and his guys were walking toward them. Dayton stepped in front of Allyson as he set his coffee aside on the top of the machine.

"Just chill," Bradford said. "I'm not here to start up."

"Then what *are* you here for?"

"That Zara girlfriend of yours and a bunch of those space cases moved in and claimed the Rust Pile last night."

"She's not my girlfriend."

"Oh yeah? Well, she kicked all the other kids out of there."

"The Rust Pile?" Dayton said. "Who cares? You guys don't even like that place."

"You don't get it," Bradford said. "If they take over the Rust Pile, pretty soon they'll want the entertainment center, the mall, and everything else."

"That's crazy," Dayton said. "That would never happen."

"It's already happening, spaceboy. They're coming to the Rust Pile on Friday after school. We're going to stop them. Are you with us or not?"

Dayton felt a chill go down his spine.

Allyson peeked around Dayton's side. "Let him talk to them," she said.

"Spaceboy has a choice to make," Bradford said. "It's them or us."

"This has gone too far—" Dayton started.

"See?" Bradford said. "He won't fight for us."

"Oh, I can fight. I proved that already. Do you want to get us all kicked out of school?"

Behind Bradford, the desi guys looked restless.

Bradford ignored the question. "Call it what you want. You side with them, you're going down." The klaxon sounded; first period was about to start. He broke off and walked away with his guys.

Allyson stepped out to face Dayton. "I'm going to find out more. Karen should have netlinked me or called or something."

"It'll be all right," Dayton said as he leaned in to kiss her. But he wasn't feeling so sure.

***

At 6 p.m., Dayton said goodbye to Margaret and promised he'd be back by seven-thirty. He headed for the Rust Pile. By the light of the drumfires, he could make out the rocks, food wrappers, half-buried cables, and rusting machine parts. This place was not worth the drama.

He walked past broken-down vehicles, burnt-out engine blocks, and some wiry sawhorse-looking things so pitted and rusted he couldn't tell their original purpose. The path leading up was worn from many footsteps. Here and there was crumbling cement with rusted metal posts shooting out at twisted, broken angles. As he neared a bonfire in the center, out of the corner of his eye, he saw Zara's grav bike. It was parked with three or four others.

"Hey, Dayton," echoed a voice from the crowd. Turning, he saw Ethan, a shuttle pilot from *Venture* who was attending a school across town. Behind him were four pilots and techs from other duty cycles.

"Glad to see you." Ethan crossed his arms in front of his face. "How've you been? I heard from Zara you went over to the other side."

"No," Dayton said fiercely. "I haven't gone over to anybody's side. I just came up here to talk some sense—"

"That's where you should have stayed." Zara muscled her way to the front of the crowd.

"We've served together." Dayton approached Zara. "This is messed up."

Zara laughed. "It's because we served together that you haven't been scragged."

The others in the growing crowd shouted in support of Zara. Even Ethan seemed caught up in the mob.

"You can't fight this entire world," Dayton said.

She stamped one foot angrily. "This entire world won't accept us. We finally have something of theirs, and we're going to keep it."

"You just don't see it, do you?" Dayton's volume went up a couple of notches to match Zara's. "All you are doing is confirming the rumors about us." He threw his hands in frustration.

"Get out before you get your arms and legs broken," Zara shouted. Many in the crowd stepped up behind her. "Get out, *Traitor*."

The crowd began to chant those words.

"Trai-tor!

Trai-tor!

Trai-tor!"

A few tried to push Dayton, but he kept his balance and retreated to Old 21. Spray-painted across the front was the word TRAITOR in giant black letters. Who would do this? A space kid? A lump rose in his throat. He opened the gull-wing door and climbed in.

"Hey." Trenton banged on the operator's side door. Dayton didn't want to hang around any more than he needed to, but he cracked open the door.

"I'm sorry," Trenton said. "This whole thing is way past the talking stage."

Dayton shook his head and looked back at the bonfire, where the rest of the *Venture* kids were shouting and throwing things into the raging flames. "You're wrong."

"My friend, you need to sit this one out." Trenton walked back to the bonfire.

I am alone, Dayton thought. *Stuck between two worlds. Neither of them wants me.*

As Dayton pulled Old 21 into the air, bottles and rocks

bounced off the side. He accelerated higher until projectiles couldn't reach him anymore.

***

The holo-image of the clock popped to 12 a.m. It was midnight. Dayton sat, as he had for uncountable hours, in his room. He lay back on his bed but couldn't relax. He'd gotten used to the foamfit mattress that cradled his body exactly, but it gave no rest tonight. His mind reeled from what had happened a few hours ago.

Beep!

The comm unit went off. He reached over and grabbed it. It was Allyson. Apparently, he wasn't the only one losing sleep over this.

Hey, Day. You up?

Dayton flipped open the expanding digital keyboard and responded.

Ayup. U can't sleep either?

Naw, stressed. Can't believe it's like this.

Been racking my brain for no answer. U have ideas?

We need 2 go 2 Ramirez with this.

Yeesh. I don't wanna be a tattler.

We have a choice?

Prolly not. Just feels bad doing that.
He's in office till 3. U wanna see him?

Hmmmm. Yeah, I guess. Not thrilled 2 do this.

OK, I'll B there. Will U?

Yah. Just as long as I am not the only one doing it.

Me too. But we see this off tomorrow. Sleep tight.

U 2.

The comm blipped off.

He drifted in and out of a light doze, his overworked nerves never quite releasing his body to sleep. He looked at the time once again. The holoclock read 4 a.m. He'd have to get up in two hours for school.

Two hours before the longest day of his life.

***

He wasn't sure what woke him. From outside the window, it sounded like the *whoosh* kind of engines those grav drones had. Probably a package delivery bot. He felt oddly refreshed but knew something was wrong. He glanced over at the holoclock: 12:30 p.m.

He bolted upright. How could this have happened? He'd forgotten to set the alarm. He sprinted for the bathroom. At the sink, he squirted tooth foam into his mouth, then waited for the twenty seconds while the scrubbing, bubbling foam did its job on his teeth. That would have to be all his prep for the morning. No time for a shower. No time for breakfast. He had to get to school. What was he going to tell his teachers?

He glanced at his comm unit, pulsing with a red message indicator light. It held texts and voicemails from Richard, Scott, and Trenton. Several from Allyson alone. She must be wondering where he was. Why hadn't Margaret woken him?

Out in the hall, he listened. A faint sound was coming from the living room. Was it sobbing? He walked softly toward it. As he walked in, Margaret was sitting on the couch, holding a holopic disc with the image of a young man rotating on it. Her eyes were red and swollen. Dried rivers of tears marked her cheeks, and she sniffled.

"I'm sorry," Margaret said between deep breaths. "I didn't want you to see me like this. I thought you left early this morning."

"Uh, look," Dayton said. He struggled to put together the right words. "If this is about me not being at school, the holo-clock didn't go off and—"

"I'm sorry," Margaret said between deep breaths. "I didn't want you to see me like this."

"If this is about the robots ..." He struggled to put the right words together.

"No, it's not that," Margaret said. "I've been so rough on you. It's just that today would have been his twenty-fourth birthday." She motioned with the holodisc.

"Who is that?" Dayton said. His words came out a lot more monotone than he would've wished at that point.

"Dennis." She wiped a fresh round of tears. "My son, your cousin, actually. You never got to meet him."

"Oh," Dayton said. He didn't want to say anything. But that word just slipped out. He was out of his comfort zone on this one. "I'm sorry."

"It was four years ago," Margaret said with a stuffed nose. "He was a dock worker at the spaceport. The same place you go to? A cargo robot's lifter arm broke and dropped a twenty-ton cargo pod right on him."

Dayton swallowed hard. "Killed?"

"Instantly."

Killed by a robot. Now, it made sense. Margaret's hatred of robots and technology in general. Her loss had evolved into a hatred of modern conveniences. He took a seat next to her on the couch. "I understand what you're going through."

"How could you?" Margaret snapped back.

"I lost my mother," he said simply.

"I'm sorry," Margaret repeated. Her tears burst forth as she struggled to rein them in. "I didn't mean to …I just wish robots had never been invented."

Dayton drew in a deep breath. He groped for the right words, tone, and everything else.

"Accidents happen everywhere. You drive a car. If Dennis died in a car accident, would you blame all cars?"

"I suppose not," Margaret said, grabbing a tissue to clean up her soaked face.

"I don't blame the thing that caused the accident. If that were true, I'd never board a spaceship again."

"You know what? Dennis was a lot like you. I don't think he'd blame all robots for what happened to him." She let out a great sigh and stopped crying.

"How about a cup of tea?" Dayton asked. He knew she liked that.

Margaret nodded.

TWENTY-THREE

At three o'clock, with half an hour to go before Principal Ramirez left the office, Dayton sent a quick comm to Allyson, saying he was on the way. He fired up Old 21 and took off from the garage bay. In zero time, he found himself in lunch-hour traffic over Los Angeles, zipping over, around, and under every slow-moving air car, and there were plenty of those. Why had everyone decided to go so slow right at that moment? His parameter alarm sounded, the sensor he had tuned into the enforcers' radar. Dayton's heart jumped. He was going unusually fast. Bobbing in and out of traffic probably wasn't the best idea in the world. He saw a black-and-white come in behind him, sirens flashing in the red-white-and-blue pattern.

His eyes searched the ground for a place to land. Would this mean a ticket? That was certainly something he didn't need right now. Would his Agency license get him off the hook for not having a regular civilian license? His heart thumped in his throat.

The black-and-white came up squarely behind him.

And then ducked around him and kept on going.

Dayton blew out a lungful of air. He had gotten lucky.

All the same, he slowed to traffic.

His comm unit blinked in the seat beside him. There were calls and messages waiting. But the school's dampening field was still on. Wonderful. Now, he had to track everybody down manually. And a lunch. No, scratch that. Lunch was way over already.

A few moments later, he flew over the school parking lot. It was a good angle, but one that showed no open parking spaces. Yeager High never had enough spots anyway, and student parking spilled over into the nearby housing tracts.

Walking to school most days, Dayton never had to worry about it.

Until now.

And the housing tracts were no help, either. Every spare piece of curb was taken by student cars. He went another block out. Nothing.

He went two blocks out. Still nothing.

Finally, three blocks away, he maneuvered Old 21 into a sliver of a spot close to a no-landing zone. He inched forward, then back, narrowly tapping the ground car behind him. He landed, got out, and found his front grav pod was still over the line.

He didn't need this.

He nudged Old 21 back just a hair. And got out. And checked.

Still over the line.

Just a few more micrometers.

Agh! Still not quite there.

Part of him just wanted to leave it. After all, it was a slight bit over the line in a massive housing tract. What were the odds? No, scrap that. He'd gotten lucky with the black-and-whites once. Would he luck out again? He doubted it.

Finally, on the fifth try, he successfully positioned Old 21 into a legal parking position.

Grabbing his student pod, he ran down the street. At the first corner, he turned and found the long stretch of the next street. Sweating, he made it to the next corner. Again, another street. How far back did he park? It seemed so much shorter from the air.

Dripping in sweat, he sprinted to the end of another block. Things were getting familiar now. Another black-and-white slid down the street. It stopped as if wondering why Dayton wasn't in school.

Not now. Nothing said *guilty* to an enforcer like a teenager running.

But it kept going, apparently satisfied that Dayton was headed toward the school.

Finally. The main entrance to Chuck Yeager High School. He made it past the big front doors when he heard the tell-tale beep on the truancy scanner. He had an absorption grid plugged into his comm unit. Why hadn't he thought to turn it on before he walked in?

Perfect. Just perfect.

The monitor bots were on him, whirring and scanning. BLIP! One spat out a detention slip.

BAH! He grabbed it and took off at a jog down the hall. The klaxon sounded, and there was the sound of everyone scrambling to their feet inside classrooms. Then, they poured into the halls.

"Hey," one of Bradford's desi guys approached him, wearing a big smile. "You need to come with me. Allyson needs to talk to you."

"She does?" Dayton checked his comm. No messages from her saying that. "She didn't comm me about anything. What are you talking about?"

"She's not going to comm you," the boy—Dayton didn't know his name—rolled his eyes. "No one comms when there's a fight. She just asked me to come grab you."

"All right," Dayton motioned for the desi kid to go first. "I'll follow you."

"Righteous," the desi said and walked ahead.

This was suspicious, and there was no way Dayton was going to turn his back on this kid. They came to a restroom at the end of the hall. It was Hall E, which had no lockers, and right now, no one was around. Dayton's adrenaline kicked in. This would be a good place to get jumped.

"She's inside," the kid said, smiling like a used flyer salesman. "Go on."

"The boys' bathroom? Really?" Dayton said.

"Yes," the desi said. "Where no one would look for her."

"You first."

"Okay, fine," the kid said as he threw up his arms. "You want me to go first, I'll go first."

The restroom, like the others in the school, had a door that swung inward for entry and one that swung out into the hall for exiting. The desi went in, and Dayton propped the heavy restroom door open wide. He walked in.

No one was inside.

No sooner had his brain registered that fact than the desi kid bolted out the exit door. Dayton swung into action right behind him, running for the safety of the empty hall. They zoomed around the corner at top speed and ran smack into Bradford and three more of his desis. All five of them pushed Dayton back into the bathroom, and the door slammed shut.

The electronic locks on the bathroom doors clicked.

"What the—" Dayton said as he slammed his body into the exit door. It held firm.

"Like we said," Bradford's arrogant voice came from the other side of the door, muffled by the grating squares at the bottoms of the doors. "We can't trust you, Outworlder. You're going to stay here till this whole fight is over."

"Bradford!" Dayton shouted. "I'm the one trying to stop this whole thing. Let me out of here."

"You think you're such a hero." Bradford spit the words out. "You stole Allyson with your crazy talk and spacer mind tricks."

"I didn't steal her," Dayton said. "You two were broken up."

"We were on a break," Bradford screamed. "Couples do that. Take breaks, but you don't get that, do you, spacer? You don't just jump in and hijack someone like that."

"She was done with you. You lost her before I even made a move."

"Shut up," Bradford's voice echoed into the bathroom. "Maybe I'll just leave you here."

With some laughter, the desi voices receded into the halls.

Dayton slammed his open palm on the door, and it reverberated but held solid. Stupid. Stupid. Stupid.

He got down on all fours on the floor. "Hello?" he yelled through the square grates at the bottoms of the doors. No answer.

He turned to look at his surroundings. Three sinks on a counter, two sonic hand scrubbers, three waterless urinals, and three toilets concealed in their partitions. From the looks of the sink and the lemony smell of the tiled floor, the janitor bots had already been here, meaning no one would be opening that door till Monday, assuming Bradford came back for him. Which he doubted.

The bots had scrubbed the place well, though some of the graffiti on the toilet stalls had been carved into the sheet metal with sharp objects. Even through the dim light, one graffiti message stood out more than the rest:

I WANT TO EAT MY HEAD.

The stinging, lemony scent of the cleaner gave him an unpleasant reminder that he wouldn't die from infection here anyway. The place was still disgusting.

When the sun went down in a few hours, the solar panels at the top of the building would stop feeding power to the already-dim lights in the bathroom.

Dayton's mind flashed with possible escapes. He could flood the toilets or sinks. That would alert the janitor bots, and they'd come to open the doors to investigate. That assumed the sensors still worked, and it was Dayton's technician's eye that told him they weren't operational. School budgets being what they were.

The halls did echo. He could bang on the grates till he attracted someone. He might even bash the grates open. No, that wouldn't work. Those grate squares were just too small to wiggle through. And there was no one left around here on a Friday afternoon in any case.

Okay, he thought, *what is my current loadout?* He dug into his backpack. His eduTablet. Gym clothes. His holo link for his edu tablet. A stylus. Some conventional pens.

Dayton fished in his front pocket and came up with his comm unit. It was one of the new Arcturus Alpha ones really popular with Earthers. He tapped it.

And nothing.

The school dampeners were still on. The dampening field was projected over the campus to prevent students from "wasting" their class time. Unfortunately, no one turned the field off after class let out. He dug again into his backpack, hoping maybe his shipboard communicator was in there. It would have the range and power to break through the dampening field. That communicator usually sealed the deal. So, he dug and dug.

Then he felt it. His multi-tool.

A simple-looking black metal tube, Dayton pointed the front end of the tool toward the lock on the exit door to the bathroom and pressed the sensor button, and a pair of mono-filament strands shot out from the front of the multi-tool and snaked into the electronic lock of the bathroom.

With a tiny scratching sound, the filaments detected the inner workings of the lock, and the tool displayed a schematic on the tool's centimeters-wide display screen. It was a simple lock. That would make sense. Why install a high-security lock on a high school bathroom? The lock responded with a loud, snapping click. Dayton pushed, and the door gave way. He was out.

Charging through the empty halls, around each corner, he expected to run into Bradford or his desis, but in each case, he only saw more empty school. He punched through the building doors and entered the central courtyard. It also was nearly deserted, with only the janitor bots jerkily making their way between empty classrooms. The whine of vacuums and floor buffers echoed through the trees, but there was no sound of anything else.

Dayton ran, gulping lungful after lungful of this dense air until he came to the edge of the small hillside across from the Rust Pile. Down below, he could see the masses of high schoolers milling around in a sprawling mob.

And out by the fence, some distance away, Dayton could make out the shipboard-clothing-clad figures of the Outworlders. The Rust Pile brawl was going down, but it hadn't happened yet.

It might fizzle out. Stuff like this usually did if action didn't happen right away. Nobody ever wanted to start something, but once someone did, it took off. Plus, Zara was there. That girl was mad. She'd been that way all along. She HATED the Earth and everyone in it. It was like a part of her person now. If anyone would push things to a complete fight, it would be Zara. He had to stop her.

Dayton made it to the bottom of the hillside to the intense stares of the Yeager students. The whole school had turned out. There were hundreds. Most kept to the back of the crowd and seemed relaxed. They were probably just there to watch. But there were dozens up front. These kids had an intensity, ready for a fight. Some walked it off, storming in circles and swiping at the air in practice punches. Others just stood there, fists balled, waiting for the chance to erupt. None of them smiled. They stared straight ahead like mad dogs.

Dayton plowed ahead, brushing past them. He had to get to the front. He'd seen situations like this before with miner's strikes and food riots; the angriest ones always came to the front.

Allyson ran up. "I heard they tricked you. They wouldn't tell me where you were. I was so afraid."

"I know," he grabbed her hand. "But they can't hold me. I have something I need to do here."

"Oh, look who made it out alive," Bradford strutted forward when he saw Dayton. "Come to fight with your space-case friends?" His arrogant smile was for all to see. He was closely followed by his gang. Bradford threw his hands up as if somehow prepared to fight, but without understanding how to.

Dayton reached out with lightning reflexes and grabbed Bradford's forefinger. He twisted it at an unnatural angle. Bradford knelt, grimacing in pain.

"Shut up," Dayton said. "I've had it with you." Releasing his grip, he punched Bradford in the stomach.

Already on his knees, Bradford keeled over as the wind left his body and collapsed on the dirt.

"That's for locking me in the bathroom." Dayton turned to Bradford's desi followers, who outnumbered him four to one. "Come on, who's next? Let's go, guys. Who wants some more?"

The clones stood there, afraid to move forward. By now, the crowd circled them as Bradford struggled to his feet and backed away. Clearly, he didn't want any more of what Dayton had to offer.

"Very nice," an amplified voice said. It was Zara up ahead, using the megaphone built into her comm unit. "Hey, everyone, Dayton's back."

"No!" he shouted. At first, he wasn't sure if his own megaphone wasn't on; his voice had such volume. "I'm done with all of this. This is ridiculous. You are fighting over a rusting rail yard. People, we can do better than this."

"TRAITOR," Zara boomed over her digital megaphone. "Flatline him."

Several of the ex-crewmembers, old crewmembers of Dayton's, looked at each other. Each waited for the other to go first.

"Do it. He's a traitor. Show him what we do to traitors," Zara urged.

Again, the looks. Again, the doubt. They were mad. But mad enough to attack their former survey pilot?

"You guys are useless," Zara resounded. "Get him. Get Dayton Murdoch!"

"No!" Trenton's voice echoed across the field. His squat,

muscular form trudged forward, stopping in between Dayton and Zara and the unwilling attackers. "First one of you that takes a shot at Dayton has to deal with me. I don't think a lot of you know what a heavy-worlder can do when they get pissed. Well, you wanna find out?"

If the *Venture* kids wondered about attacking Dayton before, they completely collapsed now. They went back into the *Venture* crowd.

Scott and five members of the grav ball team stepped up to face the Chuck Yeager students. "Yeah, no fighting on this side either," Scott said. "Everyone, stand down now."

"I think you really had a good speech going," Trenton said as he smiled at Dayton. "Go on."

"As I was saying," Dayton continued. "A lot of you on the spacer side say I'm too much of an Earther. Then the Earth-born say I'm too much of a spacer. But we both want the same thing, don't we? We want the world to be cool with who we are."

Dayton walked up to Allyson, who met his gaze. "This is a small world," he said. "But it's kind of big too. And you know what? There's plenty of room for all of us."

"You're selling out," Zara's enhanced voice boomed. "And now you're trying to convince the rest of us." She splayed both legs stubbornly. "I will never forget who I am."

"I won't either," Dayton said. "I am an outlander. But space is over for me, for now. Earth offers lots of chances. Exploring them doesn't make me any less of a spacer than you are."

Kids on both sides looked at each other and the ground and then wandered around. No one was in a combat stance or even looked like they wanted to fight anymore. Maybe it wasn't the great come-together moment he had dreamed of, but he'd take it.

"Everybody, just go home," Dayton said. "No one here is a threat to anyone else. Just leave."

Slowly, the two groups began a long, fractured retreat from

one another. The *Venture* kids headed for the fence. Earthers trudged in the other direction.

"Well," Trenton approached Dayton, a smile on his face. "That could have gone down worse. Nice speech, by the way."

Allyson came to his side, grabbing and holding onto his left arm. She looked amazed and thrilled all at once.

"Nice one," Scott shook Dayton's free hand while the grav ball players patted Dayton on the shoulder.

Even Richard appeared from the pack with a big grin. "Let's grab some food."

Dayton pulled Allyson close as they walked toward the hill. "Trenton, you want to come with us?"

Trenton nodded. "What about Zara?" he whispered.

"She'll come around," Dayton answered. "She has a lot of anger to let go of first, though. Maybe you can help her."

The group left the Rust Pile and headed out. Life was going to be different now, but that wasn't necessarily a bad thing. Hey, at least he didn't have Milly yelling at him. And friends, yes, he had some good friends, new and old.

High above them, unseen by the naked eye, ships moved. Cargo was delivered. Exploration happened. Dayton pulled Allyson close to him. All that space stuff, yeah, that could wait. He had at least a couple more years on Earth.

He planned to make the most of it.

Not a bad way to start a life.

THE END

ABOUT ATMOSPHERE PRESS

Founded in 2015, Atmosphere Press was built on the principles of Honesty, Transparency, Professionalism, Kindness, and Making Your Book Awesome. As an ethical and author-friendly hybrid press, we stay true to that founding mission today.

If you're a reader, enter our giveaway for a free book here:

SCAN TO ENTER
BOOK GIVEAWAY

If you're a writer, submit your manuscript for consideration here:

SCAN TO SUBMIT
MANUSCRIPT

And always feel free to visit Atmosphere Press and our authors online at atmospherepress.com. See you there soon!

ABOUT THE AUTHOR

NEIL V. YOUNG is a science fiction, fantasy and horror writer with many honorable and silver honorable mentions and a Finalist in the annual Writers of the Future Contest. His work has appeared in dozens of magazines and websites, including *Challenge Magazine* and *69 Flavors of Paranoia*. He lives in Orange County, California. He has served as a contributing editor for several Long Beach and Los Angeles-based writers groups, as well as the Vice President of Programming for the Southern California Writers Association. He currently works as a technical writer for an internationally-leading dental implant company.